THE
OSIRIS CURSE

THE
OSIRIS CURSE

A TWEED & NIGHTINGALE ADVENTURE

PAUL CRILLEY

an imprint of **Prometheus Books**
Amherst, NY

Published 2013 by Pyr®, an imprint of Prometheus Books

Cover illustration © Cliff Nielsen
Cover design by Grace M. Conti-Zilsberger

Inquiries should be addressed to

Pyr
59 John Glenn Drive
Amherst, New York 14228–2119
VOICE: 716–691–0133
FAX: 716–691–0137
WWW.PYRSF.COM

17 16 15 14 13   5 4 3 2 1

Library of Congress Cataloging-in-Publication Data

Crilley, Paul, 1975-
    The Osiris curse / by Paul Crilley.
        pages cm. — (A Tweed & Nightingale adventure)
    ISBN 978-1-61614-857-7 (hardback)
    ISBN 978-1-61614-858-4 (ebook)
    [1. Science fiction. 2. Secret societies—Fiction. 3. Mystery and detective stories. 4. Adventure and adventurers—Fiction. 5. London (England)—History—19th century—Fiction. 6. Great Britain—History—Victoria, 1837-1901—Fiction.] I. Title.

PZ7.C869276Os 2013
[Fic]—dc23

2013022384

Printed in the United States of America

For Caroline, Bella, and Caeleb,
my amazingly cool family.
I love you all.
You guys keep life interesting.

ACKNOWLEDGMENTS

Thanks to Lou Anders for editorial support, Phil Athans for grammatical support, and everyone else at Pyr for general support.

And thanks to all the bloggers and booksellers who spread the word about the first Tweed and Nightingale adventure. You guys rock.

CHAPTER ONE

Death stalks the streets of London.

The winter wind, sensing its presence and feeling some distant, ancient kinship, soars above the frozen city, tossing snowflakes through the oil-black sky as it searches for its location.

The wind drops lower, gusting through the frosty streets. It skims along the pollution-scummed waters of the Thames, reaching beneath London Bridge to blacken the toes of the homeless huddled together in a pathetic attempt to escape its touch.

It flies over the dome of St. Paul's Cathedral, then along the Strand, where automatons with the souls of humans go about the work of their masters. It flicks the snow around, sending it in confused, whirling gusts as it searches for the death it can taste in the very air.

There. The wind pauses, a lull in the freezing January night.

Then is drops.

An odd pair walk calmly through the streets. They are dressed in strange fashions, the man in a dark purple suit with a mustard yellow shirt, a white handkerchief poking out of his breast pocket. He carries a cane, which he swings out and around with every step. He is wearing a fedora hat pulled low over his face.

And his face . . .

Cold as the breath of winter herself, all angles and cruel bones, grey eyes so pale as to be almost white. It is only when he turns to check on his companion that any flicker of emotion is seen, a fire kindled behind the eyes, a fierce familial love.

His companion is a woman, although her like has rarely been seen in London. No hint of subservience. No inkling of what men would call the weakness of the fairer sex. If anything, the hard lines of her face are even crueler than her brother's. She moves slowly, her eyes, so brown as to be almost black, scouring all with their gaze.

She is also wearing a suit, and it is for this reason that she attracts so many hostile stares, stares that nervously flick away when she turns her dead eyes upon them. Her suit is a deep, dark crimson, the color of dried blood. She does not wear a hat. Her blond-white hair is scraped back from her head and tied with a piece of leather.

The two move slowly along the Strand. The theaters are finishing up, the rich and the privileged huddled beneath fur coats and gentlemen's jackets while they wait for the automata to bring the hansom cabs along the slush-covered cobbles.

They watch these crowds as they walk, staring at them with an intensity that few could miss. It is as if they are studying them, the people of London nothing but specimens in a laboratory.

The two are passing a dark alley when three men step out of the shadows to confront them. One has a pistol, and the other two raise rusty knives. The men are wearing tattered clothes, their faces smeared with dirt.

The wind swirls around the tableau, ruffling the greasy hair of the assailants, throwing snow up around their leaky, hob-nailed boots.

"Give. Come on. Everythin' in yer pockets," says the man with the pistol.

The man in the purple suit raises a delicate eyebrow. "Don't be absurd."

The three muggers look uneasily at each other. This isn't how it is supposed to go. The mark should hand over everything, usually begging for his life as he did so. He wasn't supposed to say *no*.

The man licks his cracked lips and swings the gun to point at the woman. "Do it. Or the moll gets it in the head."

The man in the purple suit shakes his head sadly, making a tutting noise. "Silly man," he says. He turns to the woman. "Sister?"

"I'll handle it," says the woman. And she licks her lips and smiles, showing odd, almost translucent teeth.

The attackers wonder if they have perhaps bitten off more than they can chew. They raise their weapons all the same, but before they can do anything more the woman is moving, a blur of teeth and nails. She smacks the gun out of the way, driving her fingers into the man's throat. He coughs, gagging. Blood wells from his mouth as he drops to his knees. The woman whirls, her leg coming up. It connects with the second man's head. There is a loud crack, his head jerks to the side, and he slides to the ground, sightless eyes staring up at the brittle stars. The third lunges forward with his knife, but she easily bats it aside. She grabs him by the shoulders and drags him into the darkness of the alley. He screams, a terrible cry of pain and horror that fades to a wet gurgle before eventually stopping.

A moment later the woman steps back into the light. She uses her pinky to wipe the blood from the side of her mouth, then straightens her suit and smiles brightly at the man. She holds her arm out.

"Shall we, Brother?"

"Indeed, Sister. Let us finish this."

They move away from the alley, stepping over the pools of blood now staining the freshly fallen snow. They turn onto Cromwell Street, moving through the dim light given off by snow-obscured Tesla globes. They stop outside the Natural History Museum, craning their heads back to take in the tall spires that flank the front entrance.

"Inelegant," says the woman.

"Agreed. It will have to go."

There is movement from the shadows along the side of the

building. A figure appears, wearing a dark cloak with the hood pulled low over its face. The figure approaches the siblings, then drops to his knees, the cloak billowing out in the snow around him like a pool of liquid.

"Masters. The Hermetic Order of Osiris is here to serve. As ever it has been. As ever it will be."

The siblings exchange amused looks, but the kneeling figure does not see.

"Rise, loyal one."

The figure in the cloak straightens.

"The guards are dealt with?" asks the man.

"All dead, Most High One."

"And he is here?"

"He entered at five o' clock this afternoon."

"Take us to him."

The acolyte bows and leads the siblings behind the museum. There are small huts and sheds scattered around the lot. The acolyte heads directly for one of them and holds the door open. Inside, the siblings are confronted with a hidden door that has been propped open with the broken arm of a statue.

"He is alone?" asks the woman.

"He is."

"Follow us."

Beyond the hidden door is a set of stairs leading deep underground. The siblings follow them down, finally emerging into a huge, echoing factory. The ceiling is distant, the walls lost in shadow. There are half-constructed machines cast haphazardly around, some in the process of being dismantled, others in the process of construction. There is a high-pitched whining coming from somewhere up ahead, and a moment later a massive dome of electricity bursts from the roof and grounds itself in metal plates in the floor.

The siblings walk forward, unconcerned, and after a moment can make out a man inside this dome of lightning. He is seated on a chair reading a newspaper.

The lightning abruptly vanishes. The air tastes of tin. The man notices them for the first time and gets to his feet, angry.

"Who are you? You cannot come in here!"

The man in the purple suit draws a pistol. It is plated with silver, gleaming in the light. It has engravings of lizards on the barrel.

"Sit down, Mr. Tesla."

Nikola Tesla looks nervously at the gun, then slumps back into his chair. He smoothes his mustache down. "What is it you want?"

"Justice, Mr. Tesla. We want justice."

Tesla frowns, uncertain. "Justice? Have I wronged you in some way?"

For the first time there is a slip of control in the siblings. Both of them stiffen, angry. No, *furious*.

"Have you *wronged* us? Mr. Tesla you have wronged many, many thousands. My people are dying because of you."

Tesla is shocked. "What is this? I have done nothing!"

The woman steps forward. "Nothing? You say you have done nothing, you whose inventions are responsible for so much pain! You are evil, Nikola Tesla."

"I am no such thing. What pain? What inventions are you talking about?"

"All of them," says the man, and he fires the gun.

The bullet hits Tesla in the chest. He cries out and falls backward over his chair. After a moment, he pulls himself to his knees. He touches the blood on his chest with a trembling hand and looks accusingly at the siblings.

"You . . . you *shot* me!"

The man fires again. Tesla jerks backward and lands on his back.

His sightless eyes stare up at the distant ceiling. The man puts the gun away and gestures for the acolyte to come forward.

"Do it," he says.

The acolyte nods and hurries to the body. The man and the woman turn to face each other.

"It is begun," he says.

"It is begun," she repeats, satisfaction evident in her words.

CHAPTER TWO

"Nothing's happening," said Octavia Nightingale in a bored tone of voice.

Tweed glanced up from the newspaper he was reading. "It will. It's statistically proven that more crimes are committed between two and three in the morning." He frowned thoughtfully. "And on a Tuesday, strangely enough."

"Tweed, it's *Thursday*," said Octavia in exasperation. "And it's *after* three. The only suspicious people lurking around in the dark are *us*. All the villains are in bed. Where it's warm. And dry."

Tweed sighed and pushed the muddy slush around with his boot. She had a point. He fished out his pocket watch and flicked the cover open.

3:25.

In the morning.

In mid-January.

Tweed slipped the watch back into his pocket. He'd give it another half hour then call it a night. By the time he got home and into bed it would be after five, and that meant he'd sleep most of the day away, which was a bonus. Loneliness tended to be worse during the day. Sitting alone in the house, listening to the huge grandfather clock in the hallway—that was when he started brooding, contemplating who he really was, how he had been created.

He shied away from the thought, shivering and pulling his greatcoat tighter around his body. No. Much better to keep occupied. It kept the dark thoughts at bay.

He tilted the newspaper toward the street light outside the alley. "Listen to the rubbish they print nowadays," he said, hoping to distract Octavia. "'The airship *Albion*, widely acknowledged to be a triumph of design and engineering, is due to make her maiden voyage this very Saturday. The *Albion* is a first of its kind, a luxury airship capable of carrying over a thousand guests. Kept afloat by one hundred sturdy gasbags and powered by Tesla Turbines, the mile-long airship was built in the factories of Dundee and towed to London by the Royal Navy's own airships.'"

"What's wrong with that?" protested Octavia. "It gives background information."

"Ah, I see. Is that's what it does?" Tweed found his place again. "'The launch of the *Albion* is the hottest event of the social season. Those who can afford the tickets will travel to Egypt, where they will rest for a few days in Tutankhamen's View, the controversial hotel built inside the refurbished Great Pyramid of Giza. The *Albion* will then tour Europe before returning to England, where a welcoming party will await the *Albion*'s proud cresting of the chalky cliffs of Dover.'"

Tweed glanced at Octavia. "*Can* an inanimate object be proud?"

"Be quiet," said Octavia.

"I ask merely for information. As you're always so keen to point out, my education is sorely lacking. I just wondered, what with you being so clever and everything, whether I should write a letter to *The Times* and complain about one of their reporters taking such artistic license with the English language." He frowned. "What *is* the reporter's name, anyway?" He squinted at the byline, then looked at Octavia in mock surprise. "Why, this journalist, this . . . *butcherer* of the English language, has the same name as *you*, Nightingale. You should sue."

A handful of slush hit him in the cheek. He spluttered and wiped it away, then grinned at her. "Bet you've already cut this out and framed it, haven't you?"

Octavia said nothing.

"Where is it? Above your bed? No—above your desk, yes?"

"Possibly," said Octavia reluctantly.

Tweed tucked the newspaper into one of his voluminous pockets. For all his teasing, he really was proud of Octavia. Even if she was only a junior reporter given the task of rewriting press releases, she was still the youngest person ever to have that kind of job at *The Times*. He would keep the article himself as a memento.

To remind myself how terrible I'm doing in comparison.

The thought slid into his mind, dark and insidious. He tried to push it away, but it wouldn't budge. And why should it? It was the truth, after all. Octavia had a job, a life, proper friends. He had . . . well, he had nothing much, to be honest. An empty house that depressed him. A father who was never there. One friend who was so busy at work he only saw her when they trained together, which was only for a few hours every other day.

He was wallowing in melancholy. Which was *incredibly* annoying. For himself and for others.

More than that, he feared his melancholy was turning to depression. He spent most of his time sleeping, and when he woke up it was with a heavy ball of lead in his stomach that wouldn't shift no matter what he did. He found his thoughts turning to the future, a future where he wasn't sure he had a place. What could he do, after all? He had no real skills. No *honest* skills, anyway. A life spent running cons with his father had ill-prepared him for a life on this side of the law.

Worse than all that, though, (and it was here his thoughts always led), he wasn't sure he was actually a real person.

Well, he *was*. *Technically*. But the truth was, he had no soul of his own. *His* soul used to belong to Sherlock Holmes. Tweed, in fact, *was* Sherlock Holmes. The man's soul had been drawn from his body after he died at Reichenbach Falls and placed inside a nine-month-old clone of Holmes. That clone was Tweed. The insertion into so young a body wiped Holmes's memories, giving baby Tweed a clean slate, a fresh start.

But Tweed couldn't avoid the fact. He wasn't his own person. He was living in someone else's body with someone else's soul. A cuckoo who had raided someone else's nest to make his own life.

What kind of existence was that? He didn't *belong*. He felt as if he hadn't earned his place in the world, that he hadn't earned his right to *exist*.

"Just admit it, Tweed," said Octavia, breaking into his thoughts. "You were wrong. If it was going to happen tonight it would have happ—"

The wall of the building opposite them exploded outward, bricks and stones tumbling into the road. There was a metallic grinding noise, then a burst of steam that came from nowhere, mixing with the dust clouding the air. The sound of heavy, clanking footsteps stomped into the road and moved slowly away from them.

The only problem was, there was nothing there.

Tweed and Octavia stared. An empty street. A ragged hole in the wall. A slowly dissipating steam cloud, and grey dust settling into the snow. That was it.

"That's . . . rather odd," he said.

More bricks flew suddenly out of the wall, and those already lying in the snow burst apart, reduced to rubble and powder seemingly of their own volition.

Again, they heard the hissing of steam and the *thunk thunk* of heavy footsteps.

"Look!" whispered Octavia.

Tweed glanced along the street. Large footsteps were appearing in the muddy slush that coated the road. Two sets, moving away from their location.

Tweed lifted his gaze higher and squinted. He could just make out a distortion, a portion of air that twisted slightly, bent and shivering, like light refracted through thick glass. He followed the outline of the anomaly, tracing it as it formed the shape of what he knew to be a rather large, rather dangerous automaton.

Hah! He had been right after all.

"They've got some kind of invisibility thing going on," he said. "Like in Wells's book. Look how the air is distorted above the footprints."

"I can see," said Octavia grumpily.

Tweed grinned at her. "You owe me a florin."

"Not yet I don't. It might not be Harry Banks's constructs."

Over the past month or so there had been a series of bank robberies, crimes so filled with mayhem and destruction that Tweed had reckoned it couldn't be the work of a human. Even a *gang* of humans wouldn't be able to cause so much damage.

But Tweed had figured it out. He had come to the conclusion that it was Harry Banks, the man who had betrayed them to Lucien a few months back.

Why had Tweed suspected the man in the first place? Because he had been into Banks's gambling den, had witnessed massive automata fighting each other in illegal boxing matches. Harry had a scam going, where the automata were controlled from a hidden room by real boxers strapped into pneumatic rigs, their movements and punches transmitted to the constructs so it looked as if the punters were betting on illegal automaton fights.

When Tweed had seen the chaos at the first robbery, how the vault doors had been ripped from their hinges, the walls of the banks simply bashed down, he'd immediately thought of Harry Banks.

Octavia disagreed. If ten feet tall automata were smashing down walls and making their escape through the streets of London, *someone* would have seen it.

Now they had their answer. Harry Banks had somehow found a way to make his automata invisible. That *had* to be Ministry technology. Which meant Banks had stolen it, or rather more worryingly, that there was a leak in the government department.

Tweed made a mental note to mention it to his dad. Barnaby Tweed was the man in charge of the Ministry now. He would have to look into it.

But that was for later. Right now they had a bank robbery to foil.

"Come on," he said, slipping out of the alley. Once he got used to the strange rippling effect in the air, it was easy enough to keep an eye on the constructs. The robbers moved slowly, trying to keep as silent as possible, pausing when they heard a noise, then moving on when the coast was clear. They kept to the back streets, traveling along a path where all street lights, both gas and Tesla-powered, had been put out of commission.

"You wanted to know how I knew which bank would be hit next?" Tweed whispered.

"I wouldn't say *wanted* to know. But I'm mildly curious, yes."

He nodded at the street lights. "I visited the other banks—the ones that had already been robbed. The street lamps along the most likely escape routes were all broken. I've been checking the other banks every night, looking for one with a similar pattern."

Octavia narrowed her eyes. "Are you *honestly* telling me you spend every night walking around checking all the banks in London?"

"Don't be ridiculous. How would I do that? I'm not Atticus Pope, you know."

"Yes, I *know* you're not Atticus Pope," said Octavia. "Because Atticus Pope isn't actually real."

"Some people think he is," said Tweed defensively. Atticus Pope was a popular character who starred in his own pulp novels. Crime fighter, investigator, all round bad-guy catcher. Tweed loved the books. He was currently reading *Atticus Pope and the Men from Mars*.

Octavia gave Tweed what he had come to call "the look." He reckoned it was a skill passed down through the female bloodline or something, because he had seen Jenny Turner give her husband, Carter Flair, the exact same look on numerous occasions.

"If you really want to know, all the robberies were close to each other. I've just been checking the banks that fall within a two mile radius of the others."

"Clever boy. How many were there?"

"Eight."

"Eight! And you've been checking them for how long?"

"About three weeks," said Tweed, peering around the corner of a red brick warehouse. A shadowy alley filled with moldering crates and rotting garbage stretched ahead of them. He could smell decaying vegetables, the sickly sweet smell of fruit well past its date.

He frowned as he scanned the alley. "I can't see them," he whispered.

"Let me look."

Tweed bit his tongue. Octavia *never* trusted anything he said. She always had to see for herself.

"I can't see them either—No wait, there they are."

Tweed leaned around Octavia's shoulder, noting absently that her hair smelled rather pleasantly of oranges. He saw the ripple in the air, the heat wave effect that betrayed Harry's automata.

Except . . .

"There's only one," said Tweed.

There was a slight noise behind them.

Tweed and Octavia whirled around to find the second automaton towering over them, its invisibility cloak switched off. The construct was terrifying, a hulking, broad-shouldered figure about twelve feet tall, its dark blue paint chipped and battered. The automaton had been modified since Tweed last saw it fighting in the ring. A glass-covered cage had been built into the construct's chest. A thin man sat in this cage, strapped into a cracked leather seat. His hands hovered over a set of controls.

"Boo," the man said.

He twitched the control and the automaton swung its massive arm. Tweed and Octavia ducked. The arm smashed into the corner of the wall, gouging a huge hole out of the building.

Tweed and Octavia scrambled to their feet, darting to either side of the construct. It whirled around, following their movements a lot faster than Tweed expected. Not only outside modifications, but internal as well.

He looked frantically around, but there was nowhere to go. Running away was suicide. The thing would be on top of them in an instant.

Which only left . . .

Tweed ducked beneath the sweeping arms for a second time.

"Keep still, damn you," snarled the robber. "Let me knock your head off!"

Tweed spun in a circle and ended up at the rear of the automaton, reaching up to grab the armor plating across its back. He did this at the exact same time as Octavia.

"My idea," she said. "I get to drive."

"I was here first!"

Octavia heaved herself up onto the automaton, scrambling up along the thick pipe of the spine. Tweed followed, pulling himself up until he was kneeling on the automaton's broad shoulder. The driver seemed to realize something was going on that shouldn't be. He jerked around in circles, desperately trying to find them.

"Where are ye?" he shouted. "C'mere so I can squish your heads. I want to see you pop."

"Charming," said Octavia.

"I want to drive," said Tweed.

"So do I."

"Flip you for it?"

Octavia rolled her eyes, then quickly reached out and grabbed hold of the automaton's head when the construct gave a sudden leap forward, sailing five feet though the air. It skidded in the snow when it landed, then whirled around to face the way it had come, obviously hoping to find Tweed and Nightingale standing there in the middle of the road.

"Fine," she said. "Hurry up."

Tweed reached into his pocket and pulled out his lucky penny. He threw it into the air and caught it.

"Heads," said Octavia.

Tweed lifted his hand, then swore under his breath. "Heads," he said resignedly.

Octavia clapped her hands together. "Splendid. Now let's get this fellow out so we can get after the second robber. He's making his escape."

Tweed peered into the dark alley, noting the distortion in the air as the second robber decided to make a break for it.

"How do we get laughing boy out?" asked Octavia.

Tweed thought about it. "Don't move," he said. Then he took his penny and knocked it against the metal.

Ting.

He paused, then did it again.

Ting.

He kept it up, holding a slow, steady rhythm until the driver of the automaton heard it. He stopped moving.

"Hey. H-Hey. What are you doing?"

Ting.

"Hey, cut that out! This is expensive equipment here."

Ting.
Ting.
Ting.
"Enough!" shouted the driver.
Ting.
Then Tweed hit much harder.
TING!
Then he stopped.
"What was that?" shouted the driver. "What did you do?"

Octavia opened her mouth to say something, but Tweed quickly held his hand up to stop her. She frowned at him, and Tweed thought he'd probably pay for that later. She hated it when he tried to silence her, even if it *was* for a good reason.

A moment later there was the hiss of escaping air and the front part of the cage swung upward. Tweed and Octavia tried to move out of sight, but it wasn't really easy when they were perched on the shoulders of a giant automaton.

There was a pause, then the driver's hand slowly rose into view holding a revolver.

"Over to you," said Tweed.

Octavia smiled and pulled out her Tesla gun. Tweed knew she liked nothing more than finding a good excuse to use it. She pointed it at the rising hand and fired. A burst of bright blue lighting burst out of the chamber and crawled over the driver's hand. He screamed, his fingers spasming. The revolver fell into the foot well with a clatter.

Tweed peered over the top of the cage and saw the driver slumped over on the floor. "You didn't kill him, did you?"

"Of course not."

"Off you go then," said Tweed. Octavia clambered down into the driver's cage. She fiddled with buttons and dials until the front of the cage lowered itself and sealed her in.

Tweed stood up on the automaton's shoulders and pointed into the alley. "Follow that robot!" he shouted, reckoning he must look pretty heroic standing there, silhouetted against the night sky.

Then the automaton lurched drunkenly forward and Tweed sailed through the air, landing flat on his back in the snow.

He groaned and sat up, watching as Octavia tried to figure out the controls. The automaton staggered to the side, crashing into the alley wall. Tweed flinched and covered his head as bricks and dust fell around him. The automaton heaved to the left again, leaving a massive, automaton-shaped hole in the wall.

The automaton straightened up and Tweed quickly climbed back up onto its shoulders. Then he held on for dear life as they staggered forward, Octavia trying her best to keep the movements smooth and steady.

She wasn't very successful. They careened into walls, spun around in circles, and at one point the automaton fell onto its knees and crawled through the alley for a while. While it was doing this, Tweed leaned over the top of the cage.

"Are you sure you wouldn't like me to drive?" he shouted. "Only, I think you might be more dangerous than the bank robbers."

"Nonsense!" Octavia shouted back. "I'm getting the hang of it now."

She pulled back on a lever and the automaton lurched awkwardly to its feet. Tweed grabbed hold of its head to make sure he wasn't sent flying again. The construct took a hesitant step forward, then another and another, until they were moving at a steady rolling gait.

Tweed laughed and smacked the automaton's head. "Come on then! Go faster!"

They picked up speed, exiting the alley and skidding into a wide thoroughfare. Tweed scanned the street until he spotted the wavering in the air that betrayed the second automaton, then leaned over and pointed.

"Over there!"

Octavia nodded and set off in pursuit. A few seconds later the footprints ahead of them paused in the snow, then shifted and smeared as if the driver was turning around to look behind him.

Then he set off again, the footprints appearing even faster as he picked up speed.

"Come on, Songbird!" Tweed shouted. "He's getting away!"

The automaton picked up speed, stumbled slightly, then smoothed out its stride. Tweed grinned as he felt the cold wind sting his cheeks. The distortion in the air grew closer as the robber slowed beside each road and alley that branched off from his planned escape route. Then he darted down a narrow path between two tenement buildings. Sparks burst from the stonework as the automaton's shoulders scraped the walls.

Octavia followed after, moving her construct slightly to the side so it wouldn't be slowed by the walls. They were gaining ground now, only about five paces behind. Tweed raised himself to a standing position, trying his best to keep his balance. He had a plan in mind that involved him leaping suavely across the narrowing gap, landing athletically on the fleeing automaton and doing something incredibly clever to render the invisibility device useless.

Octavia, on the other hand, had her own ideas.

She put on an extra burst of speed, and as the two constructs exited the narrow lane she lashed out with the automaton's fist, smashing it into the back of the fleeing robber with a resounding clang. Tweed grabbed on tight as the jolt vibrated up through his feet and along his spine. There was a bright flash of light, the smell of something burning, and the automaton appeared suddenly in front of them.

It was similar to the one Tweed was standing on, except it was covered in flaking red paint instead of blue. As it straightened and turned toward them, Tweed saw that the driver was much larger and much scarier-looking than the one Octavia had shot.

He actually looked like one of the men who Tweed had seen operating the boxing rigs in Harry's back room. Indeed, Tweed watched with interest, and no small amount of trepidation, as the man fiddled with levers, raising the automaton's arms up into the traditional boxer's stance.

He jerked a lever forward. The automaton jabbed out with its left hand, crashing it into their construct. Tweed was lifted into the air by the force of the blow. He started to slide down the automaton's back, but grabbed hold of the neck before he fell, draping himself across the construct's back like a particularly useless cloak.

Octavia clumsily tried to return the blow, but the man brought the right arm up to block her, then jabbed the left fist into their automaton's midsection.

They slid back in the slush. Tweed was lifted into the air again, then smacked back against the metal. The robber pushed forward, raining blow after blow onto the robot.

This was hopeless. Any moment now that metal fist was going to hit Tweed, breaking bones he would really rather stayed whole. He finally let go, fell, and landed on his backside in the cold slush. He swore when he saw how muddy his new greatcoat was getting, then swore again, even louder, when Octavia was pushed back another step, the automaton's foot almost crushing his leg.

He scrambled to his feet and moved around the two constructs. Spectators had gathered by now. It was inevitable. They had moved off the robbers' escape route, and the road in which they were fighting was a normal well-lit street lined with tenements, shops, and lots of pubs. The constant barrage of clanging metal had brought the curious out to see what was going on.

Tweed quickly patted down his coat. He had a hundred pockets in the thing and he was sure he's put his own Tesla gun in one of them. He only hoped it still had a charge. He was terrible at remembering that kind of thing.

He eventually found it in an inside pocket and yanked it out, pointing it at the automaton. He hesitated. The robber had pinned Octavia's construct against the wall and was pummeling it over and over with its fists. The thick glass that surrounded her protective cage had cracked. It didn't look like it would hold much longer.

But he couldn't just fire. The electricity would hit Octavia as well.

He moved to the side, trying to see if he could get a clear shot. But there was nothing. The robber and Octavia were constantly touching. Hitting one would hit the other.

Octavia saw him standing watching. She raised her hands in a "what the hell are you doing?" gesture. Tweed responded by waving at the automaton, then holding the gun up in the air and then repeating her own gesture back at her: "What do you expect me to do?"

She set her mouth in a thin line, waiting for the tiniest gap between blows. When it came she flung all her levers forward.

The feet of her automaton flew out in front of her and it slid down the wall like a drunkard finally giving up for the night. It carried on falling and ended up on its back.

Tweed saw the driver grin in anticipation. He thought he had her trapped. He moved forward and Octavia's construct kicked out, smashing into the robot's groin. The red automaton staggered back a few steps. Not much, in the grand scheme of things, but enough for Tweed to fire his Tesla gun.

The electricity arced and crawled across the metal casing. Sparks exploded outward, flashes of white and orange light blossoming inside the cage as the instrument panels exploded. The robber frantically slapped at his harness, somehow insulated from the electricity. The belts released and he shoved the cage open. Smoke billowed out and the man tumbled to the ground as his automaton gave a screeching groan and fell flat on its face.

The robber looked around and saw Tweed. His face crumpled with rage. He pushed himself to his feet and ran straight at him.

Tweed yawned and fired again.

Nothing happened.

He looked at his gun, shook it, and pulled the trigger again. Still nothing. The man was only ten paces away.

"I'm gonna kill you, boy!" he shouted. "Kill you dead!"

Tweed thought about berating the man for this careless grammar and needless repetition of words, but he didn't get a chance because at that moment writhing blue fire struck the man from behind and he went leaping into the air like a child's jack-in-the-box.

Octavia joined Tweed as the man crashed back to the snow. He was smoking ever so gently.

"Damn," she said. "Still had the setting on high. Think he's all right?"

"Mummy," sobbed the man in a pain-filled voice.

"He'll live," said Tweed.

A cheer burst out behind them. They turned to see that the crowd had grown rather large by now. They were cheering and applauding wildly. Tweed grinned. He spread his arms wide and performed an extravagant bow.

Octavia punched him in the arm.

"Ow! What was that for? Are we not allowed some adulation? That was good work we did tonight."

"Maybe," said Octavia in a fierce whisper. "But how happy is the Queen going to be if we're linked to this? More importantly, how happy is *Barrington Chase* going to be?"

Tweed's mood darkened instantly. Barrington Chase. The name

alone brought him out in shudders of annoyance and irritation. The man had become the bane of his life lately. A member of the secret services and appointed by the Queen herself to train them in . . . "helpful skills," as she called it.

Octavia was right. Chase wasn't going to like this. Not one little bit.

Which made Tweed a bit happier. Any opportunity to wind up the self-absorbed spy was time well spent in Tweed's book.

And on top of that, they finally got their revenge on Harry Banks for betraying them. He'd go to jail for this, no doubt about it.

"I think it's probably best if I explain all this to Chase," said Tweed, gleefully rubbing his hands together.

"Good idea. I'll stand in the background. Not drawing attention to myself."

Tweed raised an eyebrow at her. "Trying not to draw attention to yourself is going to be pretty difficult when we march these things up to the front door of Ravenstone Lodge," said Tweed. "I mean, it's not like we can just leave them here, is it?"

Octavia looked around in dismay at the devastation they had caused. "I hadn't thought about that."

"Buck up," said Tweed. "I mean, what can he actually do?"

"He's a spy, Tweed. He can do a lot of things."

"Hah. But can he? Really?"

"Yes," said Octavia evenly. "He can. And I rather think he would."

Tweed hesitated. "Oh." He thought about this for a second, then shrugged and grinned. "Oh well. Who wants to live forever? Besides, it will be worth it just to see the look on his face."

CHAPTER THREE

Ravenstone Lodge was a hundred-year-old manor house that hunkered on the outskirts of London. It was a crumbling edifice covered in moss and ivy, slipping into ruin like a decrepit old man who had decided that personal hygiene simply wasn't something he was going to bother with anymore.

The house was hidden from the prying eyes of the unwelcome (which pretty much meant everyone) by expansive, rambling grounds and a thick screen of ancient trees that ran around the perimeter of the property.

At 4:43 on this wintery Thursday morning the house was in darkness. The brittle light of the full moon shone through naked tree branches, throwing gnarled and twisted shadows onto the ground. The frigid wind set the branches clacking, the shadows shifting and stretching as if they were skeletal hands trying to dig up the frozen earth.

A fox screamed in the distance. An owl grumpily called out a reply.

Then silence.

Then . . .

Clump clump. Hissss-s-s-s-s.

Clump Clump. Clump, clump. Hiss-s-s-s-s.

The owl opened one eye, glancing down from his perch in a tall chestnut tree to the lane leading up to the house.

It stared. It ruffled its feathers. Then it opened its second eye, as if wasn't sure it was seeing correctly.

Here is what it saw . . .

Two twelve-foot automata moving inexpertly up the lane, staggering and stumbling like drunkards. The automata held their arms out in front of them, and cradled in these arms were two bound and unconscious figures.

The automata moved through the rusted iron gates and onto the graveled driveway that led up to the house. They stopped before the front door and one of the automata slowly lowered its arms to gently place its captive on the ground.

And then a series of bright lights switched on, shining directly on the two constructs.

"Raise your hands in the air," said a crackly, disembodied voice. "I repeat, raise your hands in the air and do nothing more. Failure to comply will be treated as an act of aggression and will be dealt with severely."

The first automata slowly raised its arms. The second construct's arms shot upward as well. Unfortunately, the driver forgot what he was holding, and the bound figure sailed backward over the automaton's head and landed somewhere behind him.

"Don't shoot, you idiots!" shouted a young man's voice. "It's us!" And then, "Oh. Did I just—?"

The construct lumbered around in a circle and stared at the groaning figure now sprawled untidily on the gravel.

"Sorry about that."

"What were you *thinking?*" snapped Barrington Chase.

Octavia hung her head and stared at the richly patterned carpet. She could see Tweed's feet just to her right. He was moving his weight from one to the other, impatient, frustrated. She sighed. She could see how this was going to go.

"We were *thinking* about foiling a criminal syndicate that if left unchecked would have cleaned out every bank in the city," snapped Tweed.

"That's not your job, boy!"

Octavia finally looked up. They were in the library of Ravenstone Lodge, surrounded by ceiling-high shelves of books, comfortable armchairs, and dim lamp light. Normally, she loved it here. It was so peaceful. So calming. Whenever Octavia stepped through the door she felt she could just melt into the room, into the smells of leather and old books, the scent of bees wax polish and paraffin.

But right now, the usual peaceful atmosphere was marred by the fury of Barrington Chase and the mild annoyance of Henry Temple, who was lounging in a chair by the window.

Barrington Chase was a member of Her Majesty's Secret Service. A spy, and one of Queen Victoria's best, apparently. She had put him in charge of their training and education, and to say the man resented it was like saying Tweed was ever so slightly arrogant. Chase *hated* his assignment, thought it a complete waste of time. And he took every opportunity to let them both know.

Just as Tweed took every opportunity to let Chase know that he agreed.

Even at this time of the morning Chase was immaculately presented, wearing a crimson silk dressing gown and holding a large snifter of brandy. His hair was slicked back in a middle parting, his mustache perfectly coiffed. He didn't even look tired.

"I thought our job was to do what was right."

"Oh, don't be so obtuse," Chase snapped. "Your job is to learn from myself and Temple and to be ready when you are called upon. If you stray from that remit, if you behave in a manner that brings the Crown into disrepute, then that's on your own head. Something I will be telling Her Majesty when I see her later on today."

"You're *telling* on us?" said Tweed incredulously.

"I think filing a report is a better way of putting it," said Temple.

Henry Temple was also a spy, but he was the complete opposite of Chase. Unassuming, quiet, friendly, he always went out of his way to explain his teachings, to make sure they understood the theory behind the lessons.

He smiled apologetically from where he lounged in an armchair, sipping tea and looking tired. "Sorry. Has to be done. The Queen will have to be made aware of your part in all this."

"But we didn't do anything wrong," protested Octavia.

"I didn't say you did."

"*I* say you did," said Chase. "You drew attention to yourself. I'm assuming there were witnesses? Is it too much to ask that you managed to foil this robbery quickly and quietly?"

Octavia and Tweed said nothing.

"I thought so." Chase put his brandy glass down. "I've made it perfectly clear I thought this assignment a waste of time. Whatever the Queen sees in you I do not see. Whatever plans she has for you, I think she is going to be sorely disappointed. And yes," he said, "before you bring it up yet again, of course I read the Lazarus report. And whereas you see brilliant detective work I see amateurish joining of the dots and lots and lots of luck. I hope you at least took *some* precautions? No one saw you coming *here?*"

"Of course not," said Octavia.

"That is something at least."

Chase headed toward the door. "Expect to be called in for an audience with the Queen later on today," he said. "I'm sure she'll want a few words with you."

"One thing," said Tweed. "When you file your report with the Queen, tell her Harry Banks had access to technology I've never seen on the streets before."

Temple leaned forward. "What kind of technology?"

"Some sort of invisibility device. That's why no one had seen his automata before."

Temple and Chase exchanged glances.

"Not so hopeless now, are we?" said Tweed. "Looks like there's someone on the payroll selling off the government's secrets."

"Funny how we've never had that kind of problem before," said Chase.

"Well you've got that kind of problem now."

"The timing is . . . odd, don't you think?" said Chase, a glitter in his eyes.

"What do you mean?"

"Oh, you know. Change of managerial staff. New people in charge at the Ministry. *Unproven* people."

Tweed took an angry stride toward Chase. Temple quickly got to his feet and stepped between them.

"Come now. Enough of this. Chase, you should know better."

Chase glared at Temple, then swept out of the room.

Octavia released a breath she hadn't realized she was holding. After the events of last autumn, the Queen had asked Tweed's adoptive father, Barnaby Tweed, to head up the Ministry, taking over from the traitor Lucien. Barnaby turned her down straight away, but the Queen didn't let up. She said it was *because* he was so adamantly against it that she wanted him for the job. He'd worked there in the past, he'd proven himself an honest and loyal subject, and she would hear no more words about it.

In the end, Barnaby didn't really have a choice.

Naturally, there were a lot of . . . *questions* about his appointment. But there wasn't much anyone could do when it was by order of the ruler of the British Empire.

"I hate that man," said Tweed.

"I think the feeling is mutual," said Temple, patting Tweed on the shoulder. He yawned and scratched his head. "Excuse me. Think I'd better get dressed. Looks like it's going to be a long day."

He headed toward the door, but paused and turned around. "For what it's worth, I think you did a good job tonight. And I'll be filing my own report with the Queen."

Once Temple had left, Tweed headed over to the roll top desk and shuffled through the papers inside.

"What are you doing?" asked Octavia. "That's Chase's desk."

Tweed looked at her like she was an idiot. "I *know* that. Why do you think I'm looking?"

"Stop it. That could be his private letters."

Tweed grinned over his shoulder at her. "Exactly."

"*Ahem.*"

Octavia whirled around to find Mr. McAllen, Barrington Chase's butler standing in the doorway. He frowned at Tweed, who was now doing the head-tilted-sideways stance of someone reading the spines of books, (or at least, *pretending* to read the spines of books), then turned his attention to Octavia.

"Mr. Temple asked me to give this to you."

He held out a small envelope.

"Shouldn't you be asleep?" she asked, taking it from him.

McAllen's eyebrows rose. "Rather hard to sleep when automata are storming the citadel, so to speak."

Octavia flushed. "Oh. Yes. Sorry about that. It was a bit of an emergency."

"I'm sure it was, Miss."

Octavia studied the envelope. It didn't have a stamp or anything. Just her name scrawled in untidy writing. "When did this arrive?"

"Around midnight, miss."

Octavia looked at McAllen in surprise. "Midnight? *Tonight*, midnight?"

"Indeed."

"Who delivered it?"

"I didn't get the gentleman's name, miss, but he did say he was from the docks."

Octavia didn't hear anything else. She ripped the seal on the envelope and quickly read the contents. Her mouth went dry. She looked at Tweed, then back at the letter, rereading it to make sure she hadn't made a mistake.

That name you tagged came in. Can only hold him for a few hours. Get here quick.

"Tweed," she said urgently. "We need to go."

Tweed held up a book. "Look. *The Collected Sherlock Holmes*, by Dr. John Watson. Maybe I should—" He saw the expression on her face. "What is it?"

She held out the letter. He hurried over and read it, then broke into a huge grin and gripped her by the shoulders.

"Finally! A lead!" He frowned at her. "Why aren't you smiling? You should be smiling. Songbird, I *insist* you smile."

Octavia smiled hesitantly, but it quickly faded. She was too scared it would be a dead end. A false alarm.

Tweed waved the Sherlock book above his head. "What is it Sherlock says? The game's getting started?" He frowned. "No, that's not right. The game's begun? No. The game's heating up?"

"Afoot," Octavia said wearily. "The game's afoot."

Tweed frowned. "No, that doesn't sound right. No matter," he said, tossing the book onto the couch. "I'm sure it will come to me."

The London Docks never slept. No matter what time of day or night there was always a constant stream of traffic—yachts, steamboats, schooners, ferries—all of them jostling for position in the harbor, their masts like hundreds of spears thrusting up against the soot-heavy sky.

Cargo ships from India unloaded tea. Boats from South America brought in bales of tobacco. Ships from China carried richly-colored silks. And buried beneath the coffee and the spices was the trade of a more questionable cargo, one that made more money that all the tea and cloth put together: opium, the drug of choice for the London addict.

Octavia and Tweed hurried along the quayside. The air was redolent with a clashing mixture of scents and stenches. Perfumes, spices, and cloves competing against rotting fruit that had stayed too long in the hold, stale sweat, and rotting fish. Octavia wrinkled her nose. The smell hung in the air like a miasma, an almost physical presence that she could feel settling over her skin, coating it with a patina of dead ocean as they made their way to the Royal Albert Dock.

Octavia wouldn't let herself get excited. She'd already felt the sting of disappointment and didn't want to feel it again. Back in the autumn she'd finally thought she knew what happened to her mother, missing for over a year while investigating the supposed return of Professor Moriarty. All the clues pointed to the underground prison of the Ministry, the prison where Tweed's father was being held. They'd staged a rescue for Barnaby, but it was supposed to be a rescue for her mother as well.

Except she wasn't there. She had been moved some two weeks previously.

That soul-crushing feeling of being so close yet still failing was not something she wished to experience again.

It hadn't been a total loss. Stepp Reckoner had managed to get a name from the Ministry analytical machines, the name of the person who had somehow signed her mother out of prison.

Benedict Wilberforce.

They had searched far and wide for some clue as to who this mysterious person was, but they had come up a blank. It was as if he didn't exist. No birth certificate, no police record, nothing. Octavia had finally resorted to giving the name to every harbor master, customs officer, and dock hand she could find, promising a hefty reward if she was notified when someone bearing the name was spotted.

"Cheer up, Songbird," said Tweed, putting a friendly arm around her shoulder. "All your questions are about to be answered. Wasn't it a good idea of mine to pass the name around the docks? *I* think it was. I think it was a *splendid* idea."

"As I recall, *I'm* the one who came up with that. You said it would be a waste of time."

"Nonsense," said Tweed cheerfully. "I'd never say something like that."

Octavia shook her head, but couldn't help a small grin from appearing. She liked to see Tweed happy. And he was always happy when he was showing off. And when he was being arrogant, of course. That went without saying.

She been worrying about him lately. She got the feeling he'd been avoiding her, keeping more and more to himself. She supposed she couldn't blame him. Finding out you were a simulacrum of someone else must come as something of a shock. She knew he was struggling with it, struggling to figure out who he was, to understand what was truly him and what was the legacy of Sherlock Holmes. He was confused, angry. She'd seen the dark moods take him, watched him try to fight them off. All Octavia could do was be there for him.

Which she herself was finding rather difficult. The problem was—and she was incredibly embarrassed even admitting it to herself—she suspected she might just possibly be developing . . . *feelings* for Tweed.

She shied away from the thought even as it flitted through her mind. She couldn't even admit it to herself! But something was definitely changing in how she looked at him.

She actually found herself angry that the thoughts even existed. She didn't want to be a cliché, the helpless girl who falls for the boy. If anything, *he* should fall for *her*. That would be acceptable. Then she wouldn't ever have to say she ran after a boy.

Which she wouldn't do. Ever.

So she had her own things to sort out, which made helping Tweed through his own issues a bit of a problem. But she would try her best.

They dodged around workers offloading piles of coal and sailors leaving their berths, purses full of money and ready to release some pent-up frustration with the aid of "women of questionable virtue," as Tweed put it. Automata could be seen here and there, their presence betrayed by the white glow that pierced the dockside gloom— the human souls trapped in the constructs by Ministry Mesmers, the souls that enabled them to follow instructions and solve rudimentary problems. The automata carried the heaviest crates, the constructs easily doing the work of three men.

It was a practice that was slowly taking traction, despite it making a lot of workers unhappy. In the past, if a merchant tried to use a construct at the docks for any kind of manual labor, things . . . tended to happen to them. They disappeared, or their æther cages were somehow ruptured, the trapped souls that powered the automata drifting into the air and dispersing like a breath on the wind. But nowadays there was evidence of a slow change of thought. It was becoming more acceptable to use automata, especially for some of the more unpleasant tasks.

They arrived at the dock and customs office and hurried inside.

It was small and cramped inside the low building. A harassed man wearing tiny spectacles filled in paperwork at a cluttered desk. A line of rickety chairs was taken up by those who were deemed suspicious enough for the authorities to interview.

Octavia scanned the faces, wondering if one of them was her man. They all looked unkempt, and, not to be unkind, a bit desperate. Not the kind of person who could somehow check a prisoner out of a Ministry prison.

She hurried to the door at the rear of the room. It opened into a small corridor and at the end of that was the harbormaster's office. The man looked up from his desk, blinking at her in surprise as Octavia strode in.

"Where is he?" she demanded.

The harbormaster was a rotund gentleman, with whiskers curling down his cheeks and a bald head that shone in the lamp light.

"Miss Nightingale," he said apologetically. "I . . . I had to let him go."

"What?"

"You were taking too long! I sent the note at midnight. I could only keep him a few hours. It's . . . it's almost dawn. I didn't have any reason to keep him longer. I'm sorry."

Once again, thought Octavia bitterly. Once again she had come so close, only to have victory snatched away from her. It wasn't fair. It simply wasn't fair.

The harbormaster was still talking. His words started to filter back into her hearing.

". . . only released him about five minutes ago. You must have walked right past him."

Octavia straightened up and shared a surprised look with Tweed.

"What was he wearing?" he asked.

"Nice clothes, sir. Expensive. Very well-dressed man. A top hat and all. Oh, and a nice yellow silk scarf. I remember that because it had these little pictures on the silk. Tiny little lizards. And he had a walking stick. With a shiny knob on the end."

The harbormaster grinned at them proudly.

Tweed and Octavia rushed to the door and out into the corridor. But then Octavia paused and ran back into the harbormaster's office.

"Which way did he go?"

"No idea, Miss. Sorry. Ask Mr. Lysson at the front desk. He might have seen."

They hurried back through the office and stopped before the clerk's desk.

"The gentleman that was released here just now," gasped Octavia. "Benedict Wilberforce. Which way did he go?"

The clerk tilted his head down and glanced at her over his spectacles. "I have no idea. Nor do I care."

"Please—"

"Miss," he interrupted. "I am forced, under the remit of my job, to keep a watch on those that are *in* these offices. Once they leave I do not make it my business to carry on with that observation."

Octavia ran outside and looked both ways along the quayside. But the docks were so crowded she couldn't single anyone out in the teeming masses. Which way? She looked left, then right, unsure which direction to go in.

"Which way do you think?" she asked.

There was no answer. She looked around, but couldn't see Tweed anywhere. She darted back into the offices to find him sitting on one of the chairs, cross-legged, chatting to a dark-skinned man with a grey-white beard.

"Africa?" he was saying. "Really? Long trip to make. Must be glad to get back on dry land, yes? Lots of opportunities in London. What do you do?"

The man patted a folder at his feet. "I draw designs," he said in a deep voice. "Automata. Analytical Machines, that kind of thing."

"Fascinating. Can I see?"

"Tweed!" whispered Octavia fiercely.

"In a moment, Songbird. I'm talking to the nice gentleman."

Octavia watched, seething, as the man carefully lifted his folder and unhooked the leather straps, opening it up on his lap. Inside were sketches so beautiful that for a brief moment Octavia forgot her impatience.

"Sir, these are magnificent," said Tweed in awe.

"Thank you. A pity I will not get to show anyone else." He nodded at Lysson. "These people seem to think I do not have anything to offer the country. They want to ship me back."

"Nonsense," said Tweed. He stood up, straightened his jacket, and strode across to Lysson's desk. He leant over the rather amazed man, took a piece of paper, picked up a pencil, and scribbled a note, signing it with a flourish. He held it in front of Lysson's face.

"That man is a genius," he said, pointing over his shoulder. "And I wish to sponsor his application. Understand?"

Lysson just sighed, picked up a stamp, and slammed it down on some papers, handing them to Tweed. "Be my guest. I was probably going to let him in anyway."

This deflated Tweed a bit. "Oh. Well . . . Good."

He scribbled something down on the paper he had waved in front of Lysson and handed all the papers to the elderly man.

"My address. Come see me and I'll try to get you work. If I'm not there, tell my father I sent you and show him your designs. He'll know what to do."

The old man was grinning from ear to ear. "My boy. Thank you."

Tweed sat down next to him and crossed his legs. "Don't mention it. Now, tell me, did you happen to see which direction the man with the yellow scarf went?"

"He went right. And I would have told you that even if you hadn't got me into the country."

"Oh, I know. But that's not why I did it." He stood up. "Good day. And I'll see you soon?"

"You will."

Tweed turned and grinned at Octavia. "He went right."

"I heard," she said, hurrying outside and moving along the quayside. Tweed caught up with her and she threw him a glare.

"Was all that necessary?"

"Did you *see* those drawings? The man will make a fortune here. I reckon Ada Lovelace will snap him up to design her machines."

"And are you really going to get him a job?"

"I'm going to try my hardest," said Tweed, craning his neck to try to see above the crowds.

Octavia did the same but it was hopeless. The glowglobes that were strung along the quayside were smeared with coal dust and dirt, the light they gave off utterly useless unless someone was standing directly beneath them. She looked around in frustration, then hurried across to one of the automatons offloading crates from a nearby ship. Its brass body was dull and scratched. There were even barnacles encrusted onto its back. Octavia frowned. That wasn't very charitable. The owner should be reported for such treatment.

"Put that down, please," she said.

The automaton hesitated. The light of the trapped soul flickered briefly, dimming then growing stronger again. The construct put the crate down.

"Now, grip me gently and lift me above the crowds."

The automaton leaned forward and took Octavia by the waist, effortlessly lifting her up so she could see right along the docks. She squinted, trying to catch the slightest glimpse of a richly-dressed man and his yellow scarf.

"Anything?" called Tweed.

"No—*wait*!"

There. A flash of color, nothing more, as it passed beneath a glowglobe. She quickly tapped the automaton on the arm. "Put me down."

The automaton gently lowered her to the wet stone of the quayside.

"Thank you."

The automaton bowed and returned to its work. Octavia sprinted off through the crowds, Tweed following close behind.

CHAPTER FOUR

Tweed got his first good look at their prey as he left the Royal
Albert Docks and waved down a cab pulled by a battered and
dented automaton. Wilberforce really *was* immaculately dressed, just
as the harbormaster had said. He wore brown trousers with a crease
down the center so sharp it looked like it could cut wood, shiny black
shoes, a cream-colored shirt and a dark green tie kept in place with
a pin that gleamed in the light of the automaton's æther cage. The
yellow silk scarf was looped neatly around his neck, and to complete
the ensemble, he wore a tan overcoat that he had somehow managed
to keep clean of mud and slush.

The man himself looked to be in his late thirties. His dark hair
was cut short and combed in a side parting. His skin was dark, but
not as dark as the man he had just met at the custom's offices. More
toffee-colored.

Octavia hailed their own cab. "Follow them," she said to the
automaton as they climbed inside.

The snow started to fall again as they made their way through
the early-morning streets, big fat flakes that drifted in the cold wind,
piling up in gentle mounds on every available surface. The automaton pulling their cab started to steam gently as the snow melted
against the heat of his metal casing.

They passed the Victoria Docks, the Eastern Railway, then moved
along East India Dock Road. They even passed Isambard Wharf,
where he and Octavia had first met, fleeing from their attackers in
the middle of the night.

Tweed smiled at the memory, remembering how he found Octavia
rather annoying at first. Her bossiness, her refusal to acknowledge the

genius of his ideas and plans. This was something she was still guilty of, but he had gotten used to it by now. Had even come to enjoy the friendly arguments they had.

What he *didn't* enjoy, and what he seemed to have no control over, was the fact that lately he'd found himself trying to come up with even better ideas, almost as if he was trying to win her approval.

It *wasn't* that. Definitely not. But to an outside eye that's what it would look like.

But it wasn't that.

Definitely wasn't that.

They moved onto Narrow Street, following the road until it entered Shadwell and a cramped collection of docks and warehouses cradled in the downward curve of the Thames. The damp, dark area was bordered by Wapping Street to the south and Ratcliff Highway to the north.

They moved around these narrow streets for what seemed like ages until Tweed realized Wilberforce was trying to make sure he wasn't being followed. Tweed didn't think they'd been spotted. Wilberforce would be moving a lot faster if that were the case. No, this was more of a habitual path, something he had done before, and something he would do again. The steadiness of the pace, the unhesitating turning of corners told Tweed that.

It also told him something about the man himself. He liked routine. He was careful, but his habits betrayed this caution. Made it pointless.

The snow fell thicker, white flakes against a black sky. The weather muffled London, softening sounds, sights becoming blurred around the edges as the snow floated heavily to the ground.

After a few more turns, they left the docks behind altogether, heading northeast into the Strand and then into Piccadilly.

Tweed frowned as they passed the mansions and huge houses of the rich, wondering exactly where they were going. The city would be waking up soon, and he was hoping they would be off the streets by then. Traffic was light at the moment, but in an hour it was going to be impossible to keep track of their man. It was hard enough now, with the snow falling heavier and heavier. It was only the light of the automaton's æther cage that enabled them to keep on Wilberforce's tail.

They entered Kensington, and turned onto Cromwell Road. The street globes powered by the Tesla Tower looming above lit the area with the glow of sodium bulbs. The snow drifted through their orange halos, appearing from the darkness and sinking into shadow once again.

In the distance, Tweed could see the massive front of the Natural History Museum, it's terra cotta brickwork illuminated by hidden lights, the two massive spires that flanked the front steps bright against the ink black sky.

Wilberforce's hansom cab slowed down some distance from the museum. Octavia quickly leaned forward.

"Stop here," she said, and their own cab slowed to a halt. She slotted money into the automaton's head and hopped out. Tweed followed, his feet making *crump crump* sounds in the freshly fallen snow. He shivered and clapped his gloved hands together, then winced apologetically at the noise as Octavia whirled around and glared at him.

"Sorry," he whispered.

The cab turned around and headed back the way they'd come. Tweed and Octavia ducked into a recessed doorway and watched as Wilberforce headed straight toward the museum.

"What's he up to?" said Tweed. "The museum won't even be open at this time."

They hurried along the street and crouched down behind a low wall that flanked the museum steps. They peered over the top, just in time to see Wilberforce moving stealthily along the side of the building. They waited until he had vanished from view, then followed him along the wall to the rear of the museum.

At the back was a huge garden dotted with sheds, huts, and rundown workshops. Wilberforce ducked inside one of the smaller huts. Tweed and Octavia moved carefully forward, peering through the grimy window.

The hut was empty.

Tweed straightened up and yanked the door open. The room was about five meters square, empty of any kind of furnishings, and more importantly, empty of Benedict Wilberforce.

"Check for hidden doors," said Octavia.

Tweed pointed at the floor where a semicircle of scuffed flooring was clearly visible, as if something had been moved repeatedly across the wooden planks. "Way ahead of you, Songbird. One point to me."

Tweed quickly searched for the catch to open the hidden door, but it was Octavia who found it.

"And one point to me," she said, as a narrow portion of wall swung toward them.

The hidden door was part of a false wall that hid a flight of well-lit stairs leading down into the ground.

"Secret tunnels," grumbled Tweed. "Why'd it have to be secret tunnels?"

"Look on the bright side," said Octavia, elbowing him out of the way. "At least it's not dark."

She was right. The steps and the tunnel itself were well looked after, swept clean and lit with Tesla glowglobes. He counted the stairs as they descended. Seventy-five exactly. What was that? About fifty feet underground? Sixty?

The stairs ended at a door. Octavia pushed it gently open and they peered into the room beyond.

Except it wasn't a room. It was some kind of massive factory space buried deep beneath the ground. It was easily a hundred meters long, the arched ceiling supported by thick iron struts high above their heads.

The factory floor was covered with machines. Some were half-completed, their sides pulled off to reveal vacuum tubes and wiring. Some were in the first stages of construction, just massive skeletal structures, steel and wooden frames waiting to be filled. Workbenches surrounded the walls, covered with tools, gears, clocks, glass beakers filled with strange liquids, and disassembled automatons. One table was covered with the heads of the constructs, each one a different design, some fierce and scowling, others smiling and happy.

The walls were painted black, and every available inch was covered with chalk drawings: plans and equations, designs for more machines, complex calculations that Tweed couldn't make the slightest sense of.

They entered the workshop, hiding behind the machines and crates that littered the floor. Tweed could hear a loud buzzing sound, and as they moved deeper into the room, it built up into a high-pitched whine.

A moment later there was a bright flash of blue-white light and the horrendously loud crack and hum of electricity discharging. Tweed carefully peered around a crate.

Lightning crawled and spat across the metal roof beams high above. It burst and sparked, arcing downward and grounding itself in a circle of metal plates on the floor to create a lethal cage of electricity.

After about thirty seconds, the lightning flickered and died. Tweed blinked away the afterimages that bloomed in his vision, and when he could see properly again he noticed Wilberforce standing just outside the metal plates, looking around the workshop with interest.

"Hello?" called Wilberforce.

Octavia looked at Tweed, her eyes wide. He shook his head. He didn't think Wilberforce was calling to them. Something else was going on here.

"Nehi and I had a bet," said a second voice.

Wilberforce spun around. Emerging from the shadows was a tall figure. He wore a dark purple suit and was carrying a cane with a snake head handle. He was also wearing a fedora, pulled low over his eyes.

The man pointed his cane at Wilberforce. "You made me lose. And now Nehi will make me perform some tiresome forfeit."

"And what, pray tell, was the bet?" asked Wilberforce.

"She said your lot would send someone. I said you wouldn't even know we had entered London."

"Nehi always was the more intelligent twin," said Wilberforce.

The man shrugged. "Perhaps." He took his fedora from his head, revealing an angled face the same caramel color as Wilberforce. He placed the hat on the top of a machine. "She certainly didn't think it would be you who came." He brushed invisible dust from his suit. "But it matters not. You are too late, Molock. As always."

"I get a chance to speak to you, Sekhem, so I do not deem myself too late." Wilberforce (or rather, Molock? Was Benedict Wilberforce a false name?) took a step closer to the one he called Sekhem. "Please . . . for the sake of our people, do not continue on this path. It will only lead to death."

The man called Sekhem waved his hand irritably. "Death is the whole point, Molock. It will soon be time for us to emerge from the shadows and take what is rightfully ours."

"We will not allow it. We will stop you."

"And who are you to allow *anything*?" snarled Sekhem. "We are enemies, Molock. You made us so when you chose to side against our cause. You are a traitor to your people."

"It was you and Nehi who staged a coup against *me*," said Molock mildly. "Some would say *you* are the traitors."

"We did what had to be done. We needed drastic action to save our people."

"We were not just sitting idly around," said Molock, and Tweed saw that he was getting annoyed. "We had a plan."

"A plan! *What* plan? To skulk around until you worked up enough courage to politely ask them to stop? If you thought that would work then it just confirms we did the right thing."

Sekhem pointed his walking stick at Molock. There was a quiet *snick* sound and the wood separated into two halves that shot out to either side, revealing a gleaming steel blade.

"Today you die."

Sekhem lunged forward, swinging the sword in a backhand slice that was aimed at Molock's neck. Molock jerked back, the tip of the blade connecting with a shirt button, sending it spinning into the air. Sekhem swung the sword again, but Molock stepped into his reach and smacked his forearm into Sekhem's wrist, stopping the sword in mid-movement. At the same time, Molock balled his left fist and hit Sekhem hard in the face.

Sekhem staggered back, eyes wide with surprise. Then he rolled his shoulders, swinging the thin sword in complex patterns through the air.

"You're a lot faster than the last time we met," he said.

Molock shrugged. "That's all down to you. Losing the crown made me realize I had to train myself." He slid his jacket off and took up a defensive stance, weight balanced evenly between both legs.

Sekhem came straight at him. Tweed wasn't sure if it was a feint, something to throw Molock off guard, because, really, who just ran at you with a sword? Where was the finesse? The skill?

But then a moment later Tweed saw the finesse. *And* the skill. Plus a lot more that he couldn't explain.

Molock dodged the blade, spinning away from it and lashing out with stiff fingers. They caught Sekhem in the throat, and Tweed thought that was it. Fight over. A blow as hard as that, with fingers stiffened in such a way, it should have crushed the man's larynx. But Sekhem just shrugged it off and attacked.

Molock used his forearms to deflect the blows, somehow managing to turn the sharpened edge of the weapon away each time it connected, rolling his arm so that the sword slid harmlessly aside.

As Octavia and Tweed watched, the pace of the fight picked up, the two men moving with almost inhuman speed, their attacks and defenses so effortless, so smooth, Tweed felt like he was watching a graceful dance. Neither of the fighters could land a wounding blow, but they kept trying until their arms were a blur: attack, block, spin, duck, attack, deflect. On and on until Tweed actually grew bored.

"This is ridiculous," he said, pulling out his Tesla gun.

"Wait," whispered Octavia fiercely. "What are you doing?"

"I'm not waiting here all night for those two to finish. I'm tired."

Tweed stepped out from behind their cover. He raised the gun and struck the kind of heroic pose Atticus Pope always pulled on the covers of his books.

After a few seconds he realized he was still standing in the shadows and no one could see him. He thought he heard Octavia sniggering at him, but he couldn't be sure.

He muttered under his breath and walked into the light.

"Excuse me," he said.

Sekhem and Molock whirled around to face him. When they did so, Tweed actually backed up a step. It was surely a trick of the light but for a tiny moment there the two men's eyes seemed to glow yellow.

Tweed waved the gun in the air. "Stop this now. It's all very fascinating, and I'm sure if you did your little dance in Piccadilly Circus

you could charge a few crowns for the show, but it's been a long night and I really, really want to go to bed. I lit the fire before I came out," he explained. "By now my room will be the perfect temperature for a sweet, dreamless sleep."

The one called Molock looked at him as if he were insane. "I . . ." He paused, then shook his head as if trying to dislodge something. "*What?*"

But Sekhem wasn't so easily distracted. He took advantage of Tweed's interruption and swung out with the sword.

"Look out!" screamed Octavia from where she was watching behind the crate.

Molock spun and dropped, his arm coming up to block the blow. Sekhem wasn't expecting any kind of resistance, so his grip on the cane was loose. The blade fell from his hand and Molock scooped it up in midair, swinging it around in one smooth movement. The blade caught Sekhem on the hand, slicing neatly through two of his fingers.

A ring slid from one of the severed digits as they fell, skittering across the floor. Molock queasily watched it roll away, and as he did so Sekhem pulled a knife from his belt and lunged forward.

A burst of lighting arced over Tweed's shoulder, only inches from his ear. It hit Sekhem in the chest, sending him spinning backward through the air. The lighting also arced across to Molock. He cried out and jerked to the side. Tweed saw something fly from his coat pocket. It hit the electricity and caught fire, then fluttered to the ground. Sekhem landed heavily, a wisp of smoke rising into the air from his unmoving body.

Octavia swung the gun around to Molock, but he was already moving, darting behind a half-completed Difference Engine.

"Wait!" called Octavia. "I'm not going to hurt you. I'm just looking for my mother!"

No answer. Tweed indicated for Octavia to go around one side of the computer and he'd take the other.

They moved quietly, Tesla guns at the ready. Tweed could feel the engraved patterns of the brass case rubbing against his back as he slid around the machine. Then he whirled around and pointed the gun.

There was a blur of movement, and something shot up past his face. Tweed staggered back and saw Molock hanging onto one of the roof supports fifty feet above them. He flipped himself over and stood up effortlessly, then ran along the thin iron beams, leaping between them as if he had spent his whole life in the circus.

"He's going for the door!" shouted Octavia.

Tweed swore and ran back the way they'd come, keeping one eye on the roof. But he could see they had no chance. Molock was too far ahead.

The man reached the far wall and then did something astounding. He simply stepped off the strut and dropped through the air. Tweed watched in amazement as Molock landed lightly in a crouch, then stood smoothly and ran straight through the door, slamming it shut behind him.

Tweed was right on his heels. He heard something smack up against the door. He tried to pull it open but it was wedged shut. Octavia joined him and they braced themselves against the wall and pulled. The door shifted slightly but whatever was used on the other side was pulling against the wall.

"Stand back," said Octavia.

Tweed moved back as she leveled her gun and fired. The door burst from its hinges, flying back into the stairwell. Before the smoke had even cleared Octavia was sprinting through the opening, retracing their steps back outside.

Tweed followed after, arriving in the freezing cold to find Octavia standing in the snow looking around in frustration.

"He's gone!" she shouted. She moved one way, then spun around and moved in another, searching the snow for footprints.

There were none.

Tweed knew how upset she would be. She'd waited months for some kind of sign, some kind of lead on the disappearance of her mother. And they'd just let it slip right out of their hands.

"Come on," he said gently. "Let's look around downstairs. Maybe we'll find something on Sekhem's body that can help us."

He thought she was going to argue. She looked around the cluttered garden in frustration, and then her shoulders slumped and she turned back toward the shed.

They hurried down into the factory. The warehouse space receded away from them, huge, filled with clutter. It would take them ages to search all this for clues.

First things first, though. A search of Sekhem's pockets. Tweed's eyes moved to where the man had landed after the electricity hit him—

—Tweed froze. The space on the floor where Sekhem had landed was empty. Tweed carefully put his back up against a machine. Where was he? Was he watching them right now, getting ready to attack?

"What are you doing?" asked Octavia.

"Sekhem is gone."

Octavia frowned. "What do you mean gone?" She leaned to the side and peered around his shoulder. She leaned back again.

"Sekhem is gone," she said, as if stating a new and surprising fact. "Where's he gone?"

Tweed leaned in and beckoned Octavia closer. She did so, her eyes wide.

"I have no idea," he said softly.

Octavia punched him in the arm, then straightened up to look carefully around the factory. Tweed did the same, checking the ceiling struts as well.

There was no sign of Sekhem anywhere.

"Watch my back," said Tweed, moving out from behind cover. He waited, but there was no attack, no sword blade whistling through the air to slice through his neck. Nothing.

He headed to where Sekhem had fallen, inside the circle of metal plates. There was blood on the floor, and a wooden chair that was lying on its side. But there was no body. Tweed turned in a circle, surveying the space around him. There was nowhere to hide.

He paused. There was something on the ground, a singed piece of card. He remembered seeing something falling from Molock's pocket when Octavia fired her Tesla gun at them. He picked it up. There was elaborate writing on the card, but it didn't make much sense seeing as half of the card had been burnt away by Octavia's gun.

> . . . *ate:*
> . . . *uary.*
> . . . *ture:*
> . . . *m.*

Tweed tucked it into his pocket. He'd puzzle out its meaning later. He started walking back toward Octavia, kicking something as he did so. It skittered away from him, but he followed it and picked it up.

Sekhem's ring. The one that fell from his severed finger. Tweed searched around, but couldn't see any sign of the fingers themselves.

There was a sudden hum building up in the air. Tweed's teeth tingled. He looked up then darted out of the circle of metal plates.

Just in time. He was only three paces away when the lightning crackled and thrummed, arcing down from the roof into the plates, filling the vast room with brilliant light.

Tweed joined Octavia and showed her the ring. There was a symbol on the heavy face.

It was a triangle with some sort of geometric shape inside it. It looked . . .

"Egyptian," said Octavia. "That looks Egyptian."

"Any idea what it means?"

"None."

"Then we need to find out. It's the best clue we have."

CHAPTER FIVE

Octavia woke up and frowned at the ceiling.

Why was she awake? She didn't feel like she had slept at all. Her eyes felt gritty, her mind fuddled and slow.

She rolled over to check the clock on her wall. It was only eight thirty. She smiled, feeling the glorious surge of warmth and comfort that came from knowing she still had another hour or so in bed. She snuggled deeper beneath the goose down duvet.

There was a heavy knock at the door.

Maybe if I just ignore it they'll go away. She closed her eyes tightly, but the knocking came again, more insistent this time. She heard the heavy clumping of Manners, the family automaton, moving across the wooden floor downstairs. There was a pause, then the footsteps started up again, the tread becoming muted as they climbed the carpeted stairs.

Octavia muttered a very rude word under her breath. Sleep was her only vice. She liked sleep. No, she *loved* sleep. Sleep was *good*. Sleep was . . . relaxing. It soothed her spirit. Those moments when she was drifting off to sleep, the fire banked, coals red and glowing, the snow piling up against her window, were moments of pure and utter peace for her. Likewise, those moments just after waking, when the troubles of the world hadn't intruded into her mind, when she could simply . . . float on her dreams for a while longer.

And now someone was trying to take that away from her.

Manners knocked on the door.

"Miss Octavia."

Octavia shuddered. Her father had once again upgraded their

automaton, transferring the soul of Manners into a new housing, one that actually had the capabilities of speech. Most people didn't like it, but they were still upgrading their constructs. Had to keep up with the neighbors, after all.

"What?" she snapped.

"Two gentlemen require your presence at the door."

"Tell them to go away."

"I did warn them, Miss Octavia. I told them that you did not like to be disturbed when you are resting."

"And what did they say?"

"They said to tell you it is Ministry business."

Octavia frowned. Ministry business? Why on earth would the Ministry be contacting her?

The Ministry was a shadowy, secret organization, the real power behind the government. Had been for over five hundred years, apparently. With the events of last year, the Queen herself had ordered a clean up of the secretive department, but Octavia didn't think she'd have much luck with that. The Ministry was far too large, far too . . . well, *secret*, really. They wouldn't give up their independence. They might pretend to, but they wouldn't really.

Octavia couldn't help feel a flutter of fear at the thought of Ministry agents at her door. Nobody was supposed to know that she and Tweed worked for the Queen. Chase and Temple did, obviously, but they weren't Ministry. They were secret service, and were under very strict instructions not to tell anyone.

Something to do with Barnaby, then? Tweed's father. *Adopted* father, Octavia corrected. Seeing as Tweed was grown in a lab, he didn't really have a father.

"Tell them I'll be down in a minute. I'm just getting dressed."

"Of course, Miss Octavia."

The footsteps moved back down the stairs. Octavia sighed. There was nothing else for it. She got out of bed and pulled on her trousers and shirt, then slipped her waistcoat and heavy jacket over the top. She tied her black hair up at the back, pinned it in place, then hesitated at her desk. Should she take her Tesla gun? No, no point. She'd probably be searched, and there was no guarantee it would be given back to her.

Octavia slipped into the bathroom and gave herself a quick wash. She had bathed when she came in earlier this morning, but the cold water refreshed her slightly.

She headed downstairs to find two men in identical black suits and black overcoats standing in her hallway. They hadn't even bothered to take the hats from their heads—hats, she noted, that were similar in style to the fedora Sekhem had worn yesterday. *Disrespectful buggers.*

"Yes?" she said.

One of the Ministry agents, a tall man who was so thin his skull seemed to push against his skin, turned to her. "You are to accompany us, Miss Nightingale."

"Oh? And why is that?"

The man frowned. "We are not accustomed to explaining ourselves," he said softly. "Nor do we intend to start now. You are to come with us."

Octavia's eyes flickered between the two men. The second man was taller than the first. He hadn't said a word, just stared at her with cold grey eyes. She didn't like this. Not a bit. Ministry officials turning up on your doorstep was never good news. She'd read the reports at *The Times.* About people going missing in the middle of the night.

She turned to Manners. "Manners, tell my father I've been called in to the Ministry. Also, alert my editor at *The Times*, will you?"

Manners tilted his head slightly. His æther cage, where the

human soul was kept, flared, then dimmed. "Message sent via Tesla Tower to *The Times's* Babbage machine, Miss Octavia."

Octavia smiled. Instant backup plan. Two people who would know where she was going. Technology really was quite handy. She notched her grin a bit wider and turned to the Ministry agents.

"Let's get going then, shall we?" she said cheerfully. "Mustn't dilly-dally."

If the Ministry agents were at all irritated with her telling others where she was going, they didn't show it. They simply turned on their heels and led the way outside. Octavia followed, her grin falling away, shivering from more than the thick, wet flakes of snow that were falling to the ground. A Ministry Teslacoach was parked right outside her house. It was one of the new, sleek coaches powered by Tesla Turbines. The last time Octavia had been this close to one, she had been leading it on a chase through the streets of London, and Ministry agents had been inside shooting at her. For all she knew, it could have been these two very agents who had been involved in that chase.

Octavia reluctantly climbed into the back seat of the Teslacoach. The door was slammed shut and the two agents removed their hats and climbed into the front. Octavia stared nervously at the backs of their heads as they drove. Their haircuts were identical, parted in the middle and slicked down with oil.

The coach drove through the bustling city. Even the snow couldn't keep the streets of London quiet. Pedestrians still crowded the packed pavements, pickpockets still went about their work although their haul would be diminished, their fingers slow and clumsy in the cold air. They passed costermongers selling hot chestnuts, coffee and tea, or piping hot potatoes that sent steam up into the grey sky. Her stomach rumbled in jealous protest. She hadn't eaten since . . . when *was* the last time she'd eaten? Certainly not since yesterday evening.

After half an hour, the Teslacoach pulled to a stop in front of the Ministry buildings. The last time Octavia was here there had been a rather large hole in the front of the building, a hole she, Jenny, and Carter Flair had created while trying to rescue Tweed from the Ministry prisons.

The damage had all been repaired. The two Ministry officials led Octavia up the steps and through the door, then bent over to let a Babbage automaton scan their eyes. They forced Octavia to do the same. A bright red light flashed across her vision as she put her eye to the aperture. Then she had to sign in and was given a badge to wear.

"Don't take this off," said the first agent.

"Seriously," said the second. "Don't. If you're spotted inside the Ministry without identification, you will be shot on sight."

Wonderful, thought Octavia.

The agents led her deep into the bowels of the Ministry, down long, boring corridors, through open-plan offices filled with workers collating and sending out intelligence reports and instructions. They finally stopped before an elevator that took them down to the lower levels, deep beneath the ground. Octavia felt her first real stab of fear at this. The prisons were in the lower levels. Had they found out about her involvement in the attack last year?

"Where are you taking me?" she asked.

They didn't answer. The elevator doors slid open and they stepped out into a dull corridor.

"Excuse me," said Octavia, more forcefully this time. "I demand to know where I'm being taken."

One of the Ministry goons stopped before a door and pushed it open. Octavia leaned nervously forward, peering inside. It was just a room. With a table and three chairs in it.

"Sit down."

Octavia didn't have a choice. She entered and sat down behind the table. It was metal, the surface scratched and stained. The two agents sat down opposite her. One of them dropped a thin cardboard folder onto the desk. Octavia couldn't see what was in it.

"Why am I here?" she asked.

"You know why."

"No," said Octavia patiently. "I don't. Otherwise I wouldn't have asked."

The two agents sat and stared at her. It made Octavia tremendously uncomfortable, but she'd be damned if she would show them that. Instead, she just stared back, waiting for them to make the first move.

"Why don't you tell us where you were last night?" said the first agent, the one with the thin face.

Last night? Octavia thought furiously. Was this about the bank robberies? It couldn't be, surely. That kind of thing wouldn't involve the Ministry. And even if it was about the robberies, why all this secretive stuff? They should be getting medals.

No, it couldn't be that.

Which only left Benedict Wilberforce. Or rather, *Molock*. That was his real name after all.

She wasn't sure how to play this. As far as she was aware, they hadn't done anything illegal. All they had done was follow the man to a warehouse. Obviously, something else was going on here. The two men—Sekhem and Molock—had certainly known each other, but what did that have to do with her? Had they trespassed where they shouldn't have? Was Molock part of the Ministry? Was *Sekhem* part of the Ministry? She had no idea.

"Why don't I refresh your memory?" said the thin man.

He opened the folder and spread a number of photographs out on the table. One showed Octavia and Tweed approaching the museum. Another showed them moving along the side wall, and another showed them entering the shed that led down into the factory.

Octavia looked up at the agents. "Yes?"

"What were you doing there?"

"Following someone."

"Who?"

Octavia hesitated, then decided she might as well tell the truth. Or some of it, at least. "A man called Benedict Wilberforce. I'm doing an investigative piece for *The Times*, and have had his name flagged at the docks. He entered the country last night and my contact got in touch to let me know. We followed him."

The thin-faced man leaned forward. "And what did you witness?"

"He . . . confronted another man. Someone who was waiting there. Someone called Sekhem. They fought each other, but Tweed and I . . . we were spotted. So they fled."

The second man stared at her for a few moments longer, then leaned back. Then the first man pulled out more photographs.

"So when did you and your friend do this?"

The photographs were of men and woman, all of them dead. They lay sprawled on the ground with horrendous cuts and slashes to their bodies. Octavia's stomach turned. She swallowed the bile rising in her throat and averted her eyes.

"I've never seen these people before. Who are they?"

"Guards," said the second agent.

"Posted around the museum," said the first.

Octavia looked at the photographs again. "I didn't see any guards."

"You're not supposed to. They're Ministry trained. The best."

"They're obviously not the best," said Octavia, gesturing to the photographs. "Or they'd still be alive."

"What we want to know," said the second agent, "is how you spotted them. How you surprised them."

"We had nothing to do with that!" she protested. "I *told* you. We followed someone to the museum, we were spotted, they fled. End of story."

The Ministry goons said nothing, just kept on staring at her. Octavia frowned and sat back in her chair. Realization was dawning. These agents had no idea what had happened last night. They were fishing, hoping she would have some nugget of information that would help explain whatever went on.

"It's rather obvious to me that the first man, this . . . Sekhem, is the person who killed your guards. He was waiting inside. He fought Molock with a sword hidden in a cane. Those injuries look like sword wounds to me."

"Strange thing is, we've no evidence of this mysterious Sekhem. There's nothing on our security cameras."

Octavia looked again at the photographs, at the horrific wounds. Those poor people. So much blood . . .

"Then he's very good," she said.

"Or you're lying."

"Why on earth would I want to slaughter your guards?" Octavia shouted, exasperated. Then she frowned. "Why were Ministry guards posted around the Museum of Natural History anyway? That's not under your remit."

"And what do you know of our remit, girl?" said the thin-faced man.

Octavia bristled. Something about the way he said "girl" irritated her vastly. She was sick of this. "How dare you. When I was sixteen years old I worked for *The Times* as a researcher. I'm now seventeen and am a fully paid reporter for the newspaper. I know much more than you seem to give me credit for, and I've achieved far more than you ever had by my age—probably more than you ever *will*. What are you? A bully in black, that's all. You don't know what happened last night. That's obvious. You have no evidence against me. Nothing that links me to these murders. If you have footage of myself and Tweed going in, then you obviously have it of the man we were following. Plus you must have footage of us leaving not twenty minutes later. Not anywhere near time enough to dispatch your precious guards."

Octavia broke off, suddenly realizing she was probably making a seriously bad move here. Yes, they didn't have evidence, but they could still make her life very difficult. She forced herself to calm down.

"And I'll remind you both that *The Times* knows I'm here, and will very likely be following up on my detention. So either charge me or let me go."

The two agents didn't get a chance to respond to this, because at that moment the door opened and a tall man in his late fifties entered, greying hair swept back from his face, beard neatly trimmed.

Octavia sagged, feeling an intense rush of relief when she saw him. Barnaby!

His eyes flicked over her and he focused his attention on the two agents.

"Why wasn't I told about this interview?"

The thin-faced man stood up. "We didn't think it concerned you. *Sir*."

Something about the way he said "sir" told Octavia he didn't have much respect for Barnaby.

Barnaby Tweed's brow came together. "Didn't think it *concerned* me? I'm the head of the Ministry!" he thundered. "Appointed by Her Majesty the Queen. Everything that happens here concerns me. Do you understand?"

The agents said nothing.

"I said *do you understand?*"

The thin-faced man paused, then said, "Understood."

"Good. You," said Barnaby, finally looking directly at Octavia. "Leave."

The agent tried to protest. "She was at the museum—"

"I know where she was, you cretin. I also know that she had nothing to do with any of this. Something you would know as well if you had two brain cells to rub together. You should be out finding the real culprit. Not wasting time interviewing teenagers. "Go," he said, jerking his head.

Octavia quickly stood and scurried out of the office before anyone had a chance to change their minds. She hurried through the winding corridors, handing her badge in at the door and practically running outside. She paused on the stairs and took a deep breath of the cold air. She hated that place.

"Did you confess?"

Octavia turned around to find Tweed lounging against the wall. "Confess to what?"

"To all your dastardly deeds." He pointed at her. "Don't think I don't know what you get up to."

"Oh, *please*. You *wish* you knew what I got up to."

Tweed pushed himself away from the wall with his shoulders. He strolled over to join her. "Barnaby get you out?"

Octavia nodded. "Were you taken in as well?"

"Early on this morning. I think they came for you after they let me go."

"So what's going on?" Octavia asked. "Why are the Ministry interested in this?"

"I've no idea. I couldn't get Barnaby alone to talk to him. But I think we're going to find out soon enough. We've been summoned to Ravenstone Manor."

"When?"

Tweed reached into his longcoat and pulled out his fob watch. He flicked open the lid. "About an hour ago."

They jounced along the busy road in Tweed's steamcoach. He'd had it fixed up a bit since Octavia had every-so-slightly damaged it when trying to evade the Ministry, but it was still a pile of rubbish. The smoke it spewed into the air was dirty grey and stank of burning metal. The rear space, where he and Barnaby had once prepared for their fake séances, was even more cluttered now that they had stopped conning the rich and gone legitimate. Tweed now used it to refine and build more of his little inventions. For instance, he'd made his spiders—clockwork arachnids used to spy on people—even smaller, enabling them to be hidden in even more obscure locations.

"I've been thinking," said Octavia.

"Oh oh," said Tweed. "You should be careful with that. Everyone knows women shouldn't think. Overheats their delicate brains."

"Most amusing. I've been thinking about that symbol on the ring. It's definitely hieroglyphics, agreed? So we should go to the British Museum and speak to one of their experts."

Tweed didn't answer. She glanced over and saw him frowning through the dirty glass window at the street ahead.

"Is there a particular reason you're not responding?"

Still nothing.

"Have you lost the ability to talk? Are you thinking very hard? Are you contemplating my genius? Do you have a stomach ailment? Stop me when I'm close."

"You ruined my fun," said Tweed sourly.

"What fun? What are you talking about?" He didn't say anything more, so Octavia sighed and stared out the window, watching the snow-covered hansom cabs, the streets covered with wet mud and slush, the people hunched away in their coats, faces cut in half by voluminous scarves. She frowned. "Where are we? This isn't the way to Ravenstone."

"I know that."

Tweed turned the steamcoach to the left and stopped it up against the pavement. Octavia peered out of the window and saw the massive Greek pillared frontage of the British Museum.

"The museum?"

"Yes," said Tweed. "To speak to the head of Egyptology. I was going to surprise you with my cleverness, but you had to go and think for yourself."

Octavia smiled and patted his arm. "Don't worry, Tweed, I'm *always* surprised when you show cleverness."

"Ho ho," muttered Tweed. "Hear that? That's me laughing at your wit." He shook his head sadly. "You really should learn to accept the fact that I'm the thinker in this partnership."

He climbed out of the steamcoach, pulling his scarf over his mouth. Octavia followed and they hurried across the road.

"So if you're the thinker, what am I?" asked Octavia as they jogged up the stairs and moved between the massive pillars, heading in through the wide doors of the Museum.

"Not really sure yet," said Tweed, his voice muffled. "I mean, it's not as if you even make a good cup of tea."

Octavia punched him in the arm.

The office of the professor of Egyptology, a man called Cyril Bainbridge, was immaculately neat. Octavia could tell that Tweed didn't approve. He ran his finger over the mantelpiece and held it up before her eyes.

"Look," he said accusingly. "No dust."

"So?"

"So how can you call yourself a professor of Egyptology and work from an office like this? Where are the papyrus fragments he's translating? Where are the dusty books?" He waved his hand at the wall in disgust. "Not even a sarcophagus! Unacceptable. The man's obviously a fraud."

"Or just someone who likes things neat and tidy."

Octavia turned. A small man—barely five foot three—was standing in the doorway.

Tweed took one look at him and blurted out, "Goodness, you're short!"

A pained look flashed across the man's face. He smoothed down his grey hair and sat down at his desk. Octavia noted the chair was specially raised.

"Yes, I am. Sorry about that."

"Oh, no need to apologize," said Tweed airily. "It's not your fault."

"First, let me apologize on my colleague's behalf," said Octavia, glaring at Tweed. "He has an unfortunate tendency to speak without thinking. You *are* Professor Bainbridge?" said Octavia.

"Indeed." He smiled. "And no need to apologize. I'm used to it. Now, the curator said you wanted help with something?"

Octavia nudged Tweed.

"Oh. Yes." He fished around in his pocket and handed over the ring.

"We were wondering if you could tell us what the symbols on this mean."

Bainbridge plucked a pair of spectacles from his front pocket and tilted the ring, studying it in the grey light that filtered through the window. He frowned. "Where did you get this?"

"We found it."

"You found it?" He looked at them suspiciously. "Do you know Dr. Stackpole?"

Octavia shook her head. "No. Who's he?"

"Dr. Stackpole is an archeologist. Quite well thought of. At least, he used to be. He returned from Egypt recently with some rather . . . controversial claims and items. He came to me to have them authenticated."

"What are you saying?" cut in Tweed. "That he brought you a ring like this? Because we didn't steal it."

"My boy, I'm not saying that at all. No, he didn't bring me a ring like this. But he did bring me a drawing of this hieroglyph *on* the ring. He asked me if I'd ever seen it before."

"Had you?" asked Octavia.

Bainbridge shook his head. "No. Never. I got in touch with some of my contacts. In fact . . ." He looked at the clock. "I'm having a meeting here at two this afternoon with Dr. Stackpole and a translator. Either he's going to tell us what the symbol might mean, or . . ." He trailed off and looked briefly uncomfortable.

"Or?" prompted Tweed.

"Or if he thinks Dr. Stackpole forged it."

"Why would he do that?"

"To get attention, funding. He claims to have found some . . . ancient map. On papyrus or some such. He says it points to what he calls 'the find of the century.' But he needs help deciphering it."

"Have you seen this map?"

"Good lord, no. He nearly had a heart attack when I asked if I could have a look. He says he's sent it somewhere safe. So they can't get their hands on it."

"Who are *they*?" asked Octavia.

"No idea," said Bainbridge cheerfully. "He always was a bit paranoid."

"So you don't know anything about this find of his?"

"We know that it's in Egypt, which, I think you'll agree, is a rather safe bet. He's keeping his cards very close to his chest, I'm afraid."

"Would you mind at all if we came here at two? To ask your translator what it means?"

"Not at all. Always keen to encourage an interest in Egyptology." Bainbridge stood. "Would you like a tour of the museum? Be happy to oblige."

Octavia felt a stab of remorse. She'd love that. She'd always enjoyed the museum, coming here with her parents. And a behind the curtain tour would have been something special. But they didn't have time. "Unfortunately not," she said. "We have an appointment to keep. We can't put it off any longer."

"Much as we'd like to," muttered Tweed.

"Well," said Bainbridge. "Another time, perhaps. And I'll see you this afternoon."

Octavia smiled, then she and Tweed turned and left the office.

Time to face the music.

🙢🙠

"What part of 'keep out of trouble' didn't you understand?" shouted Chase.

They were back in the library at Ravenstone Lodge. Chase was pacing back and forth while Temple sat in a wing backed chair by the window, his hands steepled together.

"Just let them explain, Barrington," Temple said mildly.

"I wish they would!"

"If you'd shut up for two seconds we might get a chance!" snapped Tweed. "Because although you seem to think we all love the sound of your voice just as much as you do, I'm afraid we don't. It's quite grating. Nasal."

Octavia sighed. Temple smiled at her and rolled his eyes.

"Explain to me," said Chase. "Make me understand. Why were you following this Benedict Wilberforce?"

"Because he is involved in Octavia's mother's disappearance."

Chase looked at Octavia, a puzzled frown on his face. "When did your mother disappear?"

"Over a year ago," said Temple disapprovingly. "You should know this. It's in their files."

Chase waved him away. "And how do you know this Wilberforce is involved?"

"His name was listed as the person responsible for moving my mother from the Ministry prison."

"Why was she being kept there?" said Chase in astonishment.

"We think it's because she was investigating Lucien and the Tsar of Russia."

"So why did this Wilberforce take her out of the prison?"

"We don't know," said Octavia.

"Is he Ministry?"

"We don't think so. At least, we've not been able to find any record of him. He vanished after my mother was moved. I sent his name around the docks and left instructions that I was to be notified if he tried to enter the country again. Last night he did." She shrugged. "We followed him to the factory below the museum and witnessed him confronting another fellow—a person named Sekhem."

Temple put his tea down with a heavy clink. "Sekhem, you say?"

Octavia nodded.

"Can you describe him?" asked Temple urgently.

Octavia was rather surprised at his intensity. Temple was usually a very laid-back person. "Of course," she said. "We got a good look at him."

"Good." Temple exchanged a knowing look with Chase. "We'll get you to work with a sketch artist. We can get his face out to all the ports."

Octavia frowned. "All the ports? That's a bit much, isn't it? He hasn't done anything to warrant that kind of attention."

Temple stood up. "That factory—"

"Temple," said Chase. "They don't need to know."

"No, but they *deserve* to know. They're involved, however you may wish otherwise." Temple turned to Tweed and Nightingale. "That factory was Nikola Tesla's laboratory."

"Nikola Tesla?" Octavia looked at Tweed in amazement.

"Has he been kidnapped?" asked Tweed. "Is that why the Ministry is going so mental?"

"I wish he had been." Temple sighed. "Tesla was shot and killed there last night."

"Nikola Tesla?" said Tweed.

"Yes."

"He's dead?"

"I'm afraid so."

Octavia could barely believe it. Nikola Tesla was . . . he was the father of the modern age, even more so than Babbage or Lovelace. He was responsible for almost every technological advance the British Empire had enjoyed over the past few decades. It was his inventions that enabled them to move information wirelessly between computing devices, his Tesla Towers that supplied power to the country, his inventions that drove the new turbines.

"We didn't see a body," said Tweed.

"It was there. Shoved up against a wall. But I'm afraid it gets worse. You see, Tesla had been given new orders. To develop weapons to protect the country against invasion. With all the trouble from the Tsar, and the rumblings from Germany, it was thought wise for him to turn his thoughts to defense."

Chase turned away from the window. "He was developing various weapons. One of them was a machine that could cause earthquakes. Another was a death ray that could be built along the coast to shoot enemy airships out of the sky."

"How close was he to perfecting these weapons?" asked Tweed.

"He was in the prototype stage already," said Temple. "All Tesla's notes were taken. All his plans for these weapons."

"Do you think it's the Russians again? The Tsar trying for revenge?"

"We have no idea," said Chase.

"Can you think of anything else you might have seen?" pressed Temple. "Anything at all?"

Octavia glanced at Tweed and raised her eyebrows. He frowned, then headed over to the desk and sketched something on a piece of paper.

"We found this," he said, handing it to Temple. "It was on a ring. The one called Sekhem dropped it."

Octavia frowned, wondering why Tweed wasn't just giving Temple the actual ring. She was about to say something, but Tweed looked at her and shook his head slightly. She sighed and closed her mouth.

"Egyptian," said Temple, sounding surprised. He gave it to Chase, who inspected it with interest.

"Where is the ring now?" asked Chase.

"At my house. I didn't want to carry it around with me."

"Why would the Egyptians want Tesla dead?" asked Octavia.

"The same reason anyone would want him dead. To reduce the power of the British Empire," said Temple.

"There is someone else who knows about this symbol," said Octavia. "An archeologist called Stackpole. Apparently, he found it out in Egypt. He's been asking his colleagues at the museum to help him identify it."

"Interesting," said Temple. "We'll look into it."

"So what do you want us to do?" asked Octavia.

Chase looked at her in surprise. "*You*? What do you mean?"

"You're training us up. On the orders of the Queen. We can help."

Chase laughed. "No. I think not. Whatever Her Majesty has planned for you it does *not* involve working on Secret Service missions. You're both just children. What could you possibly do to help?"

"We saved the Queen. And the prince. And stopped a world war," said Tweed quietly.

Chase waved this away. "As I've said before, a fluke. You will both return to your homes. Your training is on hiatus until this is all sorted out."

"But Wilberforce is my only lead to finding my mother," protested Octavia.

"Bad luck. Tesla's plans are much more important. Your mother is not a mission parameter."

"A mission parameter?" said Tweed. "Do you even hear yourself speak? That's a human being you're talking about. A real person."

"I know," said Chase coldly. "But when weighed against the potential deaths of thousands should our enemies construct even one of those weapons, a single person just isn't that important."

"You can't just weigh up a person's worth!" said Tweed angrily. "What if someone does that to you?"

Chase arched an eyebrow at him. "Fortunately, I'm important enough that my worth will most likely outweigh whoever I'm measured against."

"Not if I'm the one doing the measuring," said Tweed darkly.

Octavia put a hand on Tweed's arm. "Let's go," she said softly. There was no point in staying here. They'd get no help from Chase.

"Make sure you go home," called out Chase as they stepped into the corridor. "Play with your toys or whatever it is that children do."

They left the house and headed for Tweed's steamcoach. Octavia glanced over her shoulder and saw Temple watching them, framed by warm light from inside the library. He shrugged apologetically.

Octavia climbed into the passenger side of the coach. "What's our next move?" she asked as Tweed pumped the bellows.

"You heard the man. We return to our homes like good little children and let the grown-ups do their work."

Octavia looked at him in astonishment. Tweed tried to hold his serious face for as long as he could, then he broke into a grin and elbowed her rather painfully in the ribs. "Only kidding. What do you think we do? We track down Molock and get your mother back."

He started the steamcoach and turned it so they were facing the house. "Promise me one thing," he said, watching Temple and Chase deep in conversation.

"Anything."

"If I ever start talking like that—weighing up a person's worth like . . . like pieces in some great game . . ." He turned and looked deep into her eyes. "You tell me, yes? I don't want to end up like Chase."

"You won't," said Octavia, slightly unsettled at Tweed's serious turn.

"How do you know?"

"Because you've got me," she said, and broke into a brilliant smile. "Now come on. Let's go see what these hieroglyphs mean."

Tweed's gaze lingered, watching Chase through the window of the library. His lip curled in disgust, then the steamcoach lurched forward, throwing up two streams of gravel behind them.

Professor Bainbridge opened the door to Octavia's polite knock. She couldn't help noticing he looked slightly disappointed to see them.

"Forgive me. I was hoping it was Dr. Stackpole."

"He hasn't arrived yet?"

It was two hours since they'd left Ravenstone Lodge. She and Tweed had stopped to eat some lunch before coming to the museum, and Octavia had spent the time trying to make sure Tweed didn't wallow in his anger. That kind of thing wasn't healthy.

Bainbridge ushered them in. A woman of about sixty was seated in front of Bainbridge's desk. She stood up and smiled politely as Octavia and Tweed entered.

"Hello. I'm Professor Rowe," she said, shaking hands with them both. "You must be the youngsters who brought the ring to the professor. I wonder, may I see it?"

Tweed took the ring out and handed it over. Octavia was suddenly glad he hadn't given it to Chase. Professor Rowe sat down and examined it by the desk lamp.

"Ah, yes. This makes much more sense."

Bainbridge scurried over and sat down next to her. "It means something?"

"Indeed. You see, Stackpole didn't have the complete drawing. He couldn't have seen this. But look here. The actual ring is shaped like an eye. The eye adds something to the meaning. It is part of the picture."

"So what does it tell you?" asked Tweed.

"Well, this symbol here of the man on his knees. That is a stylized hieroglyph for death. But these lines here? I think they are meant to represent the Sekhem Scepter—a symbol of power from ancient Egypt. The Sekhem Scepter encapsulates the concept of strength and might. In fact, the word *sekhem* itself was often used in relation to divine beings. The Egyptians even used it to refer to their gods. There is a rather terrifying goddess called Sekhmet, and the god Osiris was also known as the Great Sekhem." She smiled. "Which leads us to the shape of the ring." She traced the shape with her finger. "An eye."

"The Eye of Horus?" asked Bainbridge.

Rowe shook her head. "It is not as intricate as the Horus symbol. No, this indicates the god Osiris." She looked at them, pleased. "This is what puzzled me. Why the hieroglyphs inside the ring made no sense. But taken together, all three have a meaning."

"Do tell," said Octavia.

"This is my educated guess. The eye represents Osiris. The kneeling figure, death. But not *just* death. Taken in connection with the Sekhem Scepter, which represents power, strength, even wrath, I take it to mean, 'the wrath of Osiris.' The terrible vengeance of those who wear the ring. Basically, it tells all that if you get in the way of the owner of the ring you will face the curse of Osiris, the wrath of the mighty god."

"But why have that on a ring?" asked Octavia.

"Perhaps some group is using it as a means of identification. The followers of Egyptian lore always have a fascination with these types of things."

"A secret society?" said Tweed doubtfully.

"Indeed."

"Like the Freemasons?"

"More likely a group of rich socialites trying to make themselves seem important. But we'll only know for sure when Stackpole arrives."

Bainbridge frowned and checked his watch. "I wonder where he is. He was most keen for this meeting. I don't see what could have kept him away."

"Do you have his address?" asked Octavia. "We can go and see what's keeping him. Perhaps he just misremembered the time."

"I suppose it couldn't hurt," said Bainbridge. "Just be careful. As I mentioned before, he's a bit paranoid." Bainbridge scribbled an address on a piece of paper and handed it to Octavia.

"Thank you," she said.

CHAPTER SIX

"**B**elgravia," said Tweed doubtfully. "Are you sure?"

Octavia held up the piece of paper. "10 Wilton Crescent, Belgravia. Third floor."

"But . . ." Tweed gestured around them at the up market, multi-story houses. "If he can afford to live in Belgravia, why not fund his own archeological dig? He must be loaded."

Belgravia, and the areas surrounding it in Knightsbridge, were amongst the most sought-after addresses in the city. Definitely not the kind of place a lowly archeologist should be able to afford.

"Perhaps he rents," said Octavia doubtfully, heading toward the semicircle of five-story houses that curved around an expansive central garden.

"You think that would be any cheaper?"

"No, probably not."

They hurried along the cleared sidewalk, ignoring the suspicious glares they received from any of the residents of the area brave enough to be out in the cold weather.

Octavia shivered. "What I wouldn't give for some sun right now. I'm tired of all this grey."

"It's not grey," Tweed pointed out. "It's white."

"You know what I mean. The clouds, the rain. I want some blue sky, some heat. Some *sand.*"

Tweed sniffed derisively. "Why? Horrible stuff. Gets everywhere. Even into sealed boxes. I had a theory once, when I was younger. About sand. Want to hear it?"

"What if I say no?"

"I'll tell you anyway, but I'll be slightly resentful with you for the rest of the day."

Octavia sighed. "Go ahead."

"I used to think that sand was some sort of . . . otherworldly life form. Like something H. G. Wells would write about. Think about it. Sand travels across the oceans to every single land mass. It uses the native life forms to then move even farther inland, traveling to strategic areas, ready for the big day when the attack would come."

"The attack?" said Octavia.

"That's right."

"By sand."

Tweed held up a finger. "Ah. No. *Alien* sand. See, there's a difference."

"Of course there is. Remind me again why you don't have many friends?"

Tweed stopped in front of number 10, the door identical to all the other doors in the long semicircle of joined houses. Tweed tried the door. It opened into a dim, carpeted passage. He could smell bleach and tobacco.

It wasn't like a tenement house, where a set of stone steps were hidden away behind a grubby door. These richly carpeted stairs headed up from the central atrium where Tweed and Octavia currently stood. The decorative banister curled around the walls all the way to the top floor.

They climbed up to the third level, stopping at the landing in front of a black, glossy door. Octavia knocked.

No answer. Tweed reached over her shoulder and knocked harder.

"Yes, because he obviously didn't hear me, what with me being so weak and dainty, and all feminine-like."

"Don't be absurd, Songbird," said Tweed. "I'd never think that of you. Feminine. *Really*." Tweed shook his head and stepped in front of her to hide his grin. He tried the door and was rather surprised when it swung silently open.

Tweed felt his stomach sink. That was never a good sign, was it? They both stepped into the room.

"Oh," said Tweed softly. "Oh dear."

The sitting room was a mess. It had been ransacked: books pulled from shelves and tossed carelessly across the floor, chairs and couches upended and ripped apart, the stuffing yanked free like the innards of a dying animal. Every available drawer had been pulled from its place, the contents strewn across the floor. Paintings and photographs had been torn from the walls, their backings removed in the search.

Tweed pulled Octavia into the room and closed the door behind them.

That was when he saw the body.

It had been hidden behind the door when it stood open. A man, Stackpole presumably, tied to a chair. He was shirtless, his wrinkled skin a mess of cuts and bruises. The carpet beneath his feet was stained with dark blood.

Tweed stepped forward, his eyes taking everything in, just as Barnaby had taught him. Fingers, broken. Those he still had, that was. Four of them had been cut off at the knuckle. He glanced around and saw them on the sideboard, arranged in a neat line, all of them resting upright, like pillars of stone.

"Tortured," he said.

"No, really?" said Octavia.

Tweed raised an eyebrow at her.

"Sorry. A bit nervous. Get sarcastic when I'm nervous."

"Doesn't look like he talked, though," said Tweed.

"Why do you say that?"

"The place wouldn't be such a mess if he'd talked before he died." He leaned closer. The man's jaw had been broken. His eyes, staring sightlessly straight ahead, were ruptured, the whites filled with blood. There was a gaping wound across his neck. Tweed pointed to it.

"Killing blow. Out of frustration, more than anything else. Stackpole wouldn't tell them what they wanted to know, so his killer lashed out. See how the cut is uneven, off center? The killer let his emotions get the better of him."

"And what is it they wanted to know?"

Tweed turned away from the man. "I would assume they were looking for this ancient map everyone's talking about. Or his research, maybe." Tweed glanced around the room. He knew he shouldn't be feeling so elated, so alive, but he couldn't help it. The excitement was rising inside, the boredom of the past months burned away by mystery.

"You could try looking a bit less pleased about it," said Octavia shortly. "That's a human being there. He has family, friends."

"I know that," said Tweed defensively. "And we're going to catch whoever it was who did it."

"Are we now?"

"Oh yes."

"How are we going to do that? We have no idea what's going on here."

He glanced around the room, ignoring her question. "I suppose there's no chance of us finding anything, but we should at least take a look."

They spent the next half an hour searching through papers and books, beneath the couches, under the bed, even inside the cupboards. But there was nothing to find.

Tweed eventually gave up. He stood with his hands on his hips and stared around the room in frustration. Nothing. Not a single thing.

He was about to call Octavia from the bedroom when he heard a noise.

It came from outside the door. A slight scraping sound. He pressed himself up against the wall and listened. The sound didn't come again. His imagination? A tenant heading downstairs?

Tweed reached out and gripped the doorknob, turning it slowly. He carefully pulled the door open, peering out into the landing.

The blank, gold face of a pharaoh stared back at him.

Tweed blinked in surprise. It looked like the kind of face you always saw associated with Egypt. The gold face with the striped headdress. Except, the mask didn't cover the person's face completely. The lower half was visible, a mouth that was set in angry lines.

All these observations flashed through his mind in the second after he opened the door. He didn't have a chance to do anything else because the figure brought up a curved knife up and thrust it at him.

Tweed swung the door shut, putting it between himself and the knife. The blade thudded into the wood. The strange figure tried to pull it free, but Tweed yanked the door open again. The man's grip slipped. He let go of the knife and Tweed kicked him hard in the stomach.

The air *wooshed* out from him and he staggered back against the banister. He threw out an arm to catch himself. As he did so, the sleeve on his left arm rode up and Tweed caught a glimpse of a small tattoo on the underside of his forearm—the Osiris Curse tattoo from Sekhem's ring.

He heard a noise to his left. He looked and saw more masked figures running up the stairs. Tweed swore and slammed the door.

"Nightingale!" he shouted, turning the key in the lock. "Trouble!"

Octavia hurried out of the bedroom just as the window in the lounge exploded inward. Another masked figure landed on the carpet, a rope trailing over his shoulder up to the roof.

Octavia bent down and grabbed a broken table leg, swinging it into the man's temple before he could even rise. He stiffened and slumped to the floor.

Octavia headed for the door, but Tweed caught her arm. "More that way."

Their eyes settled on the rope dangling outside the window. They hurried over and Tweed leaned out into the cold air, looking up toward the roof. He couldn't see anyone else up there, but there were two more masked figures in the street, standing by the entrance to the gardens across the road.

He ducked back inside. "How are you at climbing?" he asked.

"I don't know. I've never really tried."

"First time for everything," he said, standing aside.

There was a heavy bang at the door. Octavia climbed up onto the sill and grabbed the rope. They were only one floor from the roof, so it wasn't far. But in this weather, the rope would be slippery, fingers would be stiff.

"See you up there," said Octavia. Tweed watched while her head and upper body disappeared past the window frame. There were more bangs at the door. He didn't think it would hold much longer.

Her upper legs vanished, then finally her feet. Tweed grabbed the rope just as the door crashed open. He glanced over his shoulder as five—what were they? *Cultists*? Considering what Professor Rowe had said, he reckoned that was a pretty safe bet—cultists ran into the room.

Tweed launched himself from the window sill, sailing out from the wall. He kicked his legs frantically, trying to twist around in the air as he swung back again. A cultists was waiting by the window, ready to grab him. Tweed lashed out with his foot, connecting with the man's throat.

He staggered back with a gurgling wheeze. Another tried to push past to grab Tweed, but by this time he had his feet on the wall above the window and he pulled himself up. Octavia was waiting for him on the roof. She helped him over, then quickly reeled the rope up after them.

Tweed got to his feet and looked around while Octavia untied the rope from a chimney. All the houses in Wilton Crescent were joined together, sharing a single roof. If they could get to the end they could use the rope to lower themselves to the ground and get away.

They ran, and had made it across ten houses when a cultist stepped out from behind a chimney and pointed a gun at them.

Tweed and Octavia skidded to a halt. Tweed was just in front of Octavia, blocking her slightly from view. Tweed watched the cultist's finger tighten on the trigger.

"Duck," said a low voice behind him.

Tweed had learned never to argue when someone says duck. He dropped to the ground just as the cultist fired. His shot cracked loudly in the cold air, whizzing over his head. He didn't get a chance to fire another, because he was suddenly wrapped in electricity. The cultist screamed and dropped to the snow, jerking around in convulsions.

Tweed whirled around. Octavia was inspecting her upper arm, where a small tear could be seen in her jacket. She looked up and smiled nervously.

"Close call."

Tweed paled, scrambling to his feet. He grabbed her arm and checked it.

"I'm fine," Octavia protested. "It missed me."

Tweed stared angrily into her eyes. Octavia frowned back. He wanted to say something, to tell her not to put herself in danger like that.

But he didn't. He clamped his mouth shut, grabbed her hand, and they sprinted the rest of the way to the edge of the roof. Tweed leaned over. The roof dropped down to a second building about halfway to the ground. He quickly tied the rope around the closest chimney and tossed it over the edge. It didn't make it all the way. There was a two meter gap between the end of the rope and the roof.

A gunshot echoed behind them. Tweed whirled around to find seven more cultists running toward them, firing pistols as they came. Snow spat up around them as the bullets hit the roof around their feet. Octavia quickly scrambled over the edge and half climbed, half slid down the rope. Tweed quickly followed after, dropping the final gap and landing on his backside.

Octavia was already climbing down a drainpipe. Tweed followed her, dropping onto the street below. They were on the rear side of Wilton Crescent now, shielded from anyone watching from the main road. A small lane led deeper into the Belgravia area. Octavia grabbed Tweed by the sleeve and they ran as fast as they could, not slowing until they were surrounded by crowds of people.

Tweed's heart hammered in his chest. That was too close.

They returned to Tweed's house on Whitechapel Street. Despite Octavia's protestations to the contrary, it was the safest place to be. Because although many would class Whitechapel as the home of the morally dubious—i. e., murderers, thieves, pickpockets and the like—one thing you could say about the people here was that they looked out for each other. If you were accepted in Whitechapel, you were family. And the people of Whitechapel looked after family. Any unknowns spotted lurking around would have questions to answer, questions asked with cudgels and steel-toed boots.

And anyone spotted wearing those ludicrous Egyptian masks would have a lifespan shorter than a drunk toff who happened to take a wrong turn.

Tweed unlocked the door and stepped aside to allow Octavia in. She moved along the hall and into the massive room that took up the whole ground floor of the building.

Tweed followed her. Now that Barnaby had gone all respectable, the house was pretty much Tweed's. Barnaby rarely came home before eleven and he was gone long before Tweed managed to crawl out of bed in the morning.

Tweed actually missed the old days, when he and Barnaby scraped through life by the skin of their teeth. When they would return home after a successful con with a fish supper wrapped in greasy newspaper and they would count the money they'd earned and wonder how long they could make it last.

It wasn't right, what they had done. He *knew* that. And he'd talked to Barnaby about stopping before the whole Lazarus affair had changed everything. But he still missed it. Simpler times.

And *exciting* times. Life was never boring. Not like the last few months.

Tweed quickly scanned the room, making sure he hadn't left anything embarrassing lying around. Octavia had once described the room as the workshop of a mad scientist who'd escaped from Bedlam. Tweed had quite liked that description. Oddities scoured from junk shops, street markets—even rubbish heaps—were strewn across the shelves and desks. Among the bric-a-brac were jars of mummified animals, a two-headed snake, a suit of black armor, and a huge paper dragon head that hung from the ceiling, scavenged from the Chinese quarter recently when they celebrated their New Year.

His latest project—a model of the new Big Ben made completely from matchsticks—took pride of place on the table in the center of the room. It had taken him ages to finish it.

"That's new," said Octavia, bending down to study it.

"I know. Amazing, isn't it?"

"It's certainly . . . *something.*"

Tweed lit the lamps, then stoked the fire, adding a few more logs to get the warmth spreading through the room. He looked over his shoulder and saw Octavia inspecting the model with a look of distaste.

"Your problem is that you don't know good art."

"Oh, so this is art, is it?"

"Indeed it is."

Octavia straightened up and pointed at the couch where Tweed usually slept. Facing it were four wooden chairs, and on those chairs were the old ventriloquist dolls that Barnaby collected.

"Have you been talking to these dolls?"

She said it as a joke, but Tweed's face flushed and he quickly moved them away, putting them back on their stools beneath the window.

"You *have*, haven't you? You've been speaking to the dolls. Oh, Tweed, that's not healthy. You know that, don't you?"

"It's not as if I expect them to talk back," he said defensively. "It just gets a little . . . quiet around here. That's all."

"Have you considered a pet?"

"I . . ." Tweed frowned. He hadn't, actually. Why hadn't he considered a pet? Nothing too messy. A parrot perhaps. Something like that.

"Thank you for the suggestion. I'll take it on board."

"I'm glad," said Octavia, "because, seriously, this is . . . it's *odd*, Tweed. Even for you."

Tweed decided he didn't want to talk about that anymore. Instead, he wheeled a massive blackboard into the middle of the room.

"Are you ready?"

"What are we doing?"

"Discussing what we know. Trying to figure some things out."

"Oh. I see. Go ahead, sir."

Tweed looked down at the chalk in his hand and the blackboard behind him. "Funny."

He turned and wrote on the board.

Tesla killed. Death ray plans stolen.

Tweed tapped the board. "Obviously these plans have been taken for nefarious purposes, agreed?"

"Agreed. But it wasn't just death ray plans. It was blueprints for different weapons."

"Point noted." He wrote: *Sekhem*, circled the name, and drew a long arrow to his first point.

He looked at Octavia. "Yes?"

She nodded.

"And we are thinking Sekhem is part of a secret society, one that uses that Osiris symbol as a means of identification."

Octavia nodded. "And they are the same people who killed Stackpole. They're linked by the Osiris symbol. They tortured him to find out about this map he had."

"Agreed. So what's so special about it? It can't just be about money, can it? Selling ancient treasures?"

"Why not? People have done less to get rich. Egyptian artifacts would sell for a pretty penny."

"But that has absolutely nothing to do with Tesla's blueprints for super weapons."

Octavia frowned. "True."

Tweed wrote down: *Molock?* Then he added another few question marks and underlined them for good measure.

"Thoughts?" he said. "Because it's pretty obvious that Molock and Sekhem were not the best of friends. Did Molock want Tesla and the plans for himself? Is Molock a part of this cult as well?"

"And how does this relate to my mother?"

"Of course! I'd forgotten that!" In response to Octavia's dark look, he added, "Sorry. So—how does this relate to your mother?" Tweed paced in front of the board. "Did she perhaps know something about this secret society?"

"It's possible. I mean, there was no mention of this group when we were looking into the Lazarus affair. But it's obvious there's *some* link. Molock took my mother out of the Ministry prison using a false name. He turns up here on the night Tesla is killed and the plans for his super weapons stolen."

"It was Sekhem who brought Molock back to London," said Tweed. "He said as much himself. Molock found out what he was planning and wanted to stop him. But why?"

Too many question marks and not enough answers, thought Tweed. He drew the symbol of the secret society on the board.

"We need to find out what this is. Who these cultists really are. What they stand for."

"I agree. Only, not right now. I need to get to *The Times.* I have a story about some missing scientists that needs to be proofed. "

After Tweed dropped Octavia off, he headed back to Stackpole's flat. He wasn't sure why. It was a hunch, a feeling that they had missed something.

There was no sign of any cultists around Wilton Crescent, which was something of a relief. Tweed entered the house and climbed the stairs to Stackpole's flat. The door was closed, but when Tweed gave it a little shove it swung open.

Tweed slipped inside and pulled the door closed behind him. He did his best to ignore the body to his right and moved to the center of the room. The curtains were billowing in the cold breeze. Glass crunched underfoot. Tweed slowly turned in a circle, letting his eyes unfocus, just letting them fall wherever they would.

He stopped.

There was something different. On the floor behind the door

was an expensive-looking yellow envelope. That hadn't been there earlier on! Tweed hurried over and picked it up. Stackpole's name and address were written on the envelope in elaborate handwriting.

But something about the handwriting made him pause. He'd seen it somewhere before.

Tweed headed to the desk. He picked a random sheet of paper and held it next to the envelope.

It was the same handwriting.

Stackpole was sending himself letters. Why?

Tweed ripped the envelope open. Inside were two pieces of thick card. The first was gold-trimmed and had a lot of official looking stamps on it, plus the words:

> *The airship Albion awaits the pleasure of your company.*
> *Stackpole. H. Mr.*
> *Room 56.*

Tweed frowned. He turned the card over, then read it again. A ticket for the maiden voyage of the airship *Albion*? This just got odder and odder. Why would Stackpole want to travel on the *Albion*?

Well, *besides* the fact that it really was the most sought-after ticket of the season. But Stackpole was an archeologist. What interest would he have in that kind of thing?

Look around, Tweed.

True, Stackpole *did* seem to like living a first-class lifestyle. Tweed thought back to the newspaper report Octavia had written. Wasn't the *Albion* stopping in Egypt? Perhaps Stackpole planned on disembarking there, to find his mysterious archeological dig.

But then, why had Stackpole sent himself the ticket? Was he really that paranoid?

It's not paranoia when they're really out to get you, though, is it?

Stackpole had a sense he was in danger. He posted the ticket to himself so that if anyone searched his flat they wouldn't know he was heading back to Egypt.

Quite clever, really.

Had he done the same thing with this mysterious map?

Tweed searched the floor but there were no more letters. He checked around the desk as well, but he was out of luck.

He *did* find a whole stack of the same yellow envelopes, though.

Tweed pulled out the second piece of card from the envelope. It was a sort of introduction and welcome to those who had just mortgaged off their firstborn children in order to buy their tickets.

A voyage of discovery awaits you!
Join us for the maiden launch of the airship Albion, a true miracle of science, designed by Nikola Tesla himself.

Prepare to be filled with admiration . . .
Struck down with stupefaction . . .
You will be speechless with wonderment, and that's a promise. A thrilling adventure is yours for the taking, where the world will unfold beneath you and your life will never be the same again!

Launch date:
10th of February.
Time of departure:
12:00 p.m.

Tweed stared at the card. Something about the words tickled the back of his brain. Like he'd seen them somewhere before . . .

His eyes widened and he fumbled inside his pockets until he found what he was looking for. The piece of burned paper he had picked up back in Tesla's factory. He held it up next to Stackpole's card, lining up the words.

. . . *ate:*
. . . *uary.*
. . . *ture:*
. . . *m.*

Launch date:
The 10ᵗʰ of January.
Time of departure:
12:00 p.m.

They matched. The piece of burned card Molock had dropped was the same one that came with a ticket for the *Albion*. Which meant Molock *also* had a ticket for the airship's maiden voyage.

Tweed's mind worked furiously. Why? Did he want to talk to Stackpole? Did he want to *kill* Stackpole?

Or was it just a coincidence?

With a rush of excitement, Tweed realized it didn't matter. Molock was going to be on the *Albion* and Molock was the one who knew where Octavia's mother was. It was as simple as that.

When did the airship launch? He checked the ticket again. The 10th of February.

Tomorrow.

Tweed's mind raced. He had a lot to do tonight. A lot of preparations to make.

One thing was for sure, though. Boredom certainly wasn't going to be an issue anymore.

He and Octavia were going on a trip.

CHAPTER SEVEN

For the second day running, Octavia was rudely yanked from her sleep by someone knocking at the door. She grunted in irritation and tried to block the sounds out by burying her head beneath the pillow.

It didn't work. A few seconds later a voice was shouting below her window.

"Nightingale! Get up!"

Octavia groaned. Was she never to get a proper sleep? What time was it anyway? She rolled over and looked at the clock. 6:30! What was the idiot thinking? And on a Saturday!

You are going to pay for this, Mr. Tweed, she thought, throwing back the covers. She was going to let him know exactly what she thought about having her sleep disturbed.

She stomped out of bed, pausing only to pull on her dressing gown. She clumped down the stairs and yanked open the door.

"What do you want?" she snapped. "It's six thirty in the bloody morning."

"I know," said Tweed, utterly oblivious to her anger. He pushed past her and entered the house. "We don't have much time."

Octavia stared out at the snow blanketing the pavement, slowly counting to ten. She then closed the door and turned to face him. She frowned. He was still wearing the same clothes as yesterday. Admittedly, that didn't really mean much when it came to Tweed, but his eyes were shadowed and had a feverish glint to them.

"Have you slept?"

"What? No. No time."

"Why?" said Octavia suspiciously. "Why is there no time?"

Tweed held out a coin to her. "Flip this."

Octavia looked at the coin in bewilderment, then took it from him. She inspected it. Just an ordinary Crown.

"Call it and toss the coin."

"Why?"

"Just do it."

Octavia sighed. "Heads," she said, and flipped the coin. She let it fall to the carpet, where it landed head side up.

"Bugger," said Tweed, staring at it in dismay.

"Tweed, what is going on?"

Tweed dragged his eyes away from the coin. There was horror in his face, as if Octavia's coin toss had sealed a terrible fate for him.

"Tweed. Tell me what's going on. Right now."

"Yes. Right. Of course. After I dropped you off at the paper yesterday, I went back to Stackpole's."

"Without me?" she said incredulously.

"Yes. Sorry. But it was a hunch. I just felt we'd missed something."

"And had we?"

"No. But this was waiting on the doormat." He reached into his jacket and pulled out an envelope.

Octavia took it from him and read its contents. Finally, she looked up at him, confused. "He was traveling on the *Albion*?"

Tweed nodded. Then he took out the burned card and handed it to her. "Molock dropped this at the warehouse."

Octavia examined them both. When she realized what she was looking at her breath quickened with excitement.

"When does it—?"

"Five hours from now."

"And the coin?"

Tweed picked the coin up, examining it in disappointment. "Yes. The coin. The way I see it, we need to be on board that airship. But we only have one ticket. So I've had a busy night."

"What have you done?" said Octavia, already dreading the answer.

"Well. I tracked down the list of employees on the *Albion*, specifically focusing on the wait staff. They're the ones able to get everywhere, and *also* the ones the rich ignore the most. I found out the name of the head of the wait staff. I got his address and paid him a visit."

"You . . . paid him a visit?"

"Yes."

"In the middle of the night?"

"Yes. Please stop interrupting. I slipped some arsenic into his drinking water—"

Octavia held up a hand. Tweed frowned and stopped talking. "What?"

"You put *arsenic* into his drinking water?"

"Yes. I just said that."

"Arsenic is a poison."

"Only in large doses. I just gave him a drop or two. Enough to make him sick for a few days. Now, here's the clever bit. I then broke into the offices of the company that owns the *Albion*, and I fiddled with their paperwork."

"I . . ." Octavia shook her head in amazement. Breaking and entering. Poisoning. What was next? Murder? ". . . No, never mind. Carry on."

"I tracked down their employee records and put down a new name for the secondary head of staff. A certain E. S. Holmes."

"Which is . . . ?"

"Well, it looks like it's me now, doesn't it?"

Realization dawned. "Wait, that's what the coin toss was for? You were seeing who was going to get the cabin and who was going to have to work?"

"Fairest way," replied Tweed.

Octavia was rather angry at this. He hadn't told her *why* she was flipping the coin. She preferred to know when she was leaving her fate in the hands of chance.

She was about to berate him for this, then forced herself to stop. If she protested, he might try to settle it another way. And she might lose. Which meant she would have to work as a servant on board the *Albion*, something she really didn't want to do.

No, perhaps just this once she would let it slide.

There was a knock at the door. Tweed gripped her by the shoulders and moved her aside. "Ah. This will be for E. S. Holmes."

"Yes, about that—you used Holmes as a false name?"

Tweed shrugged. "It amused me."

"And you gave my address?"

"Had to. Couldn't have Holmes living in Whitechapel, could I? The *Albion* wouldn't hire him if he did."

Tweed opened the door to reveal a flustered looking man peering at a file while at the same time trying to straighten his spectacles.

He squinted at Tweed. "Er, hello, young man. Is your father in?"

"Father?" said Tweed, offense radiating from every pore of his body. "This is my house sir! My own!"

"Oh." The man peered at the file, then stepped forward to get a better look at Tweed. "Mr. . . . Holmes?"

"The one and only, sir. What can I do for you?"

"Er . . . it's just . . ." he tilted the file to the light. "You're supposed to be twenty-seven years old."

"Yes? And?"

"Well you don't look it."

"You should see the state of the portrait in the attic," said Tweed, and winked. Octavia rolled her eyes.

"Ah, yes. I see. A jest. I'm sorry. I don't have time for jests right now. I have a bit of an emergency on my hands. You are listed here as a secondary head of wait staff for the *Albion*. Is that correct?"

"It is indeed, sir. And proud to be."

"Well, I'm afraid you've been called to duty. The *Albion*'s head of staff has fallen sick, and you seem to be his replacement . . ."

Even as the man spoke these words he frowned, as if wondering how they could possibly be true. But Tweed stepped forward and energetically shook the man's hand.

"Sir, it will be an honor! An *honor*, I say. I'll report to the *Albion* immediately. Fret not, dear sir. I will see to it that those layabouts from under the stairs are met with a firm hand and clear instructions. You know what these cleaning staff are like. If they've not got their fingers in the belongings of the guests, they're dilly-dallying in broom cupboards and knoffling in empty bedrooms."

"Kn . . . knoffling?" said the man, clearly aghast at this heretofore unseen world of the serving staff. "What does that mean?"

"I wouldn't want to upset you, sir!" said Tweed. "A man of your status, why should your mind be sullied by such things? But don't worry, I shall report for duty within the hour. Good day, sir!"

Tweed closed the door on the befuddled man and turned to Octavia with a grin. Octavia gave him a polite round of applause.

"Not bad, eh?"

"Not bad. Now get out of my house. I've got to pack my cases." She held out her hand. "Before you go, the ticket."

Tweed reluctantly handed her the ticket and turned to the door. As he stepped outside, Octavia called after him, "And no knoffling with the staff!"

∞

The heavens themselves had cleared for the maiden voyage of the *Albion*. Londoners celebrated the break in the grey clouds, greeting the icy blue sky with joy and laughter, as if reunited with a long-lost relative.

The *Albion* had been towed to Trafalgar Square overnight. It hung above the National Gallery, mooring wires pegged around the perimeter of the large plaza. The square was festooned with bunting, Union Jack flags strung between Nelson's Column and the even larger statue of Sir Charles Babbage. The fountains had been fed food coloring, and they now spewed red and blue water into the air.

Children tried to swing on the wires holding the *Albion* steady, but were chased away by stern-faced guards. And yet even these custodians, usually so tired and irritated with the naughtiness of little ones, couldn't help but smile behind their thick mustaches and beards. It was a great day for the Empire. A great day for Her Majesty.

Octavia disembarked from the hansom cab that had brought her from her home. At least, she tried to. Against her better judgment, she was wearing a dress, a tight, uncomfortable, billowing dress. With an accompanying umbrella. Made of cloth. Honestly. What was the point? Was everyone in the manufacture of women's clothing intent on making them as uncomfortable as possible?

Octavia studied the massive airship while one of the *Albion* automatons untied her travel cases from the cab. It really was a sight to behold. It wasn't an airship in the traditional sense. It used the same idea—airbags filled with gas—to keep it afloat, but the bags were attached to what at first looked like an actual ship from the ocean.

It was how she imagined Noah's Ark would look. A rectangular structure easily half a mile long and a quarter that in width. The scale was such that many critics thought it would crash back to earth within its first hour of voyage.

The automaton picked up her bags and led her around the edge of the square, heading for a wrought iron arch that had been erected on the west side of the plaza. Beyond the arch was a long line of ornate fencing and a red carpet that led all the way to the ornithopters that ferried the passengers up to the airship.

A woman in her forties was pushing an old man in a wheelchair ahead of her. Octavia slowed her walk while the woman fumbled for their tickets and handed them over.

"Very good, madam," said the ticket checker. He looked to be in his early twenties and was dressed in a smart navy blue uniform with red epaulets down the arms and legs. His hair was swept back severely from his face. He was quite handsome, in a soldiering type of way.

He bowed when Octavia approached. "Good afternoon, Miss. And without sounding impertinent, may I just say that you've given my eyes some much needed relief?"

"Oh?"

"Indeed. I'm sure they're all very pleasant people, but you're the first person I've seen under the age of thirty-five. I was beginning to feel like a child in school again. The name's Ludgate, by the way. Edward Ludgate."

"Should you be talking so freely to one of the guests, Mr. Ludgate?"

"Oh, I think I'm safe. You wouldn't turn me in, would you?"

Octavia smothered a grin. "You are impertinent, sir. And you presume too much."

Ludgate winked at her. "Then I present my most humble apologies, Miss. Will you accept them?"

"I don't know," said Octavia. "I'll think about it."

"What's the hold up?" called a voice from behind.

Octavia turned around to see a tall, wrinkled man with the most voluminous side whiskers Octavia had ever seen sprouting from his cheeks. "All right granddad," she said in her more normal mode of conversation. "Hold your horses."

The man's eyes widened in outrage. Octavia glared at him then turned back to Ludgate and presented her ticket. He was staring at her with no small amount of wonder in his eyes. He punched a hole in her ticket, then stamped it and handed it back. Octavia returned his earlier wink. "Soldier on, Mr. Ludgate. Soldier on."

Octavia rested her umbrella on her shoulder and stepped onto the red carpet. She decided she didn't want to walk behind the slow moving people in front of her so she moved around them, ignoring the tuts of disapproval as she did so.

She sighed. This was going to be a long trip.

There were three ornithopters ready. She'd never been in one, but they were the latest craze for those who could afford it—a small passenger transport that moved people through the air at speeds of up to ten miles an hour.

But these looked as though they had been modified. At the rear of each was a metal circle—an exhaust she reckoned—leading to a secondary engine. It looked like the exhausts were hooked up to Tesla Turbines, like the *Albion* itself. That meant they would move much faster than ten miles an hour.

She moved around the long wings, climbed into the back seat, and strapped herself in while the automaton secured her trunks.

"All ready, Miss?" called the driver over his shoulder.

"Ready," said Octavia.

"Then off we go."

The driver pulled a lever and the wings started to flap. She felt the contraption lift slightly and the driver pumped another lever until they rose completely off the ground. The driver pushed power to the thrusters, sending them skimming smoothly forward. Octavia peered over the side as Trafalgar Square receded below them, the crowds cheering the ornithopter as it did a circuit of the plaza, building up enough thrust to lift it higher and higher until they drew level with the airship.

Octavia stared at it in awe. Even though the *Albion* had looked big from below, it was nothing compared to the sheer scale of it when they drew closer. The top of the ark (as she now called it) was like some huge city street. Structures dotted the deck, ornithopters coming in to land, people running around like tiny ants going about their business. The gasbags that kept the airship afloat were as long as the ark itself, segmented and kept in the shape of a cigar with wires that looked to be as thick as lampposts.

The ornithopter banked slightly and moved through a gap in these wires. It headed for an area in the center of the ship and spiraled slowly downward to land on a clearly painted red circle.

"There you go, Miss. All safe and sound."

"Thank you," said Octavia, climbing out of the ornithopter. She looked around curiously as an automaton unloaded her bags. More flying machines were landing on the deck, coming from other parts of the city. There were even smaller dirigibles bringing passengers to the airship. They were small enough to slip between the wires and hover over the landing deck while their passengers disembarked.

A young woman wearing the blue and red livery of the *Albion* approached Octavia.

"May I see your ticket, Miss?"

Octavia handed it over. The girl inspected it and smiled. "Welcome to the *Albion*, Miss Stackpole."

"Octavia, please."

"I'm sorry, Miss. Rules. We're not allowed to call any of the passengers by their first names."

"I see. Then I suppose Miss Stackpole will have to do."

The girl checked the details of the ticket again. Then she looked at Octavia with wide eyes.

"You've got one of the best cabins on the airship, Miss Stackpole."

"Have I really?" said Octavia, remembering she had a part to play. "My parents organized the whole thing. I'm supposed to be meeting them in Russia. I didn't even want to go."

She saw the attendant's eyes flatten slightly, and Octavia silently cursed herself. She knew what the girl was thinking. Spoiled rich girl, everything handed to her on a platter, too snobbish to even appreciate the trip.

Octavia didn't want to play that person. Even for a short time.

"I'm sorry," she said. "I don't mean that." Octavia thought quickly. "My parents are making me leave my suitor behind. They hope travel will broaden my horizons, make me realize I don't want to spend my life with him."

The attendant's face warmed again. She looked around furtively and leaned closer. "What's his name?"

Octavia drew a blank, then blurted out the first name that popped into her head. "Sebastian," she said. Then she did her own furtive look around, just to make sure Tweed wasn't anywhere nearby. She'd never live it down if he'd heard that.

"What's your name?" asked Octavia.

"Violet, Miss."

"Pleased to meet you, Violet. Shall we have a look at this amazing cabin my parents have paid for?"

Violet smiled. "Right this way."

Violet led Octavia through a door and down some stairs, entering a large greeting room. A bar ran along one wall. Couches and armchairs lined the others. Sunlight shone through slanted windows, casting squares of gold across the patterned carpet.

Octavia was handed a glass of champagne as Violet led her past the other guests milling around and chatting to each other. It seemed as if all of London's high society was in attendance. But not only London's. As she passed through the room she heard American, German, and French accents, and even some she couldn't quite place.

They moved through the room and into a broad hallway. Again, thick carpets had been laid down. Persian, if Octavia was any judge.

Ornately framed paintings and mirrors lined the walls. It seemed as if everything had been done to make the *Albion* appear like a stately home rather than a means of transport.

In fact, if Octavia had been brought on board blindfolded, then deposited in this or any of the other rooms Violet led her through, she wouldn't even know she was in an airship. The usual deep thrum she associated with dirigible engines was utterly absent, obviously something to do with Tesla's new turbines.

"Would you like the grand tour or would you prefer to be taken straight to your room?" asked Violet.

"Oh, the grand tour, I think," said Octavia, smiling.

Grand was definitely the correct word. It seemed that the entire upper level, (there were five), was given over to entertainment. Reading rooms, libraries, smoking rooms, dining rooms, (one of which was Egyptian themed), and restaurants, two of which served only French or Italian cuisine. A casino, a croquet pitch with a glass roof that let sunlight in, a dance hall, a card room, and finally, an opera house. Octavia stared around in astonishment, not even trying to hide her awe. An actual opera house. In an airship. It was sensational.

Violet grinned at her amazement. "It's certainly something, isn't it? Just think how those of us who work below the stairs felt when we saw it for the first time."

Octavia tore her gaze away from the tiers of seats, the ornate boxes that ringed the upper walls, the large stage that was easily the equal of the best London had to offer.

"Of course, it's not only opera," said Violet. "There are plays, melodramas, farces, comedies . . . um, what else? A company that puts on Shakespeare plays. I'm sure I'm missing something, but there's a timetable in your room so you can see if anything catches your fancy."

"Thank you," said Octavia, for the first time feeling a bit excited about the journey. Up until now it had been about trying to find Molock, trying to find out what he did with her mother. But now she was wondering if she could actually have a good time doing it. Was that allowed? To enjoy herself while trying to find the kidnapper of her mother?

She felt a wave of guilt at the thought. Of course it wasn't allowed. She was here to do a job, not to enjoy herself.

"I'd like to go to my room now, please," she said.

"Of course."

Violet pulled the opera house doors closed and led her toward the center of the airship. "There's a moveable walkway that runs around the perimeter," said Violet as they walked. "In case you're tired or simply want to rest. It's very safe."

Violet stopped at a wide set of stairs. Octavia leaned over the balcony and peered downward. She could see all the way to the bottom of the airship.

It was magnificent.

She was about to turn away when a flash of color caught her eye. She frowned, wondering what it was that had caught her attention. Then she saw it again. A purple suit.

Her stomach clenched. She leaned out over the railing to get a better look, wondering if she was seeing things.

She wasn't. Three levels down, striding along the corridor, was Sekhem, fancy cane and all.

What on earth was *he* doing here?

"Miss?"

Octavia looked over her shoulder at Violet. "Are you well?"

Octavia turned back, but the momentary distraction meant she had lost Sekhem in the crowd. She searched the floors, but there was no sign of him anywhere.

She had to tell Tweed.

They descended to level one. (The staff worked and slept on level zero, Violet informed her with a half-smile.)

Level one was where the first class cabins were situated. The corridors here were wider than anywhere else, the carpets and finishings even more expensive-looking. Original paintings on the walls, interspersed with framed photographs by new, up and coming artists who were the current toast of high society.

Octavia paused to study a photograph of a young chimney sweep, his face black with dust while an automaton stood next to him, gleaming, without a spot of coal dust on its casing.

"Do you like it?" asked Violet, nodding at the photograph.

"I think it's in extraordinarily bad taste."

Violet smiled. "I knew I liked you, Miss Stackpole."

Her cabin was larger than she'd thought it would be. A main room with a chesterfield lounge suite, a glass-topped table, a drinks cabinet, a bookshelf with all the classics set out in order of size. (All of them leather bound). Then a doorway leading to the bedroom, where she had a four poster bed all to herself, and finally a door leading to the bathroom. It even had a bath.

"Where do they keep the water?" she asked Violet.

"Tanks down below the servant's quarters. The airship will restock in Egypt."

Octavia smiled.

Well, maybe she *could* enjoy it here. Just a little.

CHAPTER EIGHT

Tweed was not going to enjoy it here. Not at all.

The day started off well enough. He packed his suitcase, left a note for Barnaby, (and another in case the old man from the customs offices showed up), then made his way to Trafalgar Square to sign on aboard the *Albion*.

The first thing he had done was report to the head of household to find out how many people the head of wait staff would be in charge of, what his duties actually *were*, that kind of thing. Of course, he wouldn't be so obvious in his questions. He'd have to find that out subtly, by using probing questions and his superior intellect.

He was in for a bit of a shock on that front.

The head of household was a tall, stern-faced man whose back was so straight Tweed wondered if he actually had the ability to bend over. Tweed was tempted to drop something on the floor just to see how he managed to pick it up.

"Ever been in the military, boy?" were his first words to Tweed.

Tweed had to admit to being slightly nonplussed by this. Was he wearing a military uniform without knowing? Had he picked up a military issue weapon without realizing? He looked down at his hands. No, they were empty of guns, rifles, bayonets, and the like.

"Er . . . no."

"Didn't think so. You can judge a person by his willingness to serve his country, doncherknow. What's your excuse?"

"Um . . . There haven't actually been any wars lately."

"There are always wars. You can find one if you look hard enough."

Tweed decided to just ignore this statement for the preposterous waffle that it was. "Yes. Good," he said briskly. "My name's Sebastian Holmes. I'm to be the new head of wait staff."

"The name's Hardstone. And no you're not, sir!"

"Excuse me?"

"Smythe mentioned his concern about your age and experience. And I must confess I agree with his assessment. I don't like the look of you, lad. Much too young. You have the look of a troublemaker about you." He stepped forward until he was in Tweed's personal space. *Way, way* in his personal space. Then he inhaled.

Tweed leaned back, not even trying to keep the look of disgust from his face.

"You will *not* be the head of the wait staff," said Hardstone. "You will instead be a *waiter*. One of the serving staff. That'll teach you some humility."

Tweed's eyes widened in outrage. "I don't need a lesson in humility! I'm perfect as I am!"

"You will report to me, boy. I am taking over as head of wait staff for the duration. I've sent a message to Egypt and hopefully a replacement can be found when we dock in Cairo. Until then, you either take on your duties like a man, or cry like a little baby. And if you choose the latter, it means you will be cleaning latrines twelve hours a day. So, which is it to be?"

Tweed's mind raced. What options did he have? He had to stay on the airship. It was their only chance of finding Octavia's mother. He couldn't let her down.

He sighed. "I'll face my duties."

"Good man! Now take your things to your cot and report to the servant's dining room at 0800 hours. Don't be late! Tardiness is a sign of the devil!"

Tweed thought about saying something in response to this ludicrous statement, but he realized it meant he would have to stay here a bit longer. Instead, he picked up his bag and slouched away.

"Stand up straight, boy!" shouted Hardstone.

Tweed straightened up, muttering curses under his breath. This was not going to be as easy as he'd thought.

The servant's dining hall was more like a huge common room. It had tables and chairs in the center of the floor space, but around the edges were comfy couches, billiards and cards tables, and a few other games that Tweed suspected none of the staff would get a chance to use seeing as they would be so busy serving the toffs upstairs.

All the staff had gathered in the room. Tweed tried to do a quick count but gave up after a hundred and fifty.

He hated to admit it, but he was slightly nervous. He stared at the other waiters, wondering who would be the first to call him out as a fake. He was trying his best to act like the other members of staff, but he found himself struggling. He'd never held down a normal job before. He'd spent his life with Barnaby taking part in cons. All this "respecting authority" malarkey was new to him. And painful.

And annoying.

And draining.

He nudged a tall fellow standing next to him. "Can't wait to get out there and do . . ." he cast desperately about, "serving stuff, eh? Waiting on all the rich people. What larks."

The fellow just frowned at Tweed, then slowly shuffled away.

"Be like that, then," said Tweed. He saw a girl watching him with an amused look on her face. "Hello," he said, waving cheerfully.

"Hello."

"Um . . ." Tweed racked his brain about what the procedure was when meeting people. "Oh yes. I'm Tw—Holmes. Sebastian Holmes."

The girl held her hand out. "Violet."

Tweed shook it.

"So are you ready to be at the beck and call of over-entitled, pompous windbags?" she asked.

Tweed raised an eyebrow. "Oh, I don't know. I've met Hardstone. He's not that bad."

Violet laughed, a surprisingly loud and rather . . . distracting cackle. It broke off abruptly, as did the low babble that had dominated the room.

Tweed glanced up to see Hardstone enter and survey his charges. Tweed narrowed his eyes. That should have been *him* entering, surveying *his* staff, *his* army of cleaners and waiters. It should have been *him* they all hated and gossiped about behind his back. Tweed had been quite enjoying the prospect of such a thing. But now, now he was one of them, a grunt in the trenches.

"I'll keep this brief," said Hardstone loudly. "We're already a man short, but we will *not* let that affect our services. Our guests have paid good money to travel aboard this airship, and we should all consider ourselves lucky we have been chosen to serve. I will brook no shenanigans. No hanky-panky. No smart comments. I want smiling faces and obedient staff who go out of their way to make sure the needs of our guests are met." He gave them all a dirty look. "Understand?"

A rumble of agreement swept through the staff.

"Good. Now. Kitchen staff. Off you go. Mrs. Deacon is waiting for you."

A third of the people in the room moved to the doors. Once they'd left, Hardstone surveyed those that remained. "And you lot are to go through every single room. A final check. I do not want to see a speck of dust or the slightest crease in bed linen. Everything in its place. Go. We have five hours till the guests arrive."

Violet grabbed Tweed by the arm and pulled him toward the closest door.

"Before he picks us for some other task."

"Like what?"

"Like making sure all the latrines are clean. I've heard about Hardstone. Cross him and you'll be on latrine duty for the entire voyage."

"Yes, he's already mentioned that."

Luckily for Tweed, he didn't plan on staying the entire voyage. At least, he hoped not. The *Albion* traveled at thirty miles an hour and it was about 2200 miles to Egypt. So they were talking about three days travel time. That's how long he and Octavia had to find Molock and force him to reveal Octavia's mother's location.

Violet led him up to the first floor of the airship. Tweed strolled along the carpet, inspecting the paintings and photographs, his arms behind his back as he took in the ambience.

"If you don't mind me saying," said Violet, glancing at him over her shoulder. "You . . . don't really seem to be of the waitering mindset."

"Oh? And what mindset is that?" asked Tweed absently. He nodded at a painting. "That's a fake. I wonder if the owners know." Tweed cast a suspicious glance both ways along the corridor. "Actually, I wonder how many more are fake. Someone could have made some serious money here." He tilted his head back, staring at the ceiling. "Say . . . one out of ten is a reproduction. Just enough to pocket some surplus money, and not enough to draw attention. Maybe even one in seven?" He thoughtfully sucked his teeth. "Of course, the supplier would have to cover himself. Use a middleman. Who I'll bet has vanished already." Tweed became aware that Violet was staring at him. "What? Sorry. Were you talking? Drifted away there."

"No," she said. "Not talking. Just . . . listening."

"Good habit that. Listening. You learn more than by talking."

"Yes. I agree."

Tweed opened his mouth, then he paused and closed it again.
"Yes," he repeated. "Er . . . should we get on? Lots of rooms to check."

The first room fairly boggled Tweed's mind. It was massive. An
elegantly furnished room that wouldn't look out of place in the Savoy.
Furniture from France, clocks from Switzerland, and some traditional
paintings from Africa, by the looks of it.

"How many people stay in this room?"

Violet looked at him in surprise. "One. It's a single."

"A single . . ." Tweed looked around in amazement. He opened
one door, peered into the bathroom, opened another into the bedroom,
then opened yet another into a *second* bathroom. He gestured at it.
"Two bathrooms! For one person! Can the rich not *walk*? Are they so
weighed down by money that they can't make it across the room to
their *single* bathroom before they soil themselves? This is ridiculous!"

Violet tilted her head to the side. "You haven't been around the
upper class much, have you?"

Tweed had. Although the contact was brief and only lasted long
enough to take their money.

"I tend to avoid things that disagree with me," he said.

"Really?" said Violet mildly. "How do you get through life then?"

"With difficulty," declared Tweed. "With difficulty and a certain
amount of sprightliness."

Violet stared at him for a few more seconds, then let out her low
cackle again. "You're very odd, Sebastian. I think I like you. Now
come on. Let's check the other suites."

"Let's not and say we did."

But they did, and it was incredibly boring. Tweed yawned his
way through their duties. (He had, after all, barely slept the night
before.)

Bedrooms: inspection of: (30.) All immaculately clean.

Cutlery: inspection of: (1300 complete sets.) all immaculately clean. In fact, some of them were a bit grubbier *after* Tweed picked them up. He couldn't help it. His hands were clean. But the silver just kept smearing from the oil on his fingers.

Dinner plates: inspection of: (1300, dinner, side, bread, dessert.) All clean.

Table cloths: ironing of. (Too many to count. Tweed's mind actually switched off from the sheer boredom. And he wasn't even ironing them. He was holding the already-steamed sections off the ground so they wouldn't crease *again*.)

Finally, it was it was time for the guests to arrive. The junior waiting staff (of which Tweed was one) had a chance for a brief rest as the guests landed in ornithopters, while the more senior staff (like Violet) escorted them to their cabins. Tweed didn't know how people did it, toiling away at an honest day's work. It was enough to turn him back to crime.

Once all the guests had arrived, their names ticked off, double-checked, triple-checked, and then checked again by the captain (Couldn't fly off without all the guests. Think of the scandal!), it was time to begin the journey.

There was a narrow balcony outside the waiter's dining hall that ran all the way around the airship. Tweed slipped outside and leaned over the railing, peering down at Trafalgar Square. The crowds had increased as the morning wore on. When he arrived early this morning there had been a tramp with a dog. The tramp, for some reason, was singing "Auld Lang Syne." Now, there were hundreds of onlookers crowding the plaza in order to see the *Albion* off.

Tweed was joined by some of the other staff. There was a heavy thunk from below as the mooring cables were released, then winched upward into the belly of the airship. The dirigible bobbed slightly. Tweed could feel the tension running through the ship as it strained to rise into the air. But there was still a central mooring line left attached. Once the others had all been wound into position, this final cable was released, and with a loud cheer from those below, the airship *Albion* surged upward.

Tweed could hear polite applause from above. He leaned over the railing and could see the bottom of another balcony about twenty feet above him.

The airship kept rising, Trafalgar Square, then London itself receding far below them. The Thames unraveled like a silvery-grey snake, heading out into the snow-covered fields and farms that surrounded the city.

Mist and clouds fell around them, obscuring Tweed's view. Most of the staff disappeared inside, but Tweed stayed where he was, thinking over his plans. They had three days. Three days in which to get information out of Molock about Octavia's mother. Chase and Temple could deal with Tesla. They obviously thought they were better suited to that inquiry, after all.

After a few minutes the grey clouds started to thin, and then with a suddenness that took Tweed's breath away, the airship burst softly through the top of the cloud bank into icy blue skies. Tweed squinted, the winter sun blinding him. He raised a hand to shield his eyes, gazing in awe at the emptiness that unrolled in every direction.

The brilliant blue all around him, the grey snow clouds below, the *Albion* in the middle, resting between two worlds.

And then the *Albion* started to move forward. Tweed felt the ship vibrate as the Tesla Turbines kicked in, the top secret technology propelling the ship forward at thirty miles an hour. Tweed had heard it could go much faster, but thirty miles an hour was the optimal speed for comfort.

Tweed sighed and slapped the delicately carved balcony. Time to get to work. And by work, he didn't mean Hardstone's chores. He meant finding out where Molock was hiding.

Tweed had thought it would be relatively simple getting to the captain's offices. (He assumed that was where the guest register or whatever it was that listed who was staying in which cabin was kept.) He imagined a small corridor at the end of which was a personal cabin. And inside that cabin a small office.

Nice and simple.

The reality was rather different. The top level of the airship was taken up with operational rooms. Offices given over to plotting their course, a mess hall for the important staff members, personal cabins for same, a radio room, logistics rooms. And on and on and on. Tweed's rather naive thoughts about where the records would be kept quickly turned to ash.

He briefly considered waiting till night time to sneak around, but then he thought better of it. He was exhausted and couldn't be bothered with all that fumbling around in the dark. Besides, he was wearing one of the best disguises available. He could go anywhere he wanted on board the airship and no one would give him a second glance. However, if he was caught sneaking around in the middle of the night, it wouldn't be so easy to explain.

"Excuse me," he said to the first person he spotted, a young man with a crisp white shirt and a pile of maps clutched in his arms. "Where is the records room?"

"The records room?" The man frowned. "What?"

Tweed thought quickly. "Sorry. I was told to go to the records room. May have misheard. It's all a bit chaotic downstairs."

"Up here as well," said the man, his frown easing slightly.

"I assume Hardstone meant the place where records are kept. Files, guest lists, that kind of thing. He wants me to sort out a room mix-up."

"Ah, I see. You want the customer files. Head to the front of the ship, into the bridge, and through the door to the right."

Tweed nodded his thanks and hurried along the dark-paneled corridor. It was much narrower up here. More like a real ship. No need to build in extra space like they did for the paying customers. This was for the workers.

Tweed had to remember to step aside when all the important and harassed staff who actually made the *Albion* stay in the air hurried past, some of them clutching creased rolls of paper, others with compasses and huge files. It all looked very disorganized to him. Surely they should have had this all sorted out before they left? It was as if they were only just now plotting their course. He supposed they had to constantly readjust, though. To make allowances for bad weather, winds, that kind of thing.

He arrived at the bridge. It was a large room right at the front of the airship, crowded with brass and wood paneled instruments. A huge globe of the world took up the center of the room. Two men and a woman were studying it, measuring distances with odd instruments and scribbling down notes in leather-bound journals. A wide window arced around the front wall, showing a view of the sky outside. In the distance he could see grey clouds towering up in their path, obscuring the pristine blue he had seen earlier. He supposed that was what all the fuss was about. To go through the weather system, or around it? And if around it, how much extra speed would they need to make up lost time?

Tweed saw the door he was searching for off to the right. But one of the crew happened to look up as he entered. His face lit up with relief and he raised his hand.

"You here to take our orders? Coffee for me."

A woman standing next to him glanced in Tweed's direction. "Tea here."

"Coffee."

"Orange juice."

"Tea."

The orders flew at Tweed from all corners of the room, and he jotted them all down in his notepad before heading to the door that led to the records room.

He slipped inside. The room was small, no more than three paces long. It had a narrow desk at one end. A shelf on the wall above it was filled with leather-bound ledgers. Tweed checked the first one. A ledger for buying food for the kitchens. Another was for house-keeping, a record of bed sheets, washing soap, silver polish, that kind of thing.

He found what he was looking for in the next book. The names of all the guests, listed in neat cursive handwriting. Tweed flipped through the pages. Over a thousand names, all linked to their room numbers. The names were listed alphabetically, which was rather handy.

He flipped to the back and skimmed through all the names beginning with W. Then he frowned and did it again.

There was no Wilberforce listed here.

He checked a third time, but he hadn't made a mistake. Still nothing.

He turned to M, just in case he was listed under Molock. No luck.

Tweed sighed and sat down at the desk, flipping back to the beginning of the book, just in case someone had entered the name on the wrong page. He read through every single entry but there was no Wilberforce or Molock listed as a passenger on this ship.

Tweed felt a rush of doubt. Had he been mistaken? Were they even now traveling *away* from their target?

But no, he had found the singed card back in Tesla's factory and it had been Molock who dropped it. He *had* to be here. He must simply be using another false name.

Which meant it was going to be very difficult to find him. He and Octavia would just have to wander around, keeping their eyes open in the hopes of spotting him. He had to tell Octavia. She would have more chance to wander the ship freely.

He put the book back and hurried through the bridge, heading down through the levels to Octavia's room. He knocked and waited. The door was opened a second later by Octavia.

"I'm afraid I didn't order room service," she said.

Tweed slipped passed her, then stared around the room in annoyed awe. "This is hardly fair," he said.

Octavia flopped onto a chaise lounge, and started eating chocolates. She looked annoying relaxed. Tweed slumped down into the chair opposite her.

She held out the box of chocolates to him. "Only the nut ones left, I'm afraid. And the ginger ones."

Tweed made a face. "Hate those."

"So how goes the life of an honest worker?" asked Octavia.

"Terrible. No wonder Barnaby tried to turn me to a life of crime. I don't know how people *do* it. And you know what the worst thing is? Having to take orders from cretins, absolute imbeciles who I am infinitely more intelligent than."

"And infinitely more modest too."

"What point false modesty?" asked Tweed. "It's a fact. I'm more intelligent than ninety-eight percent of the people on board this airship."

Octavia pursed her lips and raised an eyebrow. Tweed knew that was her disagreeing, but not really wanting to get into it at the moment. He let it go.

"And you? How goes the life of a highborn lady?" he asked.

He knew he should just tell her about Molock, but she looked rather relaxed lying there on her couch, and he didn't want to end that for her. "It seems to suit you."

Octavia stretched luxuriantly. "Oh, it does. I think I was born to be a member of the elite. All the pampering."

Tweed sighed. "Listen, While you've been bathing in goat's milk or whatever is it you lot do in first class, I've already checked the passenger manifest."

Octavia sat up, her eyes widening with anticipation. Tweed held up his hand. "Don't get excited. Wilberforce's name isn't there. Neither is Molock's."

Octavia slumped back. "Why do we keep running into these walls?" she snapped. "Every time we get somewhere it seems like we're thrown two steps back."

"It's not hopeless. We just have to keep our eyes open. He has to show his face sometime."

"And if he doesn't? What if he stays in his cabin?"

"For the whole trip? No way. Besides, if he does, there will be talk about it downstairs. The working classes are very prone to gossip, you know. Think it keeps their minds off how pointless their existences are."

Octavia frowned at him. "You'd better not mean that, Tweed. That's not a very nice thing to say."

Tweed opened his mouth to say, well, yes, he sort of *did* mean it. Just because it's not a nice thing to say, doesn't mean it's not true. But he didn't. Instead he sighed and shut his mouth.

What unholy power did Octavia have over him? Was this friendship? Not wanting to be a disappointment to her? Trying to measure up all the time? Making sure you didn't offend? He was sure that wasn't right. Friendship should be about saying what you wanted without fear of being cast out, surely? Judgment was fine. She could

125

judge him for what he said. But friendship meant he should be free to say it in front of her.

"Actually, I *did* mean it," he said haughtily. "And if you don't like it then you can stuff more of those chocolates in your mouth, because . . . well . . . *tough*."

Octavia narrowed her eyes to tiny slits. Tweed readied himself for the attack, because when she looked like that, something was coming. But whether it would be a chocolate to the head, or a verbal tirade he wasn't sure. He carefully put his hand on a nearby pillow, just in case.

He was rescued by a knock at the door.

"Thought you said you didn't order room service."

"I didn't!" she snapped. "And this isn't over."

She pushed herself up off the chaise lounge and went to answer the door. Tweed hastily stood up and grabbed a nearby silver tray. Just in case it was a member of the staff. Wouldn't do to have him spotted sitting around on the guests' furniture.

Octavia opened the door.

Tweed blinked in surprise.

Octavia blinked in surprise.

Molock blinked in surprise. "Um . . . what—?" he started to ask, but that was as far as he got, because Tweed flung the silver tray through the air directly at him. He cried out and tried to twist away, but it hit him in the side of the head, stunning him. He dropped to one knee. Tweed ran forward, but Octavia already had Molock under the shoulders and was dragging him inside the room. Tweed slammed the door shut.

"Get some ropes or something," said Octavia.

Tweed looked around. There were curtains on the walls, even though there were no actual windows. He ripped the cords that held them open and helped Octavia drag Molock to a chair. He tied the man's arms behind his back and his ankles to the chair.

Octavia and Tweed stood back, both of them breathless. They looked at Molock as he blinked and tried to focus on them. Then they looked at each other, smiles breaking out on their faces.

Octavia reached out and flicked his ear. Hard.

"Ow!" Tweed jerked away and looked at her as if she was mad. "What was that for?"

"For what you said about lower classes."

CHAPTER NINE

Octavia stared hard at the man before her, the man responsible for her mother's disappearance. He didn't look like a monster, like someone who would rip a family apart. He looked . . . harmless. A mild-mannered, thin face, a neat suit, immaculate hair. In fact, he looked slightly worried as he came to his senses and found them both staring at him.

"Who are you?" Molock asked. He frowned. "And why did you *hit* me?" he looked around. "This *is* Mr. Stackpole's room, is it not?"

"You're looking for Stackpole?" asked Tweed in surprise.

"You're not trying to *kill* us?" said Octavia.

Molock frowned. He closed his eyes for a few moments then opened them again.

"I know your voice," he said to Tweed. He stared at him for a few moments before realization dawned. "You were the one at Tesla's factory. The one who shot us."

Octavia put her hand up. "Actually, that was me."

Tweed pulled up Molock's sleeve. No Osiris tattoo. He looked questioningly at Octavia. She shrugged.

"I must admit to great confusion," said Molock. "Judging by your actions, you seem to know about the Hermetic Order of Osiris. Am I correct?"

"If you mean the crazy cult that's been trying to kill us, then yes, we do. You aren't one of them?"

"Of course not!" said Molock, shocked. "If they found me I would be dead in an instant. Look, there has obviously been some misunderstanding here. I must speak to Stackpole before he does something terrible."

"Stackpole's dead," said Tweed.

Molock's eyes widened. His eyes flicked between the two of them. "Dead? But . . . Did you . . . ?"

"*What*? No!" exclaimed Octavia. "Of course not."

"It was this . . . Hermetic Brotherhood . . ." said Tweed.

"The Hermetic Order of Osiris."

"Yeah. Them. They killed him at his home. Tortured him first."

"Why would they do that?" said Molock, confusion clear in his voice. "It doesn't make sense."

"That doesn't matter," said Octavia. "You're here for another reason. Where is my mother?"

Molock's face crumpled into an almost comical look of confusion. Octavia almost felt sorry for him. "What? Your mother . . . I don't . . ." He shook his head helplessly. "I don't know what's happening right now."

"My mother. Where is she?"

"Who is your mother? I have no idea what you're talking about."

"My mother," said Octavia softly, "is Elizabeth Nightingale. A reporter for *The Times*. She was taken to a Ministry prison and for some reason you . . . signed her out. Took her away somewhere."

"Eliz—" Molock stared at her, then he broke into a smile. "You're Octavia! Of *course*. I should have seen the resemblance."

Octavia's heart skipped when she heard his words.

He knows what I'm talking about. He really knows.

She had been scared she was following the wrong path, that her mother was slipping farther and farther away. But she wasn't. She was close. Here was proof. She took a step forward.

"So you admit to it?"

"To saving your mother's life? Yes. I do."

This time it was Octavia's turn to look confused. "Saving her life? But you kidnapped her. You've kept her prisoner for over a year."

"I assure you I did not." Molock sighed. "I see we are talking at cross purposes here. Perhaps I should explain?"

"We would like that very much," said Tweed. "Very much indeed."

"Fine. Your mother was investigating a man called Lucien—"

"We know that."

"Right. Fine. Lucien was using a simulacra of Sherlock Holmes to put some terrible plan into action. He had allied himself with the Russian Tsar and planned to assassinate—"

"Yes, yes," said Octavia. "All things we know. Skip to the end."

"The Tsar was also allied with another group. The Hermetic Order of Osiris."

Now that they *didn't* know. "Why?" asked Octavia. "What does this . . . this *cult* want?"

Molock sighed, troubled. "This is . . . very hard to explain. I can *show* you, but . . . it's difficult to know how you will react. I'm worried you may do something impulsive and . . . try to hurt me."

"Why on earth would we do that?" said Octavia.

"Because if I show you what I fear I must . . . it will change your entire outlook on life. Your whole viewpoint will shift. This is not something to be done lightly."

Octavia bit her lip. What he was saying *did* sound a bit worrying, but whatever it was he had to show them, it couldn't be *that* bad, could it? Maybe it was just a ruse for them to untie his hands.

"We're not going to untie you," she said.

"You don't need to."

Octavia glanced at Tweed and he shrugged.

"I'm game if you are," he said. "Always ready to have my viewpoint shifted."

Octavia rolled her eyes. That was a lie. Tweed was one of the most stuck-in-his-ways people she'd ever met. And at seventeen! What would he be like as an old man?

"Fine," she said to Molock. "Show us."

What Octavia saw next would stay with her forever. Not just a vague memory, but every tiny detail, every sound in the room, every color, every smell of that moment was imprinted on her very being.

At first, nothing happened. Molock simply closed his eyes and took a few deep breaths. But then his face . . . his face *rippled*, like tiny waves lapping against the shore. His whole mouth and nose sort of pushed outward, distorting. His lips receded and pulled away, his nose flattening until all that was left were two nostrils. His coloring darkened, turning brown, then olive green. The skin itself separated, forming tiny scales, little ridges that covered the face.

Tweed grabbed her arm and they both stumbled backward in shock. Tweed swept up the silver plate he had thrown earlier and Octavia grabbed her gun from the table.

Molock opened eyes that had turned yellow. On top of that he now had two sets of eyelids. The normal ones, and another set, membranous, that opened horizontally.

She was looking at what she could only describe as some sort of lizard-man.

"I told you," said Molock mildly.

Octavia's mouth was hanging open. She closed it, still keeping the Tesla gun pointed at the creature.

"What . . . what *are* you?" said Octavia in a voice she couldn't help notice was trembling. She cleared her throat. "Tell us." She waved the gun threateningly.

"There's no need for the weapon. Despite what you may think, we're on the same side."

Octavia glanced at Tweed. He had put the silver tray down. He moved slowly around Molock, leaning down to check the hands that were tied behind the chair.

Octavia followed. Molock's hands were the same as the face. Dark

green lizard skin. She hesitantly reached out and touched it. Hard.
Dry.

She moved back to stand in front of him. "Explain," she said.

Molock nodded. "I will. To start with, I am not one of your race.
I am a Hyperborean."

"A what?" said Tweed. He bent down and moved his face within
an inch of Molock's, tilting his head to the side, studying.

"A Hyperborean," said Molock, moving his face away from
Tweed. "That means I'm from Hyperborea," he added helpfully.

"I know what it *means*," snapped Tweed. "But Hyperborea is a
mythical place. It doesn't exist." Tweed reached out with a finger and
prodded Molock's face.

"Do you mind?"

"Sorry."

"And it *does* exist."

Octavia didn't know what to say. She was staring at a lizard-man.
He was staring at *them*. He was there. He was real.

"Are there more of you?" asked Tweed.

"Oh yes. Hundreds of thousands."

"And where is this . . . Hyperborea?" asked Octavia.

"Inside the earth."

Tweed snorted. "This is like an Atticus Pope story. Are you
saying the earth is hollow?"

"Not hollow. At least, not all the way. But hidden lands far
underground? Oh yes. That is where Hyperborea lies."

"With . . ." Tweed waved his hands in the air, "light? And veg-
etation? And animals?"

Molock nodded.

"And you've always been there?"

"Always."

"So why haven't we heard about you before now?"

"Well, you have, in a way. You *know* about Hyperborea."

"Legends. Stories. But not as a real place."

"That is because of the Covenant. We have always done every-thing we could to make sure your people do not find out about us. If that were to happen . . . I think a war of terrible proportions would break out. Our races are not meant to mix. We are too different."

"But what about this Hermetic Order? Do they know about you?"

"I'm afraid so."

"How?"

Molock winced. "To make you understand, I have to tell you some of our history."

"Please. Go right ahead," said Tweed. "We're all ears. Which is more than can be said for you." Tweed leaned down to inspect the small holes on either side of Molock's head.

"Please don't do that."

Tweed straightened up.

"There used to be a society that knew about us. Over time, they came to worship us, actually based their gods on us. Their whole way of life, really."

"Who were these people?" asked Octavia.

"The ancient Egyptians. Five thousand years ago Egypt was a bountiful land. Green, hot. A beautiful place. When the Egyptians first settled on the Nile Delta, they did so because we were there first. We had been there for centuries, come up from the land below. They were no more than primitives, but we allowed them to settle close by. It amused us. Made us feel superior. They looked on us as gods. Thoth, Anubis, Osiris, Amun, Ra . . . all those were members of our ruling elite, names of real people." Molock sighed. "They based their entire civilization on us."

"So what happened?" asked Octavia. "Why did you go back underground?"

"What always happens? War. Greed. Fighting. The Egyptian rulers started to curry favor, trying to gain power, gain access to technology we knew they weren't ready for. We were not that many. Our kind are long-lived and slow to breed. The Egyptians soon outnumbered us, and their entreaties became demands. Our rulers decided it was best for us to . . . retreat back into the world, to rejoin those who had stayed in Hyperborea. Once we had done this a law was passed. A very, very strict law that has been in existence now for over three thousand years."

"The Covenant," said Tweed.

"Correct. The Covenant says that our people were to stay in Hyperborea and never again—on pain of death—show our faces above ground. Our rulers saw the way the world was turning. They saw how fast humans were spreading, and knew they would not share the world with us.

"But some were not happy about returning below ground. One of our rulers, Osiris, was against it. He had no choice, of course, but once we had abandoned the world, his supporters began meeting in secret, forming a hidden cabal of like-minded individuals."

"This Hermetic Order of Osiris?" asked Tweed.

Molock nodded. "Osiris died long ago, but his ideas live on, given strength by his followers."

"And what exactly are these ideas?"

"That we should not cower underground. That the world was ours first, and it should be ours again. That we should retake it from the upstart human race, turn you all into our slaves."

"And this Sekhem fellow? And his sister, Nehi?" said Octavia. "They follow Osiris?"

"Not followers. He and his sister are the leaders of the order." Molock paused. "But with Sekhem dead, I suppose Nehi will lead them on her own now."

"Er . . ." Tweed raised a hand. "Sekhem's not dead."

"What?" Molock looked at him in astonishment. "But your weapon. I saw him fall."

"So did we. But after we chased you and went back to look for him, he was gone."

"But . . . this is terrible. I thought it was just Nehi I was up against. That Sekhem's death might give me more time. But if he is still alive, their plans will still be in place."

"It, ah, kind of gets worse," said Octavia. "I saw Sekhem. Here. Aboard this airship."

Molock stared at her, then strained at his bindings, trying to break free. "You must let me go. I need to find them. Stop them."

"You didn't tell me you saw Sekhem," said Tweed.

"I was going to. But then *he* turned up."

"And anyway," said Tweed, turning back to Molock. "Stop them doing what? He took Tesla's plans, but what are his intentions?"

"What do you think?" snapped Molock. "They're going to build his super weapons, are going to turn them against the human race."

"But . . . why? What does he have against us?"

Molock looked uncomfortable. "That . . . doesn't matter right now. What matters is stopping them. Sekhem and his people, they are now the main power in Hyperborea. The old rulers, they *believed* in the Covenant. They did not want any contact with humans. They thought, they *knew*, that any such contact would lead to the annihilation of our people. You outnumber us. We wouldn't stand a chance. But Sekhem and Nehi, they staged a coup. They ousted the royal family and took over. This was about five years ago, and since that time they have been pushing forward with their plans."

"Do all your people stand with them?" asked Octavia.

"No. There are rebels, those who still believe in the Covenant, but Sekhem and Nehi have been hunting them down and killing them. Once they have achieved this, nothing will stop them."

"And you?" said Tweed. "What's your part in all this?"

"I am—I *was*—the ruler of Hyperborea. I am the one they ousted. They would have killed me, but I had help. I escaped. Now I do my best to stop Sekhem and Nehi revealing our race to your people."

Octavia sat down in a chair. This was all so much to take in. "What did all this have to do with Stackpole?" she asked.

"Stackpole stumbled upon a hideout of Sekhem and the Order of Osiris. He found many carvings, most of them new to Egyptology. If he gained funding to excavate this site, wherever it is, he would have exposed us to the world. That cannot happen. I was hoping to convince him to forget about it."

"Then you *did* have motive to kill him," said Octavia.

"Why do you insist on thinking of me as a cold-blooded murderer?" Octavia could see Molock was getting annoyed. "Must I judge your entire race on the actions of Jack the Ripper?"

Octavia flushed, embarrassed. "Sorry."

"But what would you have done if Stackpole refused?" said Tweed.

Molock didn't say anything. He looked uncomfortable, then changed the subject entirely. "If Sekhem and Nehi are aboard, they must be returning to this hideout in Egypt."

"You don't know where it is?"

"No idea."

"You still haven't explained how all this relates to my mother."

Molock winced. "Do you think you could untie me? These cords are chafing."

"Talk first," said Tweed.

Molock sighed. "As I said, your mother thought she was investigating Professor Moriarty. She had made the connection to Lucien, and was in danger of uncovering the conspiracy with the Tsar of Russia. This conspiracy involved Sekhem and Nehi."

"How?"

"Sekhem and Nehi have a . . . very deep hatred of your Empire. They were behind the Tsar's actions, urging him onward. They want to see your Empire fall and they saw this as one way in which to do it. But when your mother came too close to the truth, word was passed to Lucien and she was taken to a Ministry prison. The Hermetic Order, they have someone on the inside, a member of one of your government agencies loyal to Sekhem and Nehi. They wanted to know how much she knew, who she had told. The plan was for this spy of theirs to interrogate her to find out."

"Who is this spy?" asked Octavia.

"I do not know. I'm sorry. All I know is that Sekhem has someone loyal to him very high up in one of your government agencies."

"Then what happened?" asked Tweed.

"My people found out. If Elizabeth had any information, anything that could help us oppose Sekhem and Nehi—remember, we did not know their plan at this time—then we had to know. So we infiltrated the prison and took her."

"Using your own name in the process," said Tweed. "Not very clever."

"Wilberforce isn't my name. It's associated with me, and that's why I used it. I couldn't resist leaving a little calling card for Sekhem and Nehi. So they would know we were still watching them."

Molock sighed. "But then we were faced with another problem. What to do with your mother. She had indeed found out about Sekhem and Nehi. She was in possession of the biggest story of her career, the most important story of all time. If we let her go, we would be exposed. She tried to convince us this was a good thing. That we should approach the Empire and ally ourselves with them against the Hermetic Order, but this is not the path forward. The Covenant still holds. If we did as she asked, my people would face death."

"So you kept her prisoner?" said Octavia angrily.

"Not prisoner. Not as such. She was given free reign of our hide-away. She taught our children to read English. To write. She taught us your history. She has been an invaluable member of our group."

"And she couldn't get a message to us?" asked Octavia, feeling betrayed. It was as if her mother had abandoned her family for another. "To her own daughter and husband? To let us know she was alive?"

Molock squirmed in his seat. "Ah."

"*Ah?*"

"Yes. Um . . . I'm afraid she did write to you. Every week, actu-ally. Telling you of the wonders she was seeing in Hyperborea. But you have to understand we couldn't let those letters get out. If they were intercepted, and someone believed them . . ."

"You took her letters?" said Octavia in a low voice.

"Well . . . sort of. Broadly speaking, I suppose you could say . . ." He broke off under Octavia's angry glare. "Yes. I'm afraid we did. Sorry."

"And she's still there? In Hyperborea?"

"She is."

"You can't just keep her prisoner forever," said Octavia. "She doesn't belong there. She belongs here, with her family."

Molock sighed. "I know, I know. But can you blame us? Your Empire has been expanding all over the globe, conquering lands, wiping out any who stand against them. If word got out about us, your government would simply see new mineral wealth. A new world to claim for Her Majesty the Queen."

"We're not all like that," said Tweed. "There are ways our people can live together. Trade is better than war. It lasts longer."

"I disagree. Why trade when you can simply take?"

"You have to tell me," said Octavia. "Where is my mother?"

Molock stared at her speculatively. "I will make a deal with you."

"No deals," said Tweed firmly. "Just tell us."

"I cannot. I would have to show you. Here is my offer. Help me stop Sekhem and Nehi. Help me capture them. Then I will take you to your mother. I promise you this on the lives of my people."

Octavia stared at Molock, then indicated to Tweed that he should join her in the bedroom.

"What do you think?" she asked.

"I think my brain is hurting," said Tweed flopping back onto her bed.

"I mean about the deal. Stopping Nehi and Sekhem *is* something that has to be done, and it looks like we know more about them than the authorities back home. If we can help with that *and* get my mother back . . . ?"

Tweed thought about it, then nodded. "Fine. I'm game if you are."

They returned to Molock.

"One thing," said Tweed. "This Hermetic Order thingy. Why is it made up of us? Humans?"

Even though his face was that of a lizard, Octavia could see the look of embarrassment that crossed Molock's features. "Um . . . Some of you still sort of look on us as gods. The Hermetic Order of Osiris has been a secret society here in your world for centuries. They are fanatical, willing to do anything for their Hyperborean rulers. Sekhem takes full advantage of their services."

"So . . . what's our next move?" asked Octavia.

"You untie me. And we see if we can't find Sekhem and Nehi before we reach Egypt."

CHAPTER TEN

Tweed spent the day wandering around the airship, acting as a slave for those apparently too rich to do anything by themselves, while at the same time keeping an eye out for Sekhem or Nehi.

After spending hour after hour tending to the passengers' needs (and being told off for forgetting to take the Captain and his crew their drinks), Tweed started to wonder how the upper class would actually function without servants. Would they remember to breathe? To eat? Or would they just lie in their beds, withering away while they wondered where Jeeves was with their breakfast?

In fact, forget strikes. Forget rising up and fighting for your rights. All the lower classes had to do was not turn up for work and the upper classes would be trapped in their bedrooms while they tried to remember how a doorknob worked.

Tweed realized he was being slightly uncharitable, but he was in an incredibly bad mood so he reckoned he was allowed a bit of nastiness. His feet were absolutely killing him. He didn't think he'd ever walked as much as he had today. Plus, he wasn't having *any* luck finding Sekhem and Nehi. Checking for two people amongst over a thousand was actually quite difficult, especially when everyone was constantly moving around, going to lunch, going dancing, watching a show, going to dinner, heading back to their cabins, etc., etc.

And time was running out. They were approaching Egypt, due to land a couple of hours from now.

It suddenly struck him that he was being incredibly stupid. What if Sekhem and Nehi really *were* purposefully staying out of sight? Octavia had mentioned such a possibility when talking about Moloch, but he hadn't really taken it seriously.

But why not?

Tweed ran down to the kitchens, and half an hour later he was standing in the corridor a few doors down from the adjoining rooms of two mysterious guests who had all their meals delivered, never once leaving the comfort of their second class lodgings.

Rather simple, when you put your mind to it. Of course, he wouldn't be telling Octavia that. She was insufferable when she was right.

Hot sunlight spilled through a porthole to Tweed's left, falling across the carpet and wall. He blinked away the sweat. How could it be so hot? Only two days ago, he had been in the freezing streets of London. Now he was south of the equator, in the middle of summer, and the temperature felt like it was over forty degrees. How did people survive such heat? It was madness.

He wiped his moist palm on his trouser leg, then took a firm hold of the Tesla gun. The corridor was clear. Now was the time. He licked his lips and headed toward the door, leaning forward to listen. Silence.

He knocked.

He waited a few seconds then knocked again. "Excuse me? *Albion* staff. We've had reports of a small fire on this level. I just want to check everything is well."

Still no answer.

Tweed reached into his pocket and pulled out a box of Lucifers he had commandeered from the kitchen. He moved a few steps away and struck one of the matches, putting the flame to a newspaper he had picked up. When the paper was burning he dropped it onto the floor and knelt down to blow smoke beneath the door.

He stood up and knocked again, more urgently. "Sir? Please, I think there *is* a fire. You must move to safety while we deal with it."

Tweed held his breath and listened. He heard a shuffling sound, then the door was unlocked and started to swing open. Tweed stood on the paper, grinding the small flames into nothing, then kicked the door hard, slamming it into the figure beyond.

Tweed strode quickly into the room, Tesla gun held ready. Sekhem was stumbling back, trying to keep his balance. Tweed closed the door and looked around. No sign of Nehi, but there was a door off to his left.

Sekhem righted himself against a couch and stared at him in puzzled surprise.

Tweed gestured with the gun. "Open that door."

Sekhem moved across to the door and pushed it open.

"Inside."

Tweed followed him through into the bedroom of the second cabin. He pointed at the bed.

"Sit."

Sekhem sat down while Tweed stuck his head out of the bedroom into the sitting room beyond. Empty. He turned back to Sekhem.

"Where's your sister?"

Sekhem held his hands wide. "I do not know. I am not her keeper."

Damn. This made things complicated.

"I know you," said Sekhem, looking at him speculatively. "You were at the factory. You and your female friend. You shot me."

"Behave yourself and I won't have to shoot you again."

An amused look crossed Sekhem's features. Tweed couldn't help but notice the man wasn't exactly scared of him. In fact, he looked totally relaxed, leaning back on the bed as if they were two friends having a chat.

"Where are they?" asked Tweed.

"Where are what?"

"The plans. The ones you stole from Tesla's workshop."

"Ah."

"Where have you hidden them?"

Tweed was watching Sekhem very carefully. He knew about facial tics and uncontrollable reactions, so when Sekhem's eyes flickered over Tweed's shoulder, he smiled in triumph. He kept the gun leveled on Sekhem and moved back a step. There was a long wooden box about the length of his forearm sitting on the dresser.

Sekhem made to stand up, but Tweed raised the gun and pointed it at his face.

"Do. Not. Move."

Sekhem sat down again and Tweed reached behind him and grabbed the box, placing it on the floor by his feet.

"That should keep Molock happy," he muttered.

Sekhem's eyes darkened. "Molock? Molock is here?"

Tweed cursed himself for speaking out loud.

"Interesting," said Sekhem. He looked at Tweed speculatively. "But I find it even more interesting that you are helping him. What did he tell you?"

"Enough. Enough to know that the face you're wearing is a disguise. Your true form is some kind of . . . lizard-man. That you are really from a place within the earth called Hyperborea."

Sekhem's eyes widened in amazement. "He told you all that? He must be more desperate than I thought."

"We had him tied up. He didn't have much choice."

Sekhem laughed. It was a soft laugh, predatory. It sent a shiver down Tweed's spine.

"And what else did he tell you? Did he tell you I'm a terrible person? That I'm a killer? A murderer? A vile terrorist?"

"Aren't you?"

Sekhem shrugged. "It's all a matter of perspective. One man's terrorist is another man's savior."

"A savior? Who are you saving?"

"My people."

"And what are you going to do with Tesla's weapon?"

"Isn't it obvious? I'm going to aim it at London and watch the city burn."

"But . . . *why*? Millions of innocent people live in London."

Sekhem leaned forward, his eyes going hard. "That's the whole point. Sometimes innocents get hurt. That's an important lesson to learn."

"But you're going to start a war. Surely you can see that? You'll be causing the deaths of your own race as well."

Sekhem laughed bitterly. "I see Molock didn't tell you everything. Typical of him. My people are *already* dying. What I do I do to save those who remain."

"What are you talking about?"

"You think me a killer. An insane, evil murderer whose only motive is to cause pain. To kill others. Don't be stupid, boy. What person is truly like that? There is *always* a reason."

"And what is yours?"

"Tell me this," said Sekhem. "What would you do to protect those close to you?"

Tweed shook his head at this sudden change of topic.

"Think. Your closest friends. You family. What would you do to protect them?"

Tweed thought about the events of the past year. Of all they had gone through to rescue Barnaby, of all they were going through now to find Octavia's mother. "A lot."

"But how far would you go? That girl from the warehouse. What is her name?"

"Octavia," said Tweed grudgingly.

"Octavia. She is a friend, yes? Perhaps something more?" Sekhem waved this away. "It matters not. What would you do for her? Would you kill to save her life? If you had no option?"

Tweed hesitated before answering. "If someone was deserving of death," he said slowly. "If it was her or that person . . . I might."

"What if the person was *not* deserving? What if it was a simple choice? Her or an innocent bystander?"

"I wouldn't make such a choice."

"You have to. Otherwise they *both* die."

Tweed shifted his weight. He felt uncomfortable, so much so that he had to actually check he was still holding the gun. It felt as if Sekhem was turning the tables on him, gaining the upper hand.

"Where are you going with this?"

"Just answer the question."

"I don't *know* what I'd do."

"Liar. You *know*. You just don't want to admit it to yourself, that you could make that kind of choice. You would let the other person die. Of course you would. *Everyone* would. There is no shame in that."

"That's where you and I differ. There is a *lot* of shame in that. Why are you asking me this? What does it have to do with you turning Tesla's weapons against us?"

"I am simply trying to show you that I am not some insane murderer. That I have my reasons. Let me ask you another question. All the advancements your kind has made lately. All of your new gadgets—the Difference Engines, the Adas, the Babbages. The airships, the lights, the coaches. How are they powered?"

"By steam. Tesla Turbines. Wireless energy."

"Ah!" said Sekhem brightly. "I *see*. Is that what it is? Tell me, what are these Tesla Turbines?"

Tweed shrugged. "They create power."

"Out of what?"

Tweed opened his mouth, then closed it again and frowned. "I . . . don't know. The Ministry doesn't let that kind of information out."

"Oh? Why not?"

"They're probably scared foreign powers might get hold of the technology."

"Ah, is *that* why?" Sekhem smiled a bitter smile and shook his head. "What if I told you something different? What if I told you that far underground, in this 'Hollow World' of ours, in Hyperborea, we have a power source. It floats in the air, just like your sun. We don't know where it came from, or who created it. But it is the same to us as the sun is to you. It gives us light. It nourishes us. Feeds us. We call it *Tak'al*—the giver of life. What if I told you that?"

"I'd say go on."

"Ah. You do not dismiss me out of hand. I like that. Good. What if I also told you that these amazing Tesla Turbines of yours, the technology that drives the British Empire, is actually drawing power from *Tak'al*, draining it. That all its energy is now directed upward, to your world, whereas it was once directed down. That my people are dying. Our crops are failing. Winter is coming to our world, and all because of Nikola Tesla and his wonderful inventions. What if I told you that?"

That . . . that couldn't be true, could it? People wouldn't stand for it. Living your life at the expense of others. "Our Queen would never sanction something like that," he said softly.

But the Ministry would, he thought.

"I once had a wife," said Sekhem in a tight voice. "My sister, she had . . ." He stopped and shook his head. "No, I will not speak of her. Many caught the sickness that the failing of *Tak'al* has brought. My wife was among them. She is gone now. But I am nothing special. Thousands of families have lost loved ones." Sekhem leaned forward. "What if I told you that I am doing what I am doing to avenge the deaths of thousands? To send a message to your people. An eye for an eye, as your famous book says. Look what you have brought upon yourselves with your greed, your obsession with progress. Look at the price of your airships, your automatons. Your comforts are purchased with the blood of my people!"

Sekhem stood up. "Now tell me," he said, his voice trembling with fury. "What would you do if our roles were reversed? What would you do to save your entire race? To avenge your family?"

Tweed stared at him in amazement. "But . . . Molock. He is one of you. If this is true, why is he trying to stop you?"

"Molock is a coward. He thinks we should hide away. That we should wait for our scientists to come up with an answer."

Tweed's thoughts raced. "Why don't you say something? Approach our government. If word of this got out, the British people wouldn't stand for it."

"Yes they would," said Sekhem bleakly. "Oh, they would feel bad. Perhaps. But once they realized that helping us meant losing their comforts, they would soon put us out of their minds."

"You underestimate us," said Tweed, his anger rising. "No person could call himself a human being and ignore something like that."

Sekhem said nothing.

"I can help," said Tweed. "I . . . I know the Queen. Let me tell her the plight of your people. I can't believe she already knows this. She wouldn't stand for it. When she found out that the Ministry was experimenting on human souls she shut them down. She is a good person."

Sekhem turned to stare thoughtfully out the window. He leaned over the writing desk, his face striped with sun and shadows from the half-open blinds. Was Tweed getting through to him?

"I applaud your faith in the human race . . ." began Sekhem.

"You misunderstand me," interrupted Tweed. "I don't have faith in the human race. At least, not like that. We are barely more than animals. We kill for money, food, love, hate. Sometimes we kill for no other reason except that we can. I frequently despair of being classed amongst the sniveling, selfish lot of them."

Sekhem glanced at him in surprise. "Then why try to convince me they would do anything but stand back and watch us die?"

"Because we are also capable of great kindness. We rally around when a neighbor loses a house to fire. We collect for the poor, even though we barely have enough to feed our own families. We go to war to help a nation a thousand miles away, because they asked us to save them from tyrannical rule. Thieves, vagabonds, and murderers will rise up and drag a man to jail because he beats his wife. Or because he mistreats animals." Tweed sighed. "We are a race of dichotomies, Sekhem, as I'm sure your people are. And I know, I just *know*, that we would not stand by and watch what you describe happening."

Sekhem turned around to face him. "You are wise, boy."

Tweed didn't know whether to be flattered or patronized by this remark.

"So you will let me talk to the Queen?"

"But you are also naive. Your Ministry is killing us. The Queen might not know, but they do. We have tried to talk to them, and they turned us away. My family has died. Thousands of others have died. What else can we do to get their attention?"

"So you'll start a war?"

"No. They started a war. We will end it."

And then he looked up. Tweed followed his gaze just as something dropped from the ceiling directly on top of him. He had the briefest glimpse of yellow, rage-filled eyes, then something hit him on the head. A harsh, white light burst across his vision, stabbing into his brain.

Then only darkness.

When Tweed woke up, the room was empty. He blinked, confused. His head was throbbing. Tiny motes of glowing dust danced in front of his face. He sat up and winced as the room spun sickeningly. He grabbed hold of the chair and felt around for his Tesla gun.

Gone.

As was Sekhem.

The plans!

He looked around frantically for the box, but it was gone as well. Tweed punched the floor angrily. He'd had them! He'd had the plans in his hands! And now they were gone.

At least they didn't kill you while you were out. Silver linings and all that.

A very small silver lining. Because Tweed had let the enemy know that he, Octavia, and Molock were on board the *Albion*.

Tweed had a sudden thought. How long had he been out? What if they had already docked in Egypt? He pulled himself to his feet, swayed for a second, then staggered over to the window. He yanked up the blinds, blinking furiously at the bright light that burst into the room.

He pushed the window open and leaned out. A few wispy clouds scudded past on a wind so hot it sucked the moisture from Tweed's eyes and mouth. He blinked rapidly and leaned out even farther. The ochre sands of North Africa drifted past below the airship. He looked to the right and could just make out a distant series of low bumps wavering behind the heat waves.

Was that Cairo? If it was, then they were close. He had to find Sekhem and Nehi before the guests started to disembark. If they escaped into the cramped streets and alleys of the city, they'd never find the pair.

He left the room. The corridor was filling with excited travelers eager to test the wares of the foreign city. What should he do? Just wander around and hope for the best? No, better to tell Octavia and Molock what had happened. Then they could search together.

Tweed burst into Octavia's room and staggered to a stop. He blinked and turned his head, taking in the chaos. Chairs had been overturned. Glasses smashed. Chocolates strewn across the carpet, and then trodden into the weave by heavy boots.

Tweed closed his eyes and took a deep breath. He heard Barnaby's voice in his head. Remove yourself from the equation. Take all emotion out of it. Think logically. Reason and deduce. Never feel and act. That was a big mistake. Feeling, and acting on those feelings, was a pathway to . . . well, to all sorts of terrible consequences, according to Barnaby.

Problem was, he was beyond all that now. His time with Octavia had made him realize just how wrong his father was. That taking emotion out of life wasn't a worthy goal. Unless you wanted to be a lonely old man who talked to himself and kept a collection of snails in the bathtub. (As Barnaby had once done.)

Sekhem and Nehi had been here. They had taken Octavia.

And Tweed was very, very angry about it.

He was just turning back to the door when he saw a note on the sideboard. It was addressed to him. He ripped it open.

Mr. Tweed. If you get this letter before we arrive at the pyramids, come join us on the upper deck for some fresh air. If you don't get this letter before we dock, then I'm afraid Mr. Molock and the lovely Miss Nightingale will have taken a fatal dive from the ship.

Tweed burst out onto the upper deck of the airship. The ornithopters were being readied, pilots warming the engines in preparation for ferrying the passengers to their hotel. The massive collection of gas-filled balloons billowed and bulged about fifty feet above him, the heavy cables fighting to keep them in check. He ran to the front of the ship. The sun was setting behind them, stretching his shadow far across the deck. He could see the Great Pyramid drawing closer, the bright sun shining full onto its refurbished cladding, glinting in the hundreds of windows that had been installed in the newly-built rooms. He searched frantically behind every piece of machinery, every ornithopter, every shed.

Nothing.

He sprinted toward the rear of the airship. At the far end of the deck was a series of buildings that served as offices for the watchmen. Tweed sprinted around the side of the buildings, then skidded to a stop.

There was about four meters of decking between Tweed and the railing that curved around the airship. Octavia and Molock were both sitting on this railing, while Sekhem and Nehi—both wearing their human faces—stood before them, guns pointed at their chests.

"You made it," said Sekhem "Good for you."

Tweed studied Octavia. She was pale and trembling, but if he knew her, she was trembling with rage and not fear. She didn't look hurt in any way.

"What are you doing?" said Tweed.

"Giving you a lesson in life."

"I don't need lessons from you."

"Oh, but you do. You see, it is the duty of all adults to teach children that life is not fair. That life is not black and white." He pointed the gun at Tweed. "I don't think you've been taught that lesson."

Tweed took a step forward, but Sekhem held up his hand to stop him. "Please. Don't. Otherwise they will both die."

Tweed stopped. He looked quickly around, searching for something, anything that could help him. Octavia and Molock were too far away to reach. He was outnumbered. He had no weapons.

This wasn't looking good.

"Now to the lesson," said Sekhem. "We talked a bit about choices earlier, remember? Of course you do. I'm going to give you the choice I was never given, Mr. Tweed. The choice thousands of my people were never given."

Should he just rush them? But if he did that, Nehi might push Octavia over.

"Pick one," said Sekhem.

Tweed tore his eyes away Octavia. "What?"

Sekhem pointed first at Molock. "Pick him, the man who probably has the best chance of stopping us killing hundreds of thousands of your kind. The man with the intel you need to possibly stop us." He tilted the gun to point at Octavia. "Or pick her. Your friend." He smiled. "You can save one of them. Who is it to be?"

Tweed shook his head. "You can't force me to make that kind of decision. I won't."

"You will."

"I won't!" Tweed shouted. "Could *you* make such a choice? If you were given the chance to save your wife or your sister, could you pick between them?"

Sekhem walked forward a few steps, his face dark with rage. "*Make the choice.*"

"No. I won't do it. There has to be another option."

"There isn't."

"There is. I won't pick which of them will die. But . . . I offer you myself in their place."

"Tweed!" shouted Octavia.

Sekhem's face registered surprise and Nehi let out a short laugh. Sekhem tilted his head slightly. "Really? You would do that?"

"I don't *want* to. But I won't play god, Sekhem. I won't sentence someone else to death."

Sekhem thoughtfully tapped his teeth with the barrel of his gun. He stared at Tweed for what felt like hours. Finally he shrugged.

"Fine. Have it your way." He reached behind him and shoved Molock hard in the chest. Nehi did the same to Octavia.

"*No!*"

Tweed barged past Sekhem and slammed into the railing. There was no sign of Octavia or Molock. Just empty sky and the sand far below.

He whirled around, but Sekhem and Nehi had vanished. Tweed turned back and stared helplessly at the sand, squinting through tears of rage.

Octavia was gone.

He had killed her.

CHAPTER ELEVEN

Octavia didn't think they would do it. She really didn't. Who pushes people off of moving airships?

But then everything happened in a blur. Nehi placed the barrel of the gun against her chest and pushed. Octavia tried to grab hold of Nehi as the air dropped out from behind her. Her fingertips brushed Nehi's shirt, but the woman took a step back and Octavia was left grasping air.

She plummeted past the hull of the airship. She tried to grab hold of something—*anything*—but there were no handholds. The sides of the airship were smooth.

Octavia twisted around to see Molock tumbling through the air a few feet away. The sight of him falling, with the sunset behind him and the ground far below, froze her heart with terror. She was going to die. This was it.

Her life didn't flash in front of her eyes, like some people said. All she thought was, *So soon? But I haven't figured anything out yet.*

A surging blast of air suddenly snatched at her, pulling her clothes and hair. It got stronger, yanking her closer to the airship. She saw vents in the hull, descending like a ladder. Every time she passed one, a great in-breath of air jerked her closer. What was this? Something to do with the Tesla Turbines? A safety measure?

Whatever it was, it was pulling her closer to the *Albion*, and as she was about to leave the airship behind there was a final pull of air, sucking her beneath the hull.

Octavia screamed as she was thrown about. She tumbled head over heels, narrowly avoiding crashing up against the bottom of the airship.

Then the wind stopped. She floated lazily for a second, then dropped.

She hit something and bounced.

Octavia looked wildly around as she came down again. She had landed on a rope net. She grabbed hold of it tightly, staring down at the desert floor hundreds of feet below. Wind whipped her hair around her face, but it wasn't the fierce sucking air that had saved her. It was the wind created by the *Albion* sailing through the sky.

Octavia took a deep, shuddering breath of relief.

Then she heard someone calling her name.

Molock.

She looked wildly around. The rope net spanned the entire length and breadth of the airship. She searched everywhere, but couldn't see any sign of the Hyperborean.

"Over here!"

Octavia turned toward the sound of the voice. Molock hadn't made it onto the safety net. His foot had become tangled in the rope and he was dangling over empty space.

The wind buffeted him, shoving him back every time he tried to pull himself up. Octavia started crawling toward him. She could see his foot starting to slip. He had managed to loop the rope around his ankle, but the wind pummeled him, blowing him back and forth like a leaf on an autumn tree.

"Hang on!" Octavia shouted. But her words were snatched away by the gale and flung out into the clouds.

Octavia found herself struggling against the air pressure. It had to be a safety feature, something generated by the Tesla Turbines. The makers harnessed the outflow of air and used it to save anyone who fell overboard.

Or were pushed, she thought bitterly.

The wind howled and shrieked in her ears. She tried to duck

lower, pulling herself forward. She was about ten feet away now. Molock saw her coming. He tried to reach up with his hand, but every time he bent upward at the waist, his foot would slide further out of the rope.

"Stop moving, you idiot!" Octavia screamed.

Molock locked eyes with her. He shouted the word, *"What?"* At least, Octavia thought he did. She couldn't hear anything over the wind.

And neither, it seemed, could he. Molock put his hands to his ears, indicating he couldn't hear her. Octavia raised one hand and pulled it quickly across her throat, indicating he should stop doing what he was doing. It was only when Molock paled even further that she realized her gesture for "stop it," could also be interpreted as "You're going to die."

She dragged herself closer. Molock finally had the sense to stop struggling. Which was a good thing, because the only thing keeping him from plummeting to his death was the buckle on his boot.

Which then started to tear, the stitching separating slowly from the leather.

Molock opened his mouth to scream. Octavia lunged forward, slipping her arm through the rope and wrapping it around his calf, bringing it back up and linking it to her other arm.

With Octavia holding him, Molock eventually managed to pull himself upright. He grabbed hold of the edge of the net, then indicated that Octavia should let go of his foot. At least, that's what she thought he was indicating. His hair was whipping all over his face, and his jacket was riding up over his head, so it was possible she was wrong. But she let go anyway, and he pulled his foot through the hole.

He was snatched up by the wind and flung over the top of the net. He somersaulted over Octavia's head, then bounced and rolled to a stop about thirty feet away. Octavia sighed and dragged herself back, flopping down next to Molock. He was gripping the rope rather tightly, his knuckles showing white against his skin.

"That was rather exciting," he said in a shaky voice.

Octavia grinned. "Don't get comfortable. We still have to figure out a way back onto the airship."

"No," said Molock. "I think I'm just going to lie right here. Forever."

Octavia looked around in frustration. She wanted to get back to Tweed, to let him know she was still alive, but she couldn't see any way off this net. After they docked it would be a different story. It would be easier to get free when they didn't have a thousand-foot drop beneath them.

The sun sank lower in the sky behind them. The heat burned against her neck as they approached the Great Pyramid (or rather, Tutankhamen's View, as it was now called). The newly refurbished pyramid, now made primarily of glass and steel, was topped with a glittering capstone that doubled as an elevator. The windows winked and glittered, dazzling her with a thousand reflections of the setting sun.

She blinked and looked away. New roads had been laid between Tutankhamen's View, the two other lesser hotels, and Cairo itself. Even from this distance she could see the steamcoaches chugging along, clouds drifting sluggishly into the heat-heavy air.

As they drew closer to the hotel, ornithopters started to lift off from the deck above them, carrying those too impatient to wait for the airship to dock.

Octavia soon realized how massive the pyramid actually was. From this distance it looked *reasonably* big. But when the ornithopters flapped their way up the face of the structure, shrinking in size the closer they got, she could truly appreciate the massive scale of it all.

"That is truly one of the most horrendous and exploitative buildings I've ever had the misfortune of laying my eyes upon," said Molock sadly. "What was the government thinking?"

"Money," said Octavia. "Some English conglomerate paid them a lot of cash to do that."

Ornithopters were soon buzzing back and forth, ferrying more and more passengers to the hotel. The *Albion* drew closer, decreasing speed as it did so, and finally drifted to a stop directly above the capstone.

Octavia peered down through the net. There was a huge central shaft cut down the center of the pyramid. From this height she could see the lights of the various levels all the way to the ground floor, the hundreds of guests moving throughout the hotel.

"I suppose we should try to flag someone down," said Octavia. "Can't stay up here forever."

"No," said Molock sadly. "More's the pity. It's actually quite relaxing now that the mind-numbing fear is gone."

They crawled slowly toward the edge. Now that the airship had stopped moving, the wind had dissipated completely. Only the balloons were keeping the airship afloat. There was still no easy way down, and it took a lot of waving and shouting before they managed to catch the attention of a rather startled pilot. He almost crashed his ornithopter into the hull of the airship when he saw them, but he managed to get word to someone on board and about half an hour later a previously invisible hatch opened in the underside of the ship and they climbed back to safety.

They were ferried to the capstone, which was actually wider than it had looked from above, easily thirty feet along each side. Octavia and Molock joined the other guests waiting for elevators to descend the central shaft into the hotel.

There had been something bothering her about Molock's story.

Well, *all* of it bothered her, but there was something that worried her more than everything else.

"Are you sure there's a spy in our government?" she asked.

It was a worrying development, because it meant one of their own people was trying to cause the destruction of London. Cult or no cult, that was just . . . horrible.

"That's what our sources told us. That Sekhem had a member of the Hermetic Order deep within your government. High up."

"But for what purpose?"

"Intelligence gathering, mainly. In this game you need to know what your enemies are up to."

"If you don't mind me saying, we don't seem to be very good at the game then."

They shuffled forward slowly in the line. Octavia's gaze drifted to the ground, where the busy roads were full of rickshaws and steamcoaches moving people back and forth between Cairo and the pyramids.

But there was one figure walking along the road in the opposite direction, heading back along the path the airship had traveled. She would recognize that hunched over walk anywhere. It was Tweed.

What was he doing, heading out in this heat?

Then she realized. He thought she had fallen to her death. He was heading into the desert to retrieve her body.

A rush of pain welled up in Octavia. She grabbed Molock and pushed her way to the front of the queue, ignoring the cries and shouts of annoyance. She shoved a young woman out of the way and climbed into the elevator. A man with dark skin pulled the door closed and swung the lever all the way to the left. The lift dropped down the shaft.

If the elevator was anything to go by, then the hotel itself was going to be ornate to the point of bad taste. Gold cherubs stared down at them from each corner, and the walls were mirrored, so that Octavia found herself looking at her disheveled reflection stretching all the way to infinity. Her hair was all over the place thanks to the wind on the safety net. Her clothes were tattered, her bodice ripped at the shoulder and across the back. No wonder she had been getting such distasteful stares from the other guests.

Octavia watched through the gate as they descended past the different levels. She could scarcely believe it used to be a priceless pyramid, the tomb of Pharaoh Khufu. Now barely anything of the original structure survived. It had been hollowed out, rooms and staircases grafted onto the interior walls. Hidden lamps cast dim light across the corridors, illuminating the Egyptian friezes that had been painted over the old, faded, original art.

It was garish and tasteless, and a huge hit with the rich.

The elevator bumped to a stop and Octavia hurried out into the ground floor lobby.

"Wait here," she said to Molock. "I need to find Tweed. We'll catch up with you later."

Molock nodded in bewilderment and Octavia moved through the lobby, passing display cases where most of the original pieces from the pyramid were displayed: the sarcophagi, the staffs, the gold and decorative headdresses.

Octavia hurried past the front desk and headed for the door, a long oblong of bright light that cast the interior of the lobby in shadow. She dodged around valets carrying suitcases and travel bags, sidestepped guests queuing up to check in, most of them grumbling about the sheer cheek of them having to wait for *anything*, and emerged into the sweltering early evening air, blinking in the light.

Octavia had seen Tweed on the north side of the pyramid, heading out into the desert. She didn't think he could have gotten far. The silly bugger was on foot after all.

She waved down a . . . well, she *assumed* it was a means of transport. A colorful rickshaw-type cab, open at the front, covered with bright beads and swirling patterns. She was about to search for some coin to insert into the automaton, but she pulled up short when she found herself confronted by the gap-toothed smile of a boy of about twelve years old. He was wearing a dirty bowler hat on his head, strands of greasy black hair sticking out of the side. His dark face was eager, his eyes bright.

"You want to ride? Pretty girl want to go somewhere?"

"Er . . . yes. I do. Thank you."

"No problem. Akil will take care of you. That is my promise."

Octavia climbed aboard and sat back in the worn wooden seat. Akil flicked his white tunic out behind him, turned to face the front, then started trotting away.

"Where to?" he called over his shoulder.

"Oh, that way," said Octavia, pointing. "North. Out into the desert."

He glanced over his shoulder at her, his brow creasing in concern. "You really don't want to go into the desert, Miss. Dangerous. Better to stay at the hotel."

"Oh, believe me, I know. But I shouldn't think we'll have to go far."

Akil picked up speed, dodging around the other cabs and screaming abuse at anyone who got in his way. He would run as fast as he could for a few steps, then lean back and let the two handles he clasped beneath his arms take his weight, lifting his feet from the ground and coasting for a while. As soon as the cab slowed down, he would drop his feet and run until he picked up speed again.

They did this for about ten minutes, heading out toward the desert on an old, hard-packed road that obviously wasn't used much at all. They were heading away from the hotels and civilization. The sun was a blood red orb, half-hidden by a sea of haze that hung low over the horizon. It reflected off the undersides of a few stray clouds, stretching out from red to gold, the sky above a deep purple color.

Octavia dragged her eyes away from the sunset and spotted a line of dust on the road ahead. She leaned forward, then broke into a grin when she saw Tweed's back.

"Stop here, if you please, Akil."

"Miss, I do not please. I cannot leave you here. It is dangerous. That man up ahead, for instance. He is up to no good. I can see it. A very shady character, if ever I saw one."

"He's harmless, Akil. Well, relatively so," she amended.

Akil reluctantly stopped the rickshaw and Octavia hopped out, gathering up her skirt and hurrying along the dusty road.

She was almost upon Tweed when he finally heard her approach and turned around.

The look on his face brought her to a sudden stop. He was streaked with grime from the road, little tracks of pale skin showing through, almost as if carved by tears. He looked utterly miserable, his features collapsed in grief and pain.

Octavia had thought she would say something witty and amusing when she revealed herself. But one look at Tweed's face chased all such thoughts aside.

They stared at each other, on this dusty road in Egypt, with the sun setting behind Tweed's back. Then he took three long strides forward, gripped her face in his hands, and just stared into her eyes, a mixture of emotions flowing across his features. Grief. Understanding. Acceptance. Relief.

Octavia didn't know what to do. She stared back, her breath catching in her throat, frozen by the intensity of his gaze.

Then Tweed gently laid his forehead against hers. She could feel his cool skin against hers.

"You're alive," he whispered.

Octavia licked her dry lips. "No thanks to you," she said softly, and was rather surprised to hear a catch in her voice.

Tweed jerked his head back and looked at her in outrage, his features suddenly reassembling into the Tweed she knew. "What do you mean?" he exclaimed.

"You know what I mean. 'No, I won't pick,'" she mimicked. "What was that about?"

"That was about me playing for time! How dare you judge my techniques! I'm a master detective," he declared haughtily.

They stared at each other in mock outrage. Then Octavia broke into laughter. But she was shocked to feel tears building up as well. She turned quickly away so he wouldn't see and started walking along the road.

"Come on," she called over her shoulder. "We've got things to do. Secret archeological digs to discover. Insane lizard madmen to stop. And what are you doing? Going for a walk."

Tweed caught up with her.

"You know I like my walks. They help me think."

"You must need a lot of walks, then," said Octavia.

They arrived back at the rickshaw to find Akil waiting. He glared at Tweed.

"Are you fine, Miss? Would you like me to deal with him?" A wicked looking knife suddenly appeared in his hand.

"Hello," said Tweed, totally ignoring the blade. "And who are you, small child?"

"How dare you! I am not a small child. The gods spit on your ancestors you son of a dog. I can cut you down where you stand."

"That's nice." Tweed patted Akil on the head and climbed up into the rickshaw.

Akil sputtered with outrage.

"He's all right, Akil," Octavia said quickly. "Just spent a bit long in the sun," she said. "Touched in the head."

Akil glared at Tweed. Tweed smiled benignly back. "Hop to it, Jeeves. I need a bath." He sniffed the air. "And so do you, Nightingale. You smell almost bad as your little friend here."

He leaned back and closed his eyes. Octavia climbed up next to him and Akil turned them around and headed back to the hotel.

Every now and then he would open one eye and look at her, as if to make sure.

"What's our next move then?" asked Tweed as they strode into the hotel.

"Find Sekhem and Nehi, I would think," replied Octavia, looking around for Molock. She couldn't see him anywhere. "What happened with them anyway? After we fell."

"They . . . left me. I was at the railing, looking for you. When I turned back they had gone. And you're wrong, our first move is for you to check into Stackpole's room so I can wash up." He sniffed. "Actually, you really *could* do with one yourself. You can go first if you like."

"How kind of you."

Tweed smiled. "See what a gentleman I am?" He frowned and looked around at the crowds milling around the lobby, some heading to the bar, others to the dining room. "Where's lizard-face?"

"I don't know. I left him to come find you."

"No matter. We can catch up later."

They headed for the check-in desk. "I'd better take it from here," said Tweed.

"Why?"

"Because it was easy enough to change the ticket to reflect a Miss Stackpole, but I haven't had time to break into the hotel reservations book to change it. They're expecting a Mr. Stackpole, so that's what they'll have to get."

"Fair point. But I advise you to go to the bathroom first to refresh yourself. I don't think they'll give you a room key looking like that."

"Fair point, well made."

Tweed disappeared to find a bathroom and returned ten minutes later with his messy hair slicked back and his face wiped clean. His clothes had been given a good dusting as well, so he looked at least moderately presentable.

Octavia joined him as he headed for the closest clerk at the check-in counter. It was long, made from mahogany, and polished so much she could see her face in it.

Tweed smiled at the clerk, a thin man with a nervous, haunted look to his face. She supposed she'd feel the same way having to deal with the rich and pampered all day.

"Greetings, my good man," said Tweed. "I've come to claim my key. Just came in on the *Albion*, don't-yer-know. Spiffing ride. Absolutely spiffing. Jolly good fun."

Octavia elbowed Tweed in the ribs. He was overdoing it. And very likely on purpose as well.

"Of course, sir. And the name?"

Tweed opened his mouth to reply, but before he could say anything, a voice spoke a few feet away from them.

"Stackpole," said the voice. "Henry Stackpole. I made reservations."

Tweed snapped his mouth shut and turned to look. So did Octavia. What she saw did not please her at all.

It was Barrington Chase.

His back was angled away from them, facing a clerk at the other end of the counter. But there was no doubt it was him.

Octavia whirled around, grabbing Tweed just as he pointed and opened his mouth. She clapped her hand over his lips, smiled apologetically at the puzzled clerk, and pulled him behind a tall potted fern.

"What the hell is *he* doing here?" sputtered Tweed, when Octavia finally took her hand from his mouth. "And why is he pretending to be Stackpole?"

Octavia stared at Chase's back for a while, thinking. "Remember what Molock said? About there being spies in the government? Members of the Hermetic Order?"

Tweed's eyes widened. "You don't think . . . ?"

"Why not?"

"Are you sure?"

"Why else would he be impersonating Stackpole?"

"I *knew* it."

"You did not."

"I *did* . . . well, not really, no. But I knew there was something dodgy about him. Who'd've thought? Barrington Chase, batting for the other team."

There was an embarrassed silence.

"You *do* know what that means, don't you?"

"Yes," said Tweed. "As soon as it came out, I realized my mistake. It was too late to stop it, though."

Octavia parted a few leaves and tried to get a better look. Chase was talking to the clerk. The man nodded and turned around to check the little alcoves that covered the rear reception wall. He took a key from a hook above one, then reached inside and pulled out a letter.

"He's got a letter!" she said.

"I can see that!"

Octavia made a mental note of the alcove the letter and key came from, then watched Chase walk away, a satisfied smile plastered over his face.

"I really hate that man," muttered Tweed. "He stole my bath."

Octavia let the leaves close and turned to face Tweed. "Is that all you can think about? Your bath?"

"I was looking forward to it."

"What do you think was in the letter?"

"Don't know—ooh! Wait!" Tweed peered through the ferns again, then turned back to Octavia with an excited look on his face.

"The envelope is yellow!"

"So."

"Don't you see? It's the map to this mysterious dig!"

"Why do you say that?"

"That's the same type of envelope he used to post the airship tickets to himself. What better way to keep the map safe than to send it here ahead of his arrival? It wasn't left lying around for anyone to find. He didn't keep it on his person for someone to steal. No, he sent it ahead. He planned on picking it up when he arrived. No one would ever know."

"Except for the people who tortured him," said Octavia.

Tweed suddenly gripped her arm as if realizing something momentous. "Except," he said, and Octavia realized he hadn't been listening to a word she'd said, "for the people who tortured him. So Stackpole *did* cave under interrogation."

Octavia sighed.

"Octavia, if Chase is the spy Molock was talking about, we . . . we only went and told him about the ring! Remember? Back at the manor? We *told* him about Stackpole, that he'd been asking about the symbol. While we were off chatting with Bainbridge, Chase was torturing Stackpole for information. He's dead because of us!"

Octavia thought about this. "And the cult members? Who showed up while we were there?"

"Chase left them there. He knew we'd go there eventually. He wanted us out of the way so word of this secret society didn't get out." Tweed clenched his fist. "And now he's stolen my bath."

CHAPTER TWELVE

Tweed was feeling a bit confused.

He was ecstatic that Octavia was alive. Obviously. Watching her fall from the airship had been one of the worst moments in his life.

But when he had seen her walking toward him along that road . . . well, his first instinct had been to grab her in his arms and . . . and *kiss* her. To hold her tight and never let her go.

He was rather surprised at this.

He liked her. *Really* liked her. But he hadn't thought he liked her in that *way*. Hadn't entertained the thought. Well, he had, *briefly*, but he had dismissed it almost immediately, because they'd only known each other for a short period of time. He respected her too much to make any sort of inappropriate move, one that might jeopardize their friendship. He valued her too much for that.

He was wondering now if this wasn't a mistake.

It was certainly something to ponder. But later. Because he had no real idea how to sort out that kind of stuff in his head. It required a lot of thinking. He had to weigh up the good points and potentially bad points, the risks involved, the changes it would bring.

And right now there were global conspiracies to foil.

Tweed had come up with two plans on that front. The first was incredibly daring and clever and was by far his favorite.

The way he saw it, the letter Chase took from Stackpole's alcove contained this mysterious map that everyone was after. Tweed reckoned Chase would read the map, memorize it, then destroy it afterward. The method of destruction with the highest probability would be throwing it in the fire. Tweed planned on using glycerin on the burned paper to soften it, then use harsh lights to read the metal left over in the paper from the ink. So Tweed's proposal was to wait for Chase to leave his room then break in and gather the burned map, use the glycerin on them, and find out where this ancient site was.

Octavia wasn't so keen on the idea. She said it was obvious the sun had baked his brain and that he should report immediately to the nearest hospital for treatment. Not only that, but where on earth did he think they would get glycerin?

Fair enough, he thought.

The next plan was simpler. They break into Chase's room, over-power him, and steal the letter.

Too dangerous, Octavia said. Also, stupid. Chase was a trained killer. He'd been a spy for twenty five years. He'd be prepared for that kind of thing.

Tweed had got rather annoyed after that and told Octavia to come up with a better plan then.

She did. Immediately.

So they waited for Chase to leave the hotel later that night then followed him.

How . . . *plebeian*! How *boring*! It was a plan befitting a five year old, lacking in cleverness and elegance.

But . . . it worked.

Which was why he, Octavia, and Molock were currently perched atop a sand-covered outcrop, staring down into a rocky valley about forty miles from Giza. The moon was full, shining silver-white light across the desert. Everything seemed so much clearer out here, the stars like diamond dust scattered across black velvet.

By the moon's light Tweed could clearly see Chase as he moved slowly along the valley wall, checking crevices and narrow paths in the rock face. He had been down there for quite a while now, so Tweed had spent the time telling Octavia what Sekhem had said back on the airship.

"Is this true?" Octavia asked Molock.

Molock looked uncomfortable. "Broadly speaking, yes."

"Broadly speaking? How broad are we talking here?"

"Not very." Molock sighed. "Fine, it's true what he said. Tesla's inventions *are* drawing on our power."

"And the sickness?"

"Also true," said Molock heavily.

"Sort of makes you see their point of view," said Tweed quietly.

Octavia looked at him in astonishment. "*Excuse* me? Those two are maniacs! A few hours ago they tried to kill me."

"I know that. I'm not saying what they're doing is right. Just that . . . I don't know . . . If my people were being killed by some sickness like that? I reckon I'd want revenge as well."

Octavia stared at him. Tweed looked away, uncomfortable. "What?" he said pushing his finger in the sand.

"I just never expected to hear that kind of thing from you, that's all," she said.

"Oh, and you wouldn't move heaven and earth for family?" snapped Tweed. "Look at what you're going through for your mother."

"That's different. I'm not killing innocent people."

"I know!" said Tweed, exasperated. "I'm not saying they're right. Just that I understand them."

"As do I," said Molock. "Of course I do. Those are my people dying. But I also think that revealing ourselves, or . . . or slaughtering thousands of you for revenge, is the wrong thing to do. I had the best Hyperborean scientists working on a plan. We were so close when Sekhem and Nehi staged their coup." He shook his head. "No matter what happens, Hyperborea must be kept secret. The Covenant has held for thousands of years, and there's a reason for that. It is the correct path to follow."

"I think you're wrong," said Tweed. "Sekhem said the Ministry knew about what was happening. That they didn't care, fine. But the Ministry is not who you should tell. Go directly to the Queen. I'm telling you, she will help your people."

"No," said Molock firmly. "I'm sorry but *you* are wrong."

Octavia nudged Tweed and jerked her head down toward the valley. Chase had stopped moving. Tweed crawled forward to the edge of the outcrop to get a better look. What was he doing?

A moment later, Chase turned to the side, took a step forward, and disappeared into the shadows.

"Looks like we've found Stackpole's mysterious site," said Octavia.

Tweed stood up and brushed the sand off his trousers. "I'm heading in."

"It's too dangerous," said Octavia. "Who knows what he's doing down there. He might be waiting for Sekhem and Nehi. He might be speaking to them right now."

Tweed put his hands on his hips and struck a heroic pose. He was perfectly aware that he was silhouetted against the full moon. He must look like a heroic explorer or something. "Songbird," he said, "my middle name is danger."

"Is it? Really? I always expected something . . . different. Like Cecil. Or Bartholomew."

Tweed's arms fell to his sides. "*Cecil?*" he said in outrage. "*Bartholomew?*"

"Can we not do this now?" said Molock.

Octavia stood up. "You're right. Now is not the time. Let's go then."

Tweed took the lead. Unfortunately, this meant he was the first to hit the patches of loose stone, the little drifts of sand that were draped treacherously across indentations in the ground. So he ended up skidding down the slope into the valley instead of walking.

The others were fine, though. They just made sure to walk wherever he didn't.

They hurried along the valley floor, moving as close to the rocky wall as possible. Tweed didn't like it. He felt hemmed in. The walls of the narrow ravine soared up above them, their jagged edges clear against the night sky. He kept expecting to see the silhouettes of cloaked fanatics appear, ready to strike them down.

Not that he was scared of them or anything. Not that. It was just, fanaticism of any kind got to him. He couldn't understand it. It was the antithesis of rationality. It was faith taken to murderous extremes, immune to reason and logic. If he couldn't reason with it, he couldn't understand it.

They soon found the spot where Chase had disappeared. It was a crevice about ten feet across, shielded from outside view by the rock folding back on itself. It was only when you were actually leaning up against the cliff face that you could see the opening.

Tweed peered inside. A dim orange light was coming from somewhere around the corner "He's lit some torches for us," he said. "How considerate of him."

They moved into the crevice. Narrow rock walls hemmed them in, but after about twenty paces it opened out into a wide, man-made corridor. The floor was covered with cracked and chipped clay tiles, the spaces between them filled with shards of ceramic. The light he had seen from outside came from wall torches spaced every ten feet or so, receding into the distance.

They moved farther along the passage. As they went, Tweed noted the murals and friezes on the walls. They reminded him very much of Egyptian hieroglyphics, only much more complex. The simplicity was still there, but there was a finer level of detail in each painting.

Molock had been looking at the paintings as well, studying them as they went. After a few minutes he let out a gasp of astonishment. He stopped, running his hands across the wall paintings.

"What is it?" asked Octavia.

He looked at her, his eyes shining with excitement. "Do you know where we are?" he said.

"No."

"This . . ." he moved along the wall, tracing the paintings with his hands. "This is where my people first left Egypt, descending back into Hyperborea. This place has been lost for millennia!"

"Huh," said Tweed. "How about that? Stackpole really *had* found something new."

"That poor man," said Octavia softly.

"It's all here, look," said Molock. He pointed at the paintings. "Ra. Osiris, Thoth. All the rulers leading my people back underground. And look here." He pointed at another section of the wall, where more traditional Egyptian figures were chasing after the others. "See how they try to stop us? How they raised their weapons against us?"

"Yes, fascinating," said Tweed. "But Molock, is right now the best time for a history lesson?"

"No. Of course. Sorry."

They started moving again. The passage eventually opened into a vast room, easily as large as the hangars where they built airships back in London. Relics and statues littered the echoing space. There were sarcophagi everywhere, some them standing up against walls, some of them fallen over, smashed against the floor. The faces on the lids were reptilian, not at all like the faces of the pharaohs on the more traditional sarcophagi.

Torches had been lit all around the walls, illuminating pottery, brass weapons, sickles. Off to their right were life-sized earthen statues, about fifty of them lined up in neat rows. Tweed wandered over to inspect them. They were holding real weapons, swords and axes gone green with age. The statues were carved with fine attention to detail, each face unique.

Tweed ran his hand over one of the statues, then fell into a sneezing fit when the dust got up his nose. He clasped his hands over his face in alarm, trying his best to sneeze quietly. The other two glared at him and he turned his back until he got the sneezing under control.

He straightened up and wiped his streaming eyes, waving apologetically at Octavia.

There was a sudden noise from the far end of the room. Tweed hurried over to join the others and they hid behind one of the stone sarcophagi, crouching down in the shadows.

"I *am* sorry, Chase old chap," said a distant voice. "I forgot to change my watch to Egypt time. I've been waiting for you for an hour now."

Who was that? The voice sounded familiar.

"What were you doing back there?" That was definitely Chase's voice, suspicious and curt. The voices were drawing closer, approaching the vast room.

"Just looking around. I got bored."

Temple! That was it. It was Temple. Tweed had a lot of sympathy for Temple. Having to work with Barrington Chase day in day out must be a nightmare. But what was *he* doing here?

"I'm not sure I believe you, Temple."

"What—Chase . . . Good God, man! What the hell are you doing?"

Tweed peered around the side of the sarcophagus. His eyes widened in alarm. Chase had a pistol pointed at Temple.

"Don't play coy, Temple. We both know what's going on here."

"Quick," said Tweed to Octavia. "Give me your Tesla gun."

"Where's yours?"

"Sekhem took it, remember?"

Octavia reluctantly pulled out her gun. "Why do you need it? Hey, wait!"

This last was directed at his back because as soon as he had the gun he stood up and moved into the open.

"Drop the gun, Chase," he snapped.

Both Chase and Temple whirled around to stare at him in astonishment.

"Tweed?" said Chase, as if he could hardly believe his eyes. "What the bloody hell are you doing here?"

"Stopping you."

"Stopping me—" He shook his head as if still not quite believing what he was seeing. "Stopping me doing what?"

"From helping the Hyperboreans build their Tesla weapons."

"Helping them do *what?*"

"Sebastian," said Temple quickly. "You *know* about the Hyperboreans?"

"We followed the clues from Tesla's warehouse and they led us here. Yes, we know about them."

"I told you to stay out of Tesla's murder," said Chase.

"We did," said Octavia, emerging with Molock from their hiding place. "We were searching for my mother."

"Octavia," said Chase. "I'm disappointed in you. I thought you had more sense."

"You're disappointed in *me?* That's rich. I'm not the one who's a member of some secret Egyptian cult that wants to hand over super weapons to the lizard-men."

"I say," said Molock. "That's a bit strong."

"Sorry," said Octavia.

"You have no idea what you're talking about," snarled Chase. "Now get out of here and let me do my job."

"Can't do that, old chap," said Tweed. "You've been a bit naughty."

"I haven't been *anything*. You're insane!" Chase switched the gun and pointed it at Tweed. "Now back off."

Temple quickly yanked his own gun free and pointed it at Chase. "Drop it, Chase. We can take you in and discuss this at the Ministry."

Chase smiled bitterly. "So that's how it's going to be, is it?"

"That's how it's going to be," agreed Temple.

A deep thrumming suddenly echoed through the chamber. Tweed felt a vibration running up through his feet. Stones and dust pattered to the ground.

"What—?" began Octavia.

Chase made a sudden lunge for Temple. Temple fired his gun, the explosion echoing around the chamber. Chase cried out and dropped to the ground, a red stain spreading across his chest. Temple glanced down at him then turned and sprinted back for the entrance.

"Wait here!" he shouted over his shoulder. "It could be members of the Order of Osiris. Come to back him up."

Tweed hurried over to check on Chase. He felt for a pulse. It was still there. Fluttering, erratic, but he wasn't dead yet.

Chase's eyes flickered open and he glared at Tweed with pain-filled eyes. "Ruined everything again, Tweed."

"Ruined your plan, you mean."

"My plan? You . . . you *idiot*. I'm not the traitor. I'm one of those who keep . . . who keep knowledge of the lizards from everyone else. That's my job. That's why I'm here. To *stop* Nehi and Sekhem from carrying out their plan."

Tweed frowned. "But . . . you were pointing your gun at Temple."

"Use your head! He's a *traitor*. He's in league with the lizards."

"But . . . how did you know about this place?"

"That's . . . that's thanks to you. You showed me the symbol. I knew it was the cult. Followed the clues here. Didn't expect to find Temple, though. But I've always had a funny feeling about him."

Tweed glanced over his shoulder to where Temple had disappeared. *Temple* was the traitor? Could it be?

"Always trying to figure stuff out on your own," said Chase weakly. "That was always your problem. Too clever to listen. Too good to think there were others with more . . . more experience than you."

"So you're telling me that Temple is a part of this Hermetic Order of Osiris? That *he* tortured Stackpole?"

Chase grinned. His mouth was filled with blood. "No. You still don't understand. That was me. I had to find out where the map was. Had to stop word of it getting out. Had to lock everything down."

Tweed wasn't sure he had heard correctly. "So you *tortured* an innocent man?"

"For the greater good. If people found out about the lizards, there would be chaos. Panic. It would shift every political boundary in the world."

Tweed sat back on his haunches. "You're insane."

"No. I do what I do to keep the status quo."

Tweed glanced up at Octavia. She had been listening to the whole thing. Was it possible? It would explain a lot of things. For instance, why the cult showed up at Stackpole's home. If Temple was a spy, he would have told Sekhem and Nehi about Stackpole and his map. They would have wanted to shut him up, especially if they had their own plans. Stackpole was just someone who was making too much noise at the wrong time.

Tweed frowned. What had Temple said before he left? It could be members of the Hermetic Order come to back Chase up. But no one had mentioned the cult to him. Not Tweed, not Chase. So the only way he could know about them was if . . .

Tweed straightened up and sprinted out of the chamber, heading back along the passage to the entrance. A bright light was spilling into the tunnel from the outside. Tweed skidded out of the crevice into the valley, then pulled up short. He shielded his eyes and stared upward in shock.

It was the *Albion*. The airship was hovering about thirty feet above the valley walls. It filled the sky, a massive behemoth, looking like a beached whale that listed slightly to the side.

What was it doing here?

Even stranger. Ornithopters were launching themselves in panicked flights from the top of the flight deck. The ornithopters went in all directions, some of them spiraling to the ground, others turning unevenly and heading back toward Cairo.

Ropes unfurled from the railings of the upper deck. As Tweed stood watching in amazement, members of the crew slid and climbed down to the valley floor, their faces panicked and terrified. Some of them didn't make it. Their hands slipped and they plummeted to their deaths on the hard rocks of the ravine floor.

Then Tweed saw Temple. He stood in the middle of the valley waving his arms in the air, ignoring everything around him. Tweed looked up and thought he could just make out Nehi and Sekhem peering over the side of the flight deck. There was a loud crackle in the air, and then Tweed heard Nehi's voice echoing through the night.

"Do it."

The speaker system aboard the airship, thought Tweed.

But do what?

A light flared as Temple struck a Lucifer match. The orange flame illuminated cruel and eager features. Tweed had never seen that look on Temple before. He had always seemed to genial. So calm.

Temple bent over and touched the match to something on the ground. There was a spark and a flare of phosphorous light. Then the spit and crackle of flame moved rapidly in Tweed's direction.

His horrified gaze searched the ground. There. Right against the stone walls. A fuse.

The flame was already upon him. Tweed tried to stamp it out, but the flame erupted on the other side of his shoe and disappeared into the cave.

Tweed ran back to the entrance. "Get down!" he screamed as loud as he could. "Bomb!"

A few seconds later there was a loud detonation, a terrific *whumping* noise that he felt first in his chest, then in his head. A second after that the shock wave hit him, blasting him off his feet and sending him flying into the wall.

Thick, choking dust billowed out of the cave. Tweed coughed and waved it away, trying to see inside.

"Octavia?" he shouted urgently. "*Octavia!*"

He waited, fear rising high in his chest. Then he heard a slight coughing sound.

"Here," she croaked.

Tweed sighed with relief. "How you doing?"

"We're . . . fine! I think. Just . . . behind a few rocks . . . Wait . . ." Her voice trailed away, then came back more urgent than ever. "Something's coming! Tweed, something's coming! Hide!"

Tweed frowned. Something was coming? Had he heard that correctly? How could something be coming?

He was almost too busy puzzling this through to remember she had told him to hide. He darted around the side of the rock that hid the crevice from view, just in time to avoid being run over by a rush of bodies. They bounded out of the cave on all fours, scrabbling over the rock, bounding across the valley floor. Tweed peered through the dust and was astounded to see they were lizard people— Hyperboreans. They looked like their true selves, though, running on all fours toward the airship.

When they arrived beneath the dirigible they launched themselves into the air, scrambling quickly up the ropes and over the side. That was when Tweed finally realized their plan. *That* was why Sekhem and Nehi were on the *Albion*, why this site was so important. Sekhem and his sister were *stealing* the airship. Tweed had no idea why, but that was what they had done. They had ejected all the crew who remained on board and were replacing them with their own. They must have been waiting on the other side of the cave walls, waiting for Temple to detonate explosives to free them.

Why did they want the *Albion* though? It had to be something to do with Tesla's plans. They wouldn't just steal the *Albion* on a whim. This was carefully planned. There was a reason.

But what?

Tweed stared up at the airship in frustration. What were they going to do? Crash it into London? No, nothing so simple. Sekhem wanted a more powerful message than that. He wanted revenge. As he said, an eye for an eye.

But . . .

Tweed stared speculatively at the underside of the airship. At the empty ropes now dangling from the railings. They couldn't build a super weapon if they didn't have the plans, could they?

He glanced to his right. The dust clouds thrown up by the explosion drifted across the valley, obscuring Temple from sight.

He grinned into the night, spat on his hands, then sprinted from cover, leaping into the air and grabbing one of the ropes.

He started off well, and if good intentions were muscles, Tweed would have been inside the airship by now. Unfortunately, they weren't, and Tweed soon slowed in his ascent. His arms started to ache, his breath came in ragged gasps.

"I . . . really . . . have to . . . get fit," he wheezed, pausing in his ascent to catch his breath. He looked down. The dust cloud was dissipating. Temple was still waiting down there—Tweed could just see his figure, dark and shadowy through the thin cloud.

"You'll get yours," Tweed muttered. He felt betrayed by the revelation that it was Temple, not Chase, who was the bad guy. He'd been so sure. When Molock had said there was a spy in the government, and then they'd seen Chase at the hotel, he'd been convinced he was the spy. Well, you would, wouldn't you? It wasn't *Tweed's* fault.

He shook himself and started climbing again. He looked up. The underside of the ship was about fifteen feet away. Nearly there.

He kept going and finally reached the railing. He pulled himself up and threw his arms over the edge. He'd picked a rope toward the middle of the airship, so that he could hopefully sneak up without Sekhem or Nehi noticing.

He levered himself over and collapsed as quietly as he could onto the wooden deck. His whole upper body was in pain, and when he tried to push himself up he found his arms were shaking violently. He hoped he didn't have to fight anyone right now. That would be embarrassing. He'd have to just whirl his torso back and forth and hope his flailing arms hit somewhere vital.

Tweed peered around. The Hyperboreans were milling around the upper deck, inspecting the remaining ornithopters, staring up at the huge gas bags that kept the airship afloat. One of them was deep in conversation with Sekhem and Nehi over what looked like a map.

Tweed climbed to his feet and dodged around crates that were lashed to the deck with thick wire. He moved quickly between them, keeping out of the bright moonlight.

He made it to the doors and hurried down the steps into the greeting area. The lights had been dimmed. They cast a weak orange glow over the dark wood of the tables and bar. Tweed slipped into the room beyond, pausing to listen.

Silence.

It was eerie. The ship was designed to be full of life and sound, people milling around, staff and waiters bustling to and fro. It wasn't meant to be empty. It felt like the ship's soul had gone missing.

Tweed realized he was just standing in the middle of the room like a statue. He shook himself and hurried through the door into the corridor beyond, heading for the wide staircase in the center of the airship.

He made his way down the steps and along the passage that led to Sekhem and Nehi's rooms. He tried the door. It was locked. Typical. He tried Nehi's but it was also locked tight.

Tweed glanced over his shoulder, but he didn't think there was anyone around, so he backed up against the opposite wall and then lunged forward, shoulder first.

He hit the wood and collapsed to the floor, groaning in pain and clutching his aching arm. He'll give the *Albion* makers one thing. They certainly built a solid door.

He stood up and tried using his feet this time. He finally got the door open on the fifth attempt, the lock splintering so that he was able to shove it the rest of the way open. He stepped inside and wedged the door shut.

He had to move fast. He pulled open the door to the adjoining room. This was where Sekhem had told him about his family, about what was happening to his people.

Tweed looked around for the wooden box, the one that held the plans.

It was on the desk.

Tweed grinned and swept it up. It was heavier than it looked. He tried to open it but it was locked. He spotted a leather satchel with some clothes in it, emptied the clothes out, then stuck the box inside.

He grinned, feeling very proud of himself. He'd done it. He had the plans.

The door leading to Sekhem's room creaked. Then there was a shout of anger. Tweed looked frantically around then dropped to the floor, shuffling under the bed just as someone burst into the room. He saw black boots hurry toward the desk, then spin around again.

"They're gone!"

"*Teska-dul!*"

Tweed wasn't sure what that meant, but he had a feeling it was a rather naughty word.

"I was here only twenty minutes ago," said Nehi. "They might still be on board."

You're not wrong there, thought Tweed nervously.

"Alert everyone. I want the ship searched."

The feet ran from the room. Tweed thought about his next move. He couldn't exactly wait here. They'd take off soon, and if they were searching the ship he'd be found eventually. No, his best bet was to get off the *Albion*, take care of Temple, then hide with the others until the airship disappeared. Sekhem and Nehi couldn't hang around here indefinitely. They'd stolen the *Albion*, after all. They would want to get over the open sea as soon as possible.

Tweed slid out from under the bed and crept out into the hallway. He paused and listened. He could hear distant shouting, and the sound of running feet.

How was he going to get out of here? He slung the satchel with the box over his shoulder and moved quickly along the corridor. He reached the end and leaned up against the wall. He peered around the corner. All clear.

He was about to step out from cover when something made him pause, a little tingle of instinct. He crouched down behind a large plant pot and waited.

A second later he heard a scrabbling sound. Then a lizard-man appeared, crawling slowly along the roof.

Tweed pushed himself back against the wall as the lizard crawled past. It paused and looked down the corridor Tweed was hiding in, sniffed the air, then carried on along its course.

Tweed waited for about a minute, then emerged from hiding. He hurried along the corridor, but then had to duck into a room as another Hyperborean came scrabbling along the wall.

This was hopeless. He was never going to get past them.

He peered both ways along the passage.

And his eyes fell on the dumbwaiter at the far end. It was used to ferry food up from the kitchens.

Perfect.

He ran along the carpet and yanked open the doors. A tight fit, but he'd manage it. He pulled himself up, then turned his shoulder and wedged himself into the enclosed space. A rope attached to a pulley disappeared up into the darkness. Tweed leaned out and pushed the button for the top deck. The dumbwaiter shuddered, then reluctantly moved upward, straining with his weight.

The ride felt endless. And it wasn't silent either. He thought the whole airship must hear the sounds of the motor that was winching him up to safety.

He finally juddered to a stop. Tweed slowly slid the doors open. Darkness greeted him. He stared out, hoping his eyes would adjust, but there was no light anywhere. Was it a trap? Were they waiting for him to step out, then they'd all leap on him?

Only one way to find out.

He clumsily extricated himself from the space and straightened up.

Nobody attacked him, which was always nice.

He tried to orient himself, but still didn't know which corridor he was in. He put his hand against the wall, using it to guide him in what he hoped was the right direction.

After a couple of minutes he saw a dim orange glow up ahead. He quickened his pace and arrived at the bottom of the stairs that led up to the greeting room.

Tweed broke into a grin. Nearly there.

He climbed the steps. Nothing had changed in the greeting room. He crossed the floor and hovered anxiously at the foot of the stairs leading to the outside deck.

The sound of approaching feet came from behind him. Tweed took a gulp of air, and scurried up the final set of stairs, emerging into the humid night air. Tweed moved quickly to the railing. He put his hand on the rope and leaned over. He felt his stomach lurch. God, it looked really high from up here.

"Don't move," said a voice behind him.

Tweed glanced over his shoulder to see Nehi pointing a gun at him. He decided he had a split second to do something unexpected, something to catch her off guard.

So he threw himself over the railing.

The wind pummeled his face. The satchel with the plans slapped painfully against the back of his head. He reached out and grabbed the rope. Pain flared as it slid across his palms. He tightened his grip and pulled it toward him, clamping it beneath his armpit. He lurched, slid some more, then slowed down. Problem was, he didn't *want* to slow down too much. He loosened his grip again, trying to descend as fast as he could, hand over hand. He looked up. Nehi was on the next rope along, descending gracefully and quickly. She was about twenty feet above him, but she was catching up fast. He looked down. The ground was still about twenty feet below him. He tried to go faster, wincing every time the rope burned the skin off his palms.

He couldn't see anyone waiting below. Where was Temple? He didn't want to land only to be confronted by a gun against his head.

No time to worry about that. When he was about ten feet from the ground he let go. A brief fall, then a sudden impact. He bent his knees and rolled in the dust, pushing himself to his feet and sprinting for the cave where Octavia and Molock were waiting. It was the only place he could go, somewhere they could defend.

He looked over his shoulder just before he ducked into the crevice. Nehi was sprinting toward him. Not only that, but some of the Hyperboreans were swarming from the airship, heading back down to back her up.

Tweed swore and put his head down, sprinting along the passage and into the huge room beyond. He skidded up short and almost collided with Octavia and Molock. They were moving toward him, Molock holding an old bronze sword against Temple's back.

"Where have you been?" snapped Octavia. "Never mind. I don't want to know. Back up. Quick."

"No can do. I've got Nehi and some lizard-men on my tail."

"Why? What did you do?"

Tweed patted the satchel. "I only got Tesla's plans back."

Octavia's eyes widened.

"Can we talk about this later?" said Molock. "That explosion weakened the structure of the cave. The roof's going to collapse any moment now."

As if to underline his point, a huge section of rock dropped down and smashed into one of the sarcophagi. Tweed flinched, waving away the dust.

"We can't go out that way. They'll kill us."

"Then where?"

Tweed could hear Nehi and the Hyperboreans approaching from behind. He grabbed Temple and shoved him hard, sending him stumbling back toward the entrance. Hopefully he would confuse Nehi for a few extra seconds. The dust would make it hard for her to see who it really was.

He turned the others around, pushing them back into the room. The Hyperboreans had to come from somewhere, hadn't they?

They stumbled through the choking dust, tripping over pottery and rocks. There was a huge rumbling sound, then a terrific grinding and crashing behind them. The whole place was coming down!

"Run!" he shouted.

They ran faster. Rocks and boulders tumbled down the walls and rolled across their path. Thick, choking dust billowed everywhere. It was hard to see anything. He could hardly breathe. He reached out and grabbed hold of Octavia's shirt, unwilling to let her out of his sight. She reached back and grabbed hold of his wrist, digging her fingers in deep.

They kept going, deeper into the darkness while the room caved in behind them. Stones fell on Tweed's head, earth trickled into his eyes. He had no idea where they were going. All he knew was the feel of Octavia's hand around his wrist, the sense that she was still close to him. They ran because they had to. Because stopping would mean instant death.

He felt a cool breeze against his cheek. It gave them renewed energy, drawing them closer. They were ahead of the dust now, in a tunnel filled with broken rocks and shards of stone. This must be the point of the explosion.

The tunnel opened out, the walls curving away to either side. Their footsteps echoed, the sounds coming back to them from distant walls.

And then there was a final, horrendous roar behind them as the roof finally collapsed. A cloud of dust exploded past them, engulfing them in a choking miasma. They pushed ahead, trying to get beyond the suffocating blanket.

They followed Molock off the path and onto a lip that ran around some sort of colossal interior cavern. It receded into the distance and dropped away into darkness. The dust cloud drifted up toward an invisible roof.

Tweed had only the briefest glimpses of all this before he felt a sharp prick in his neck. He whirled around to find Molock stepping away from Octavia, who rubbed her neck and frowned at the Hyperborean.

"What was that?" she said.

Tweed blinked. He suddenly felt very, very tired. He lifted his hands to his face and saw them blur in and out of focus. He locked eyes with Octavia and fell to his knees.

"I'm so sorry," said Molock, but his voice sounded slow and drawn out. His words came out as, "I'm-m s-o-o s-o-o-o-r-r-r-y."

Tweed's eyelids were too heavy. He thought it would probably be nice to sleep, to have a bit of a rest. Yes, that would be the best thing for everyone.

He fell forward and closed his eyes.

CHAPTER THIRTEEN

O ctavia slipped in and out of consciousness, hovering in that in-between state of waking and non-waking that she usually found so pleasant. But this time there was something sinister about it, something unsettling. She opened her eyes, blinking at the hazy, odd-colored sunlight. She told herself to get up, to pull herself back into the waking world, but then her eyes drifted closed again and she gave up the fight, sinking back into oblivion.

But that feeling of gentle sleepiness soon faded, replaced by a throbbing headache that pulsed and prodded her brain. Her tongue felt swollen in her mouth. She tried to lick her lips but there was no moisture there.

A gloriously cool trickle of water flowed into her mouth. It wet her tongue, but was then sucked away like a single drop of rain in the desert. More water came. This time she grabbed the wrist of whoever was holding the flask, not letting them go. She greedily swallowed as much as she could.

"Slowly," said a voice. "You'll get sick. Can you sit up?"

Octavia cracked open her eyes. Shards of bright light stabbed between her lids. She squinted, waiting, and after some moments tried again.

A dark green face appeared before her. She jerked back before realizing it was just Molock in his natural, Hyperborean state.

"Apologies," he said. "I didn't mean to startle you."

Octavia waved this away. She tried to sit up, but felt weak and dizzy. "What . . . what happened?"

"Ah," said Molock. "Um . . . yes. About that."

His tone was embarrassed and contrite. Octavia forced her eyes open wider and looked directly at him. "What?"

"Well, you see, it's a law in our world. No outlander has ever been allowed to see any entrance into Hyperborea. It is forbidden. So . . . I may have drugged you a bit."

"You *what?*"

"Just a little bit. At least, that's what it was supposed to be. But . . . the thing is, our physiologies are a bit different. A tiny dose for us turned out to be quite a large one for you and Mr. Tweed."

Tweed! Octavia quickly looked around and saw him sleeping on a wooden floor. She felt his pulse. It was beating strongly.

Octavia sat back with relief, for the first time looking around. They appeared to be in some sort of boat. Actually, it was more a long skiff, constructed from what appeared to be brown clay, or perhaps even stone. Angular pictures had been carved into the surface.

She stood up and braced herself against the side of the skiff. She looked over the edge, expecting, as one would, to see water.

Instead she saw empty air, and far, far below them, dark green jungles.

The skiff was skimming through the sky just like a Tesla-powered airship. She looked in amazement at Molock.

"How are we flying? Do you have Tesla technology?"

"Hmm? Oh, no, no. I'm not sure of the exact science, but I think it has something to do with mercury suspended in some sort of closed system and spinning rather fast." Molock frowned. "I *think* that's what my scientists told me."

The heat against Octavia's skin was heavy and humid. She was sweating already, beads of perspiration forming on her arms, her back.

She looked up at the sun. At least, she *thought* it was the sun. It certainly looked like the sun. Except it was a lot smaller, and shone with a whiter light.

"Is that . . . ?"

"That is *Tak'al*. Our source of life."

"What *is* it?"

"I've no idea. No one does. Anytime we try to get close to it, we're pushed away. It's as if it has some sort of magnetic properties that oppose us. The harder we try, the more power we use, the more violently it repels us."

A wave of dizziness washed over Octavia. She frowned.

"How long have we been out?"

"Ah . . . About two days. Yes. I think that's about right. Two days."

"Two days!" Octavia shouted. "You've had us drugged for two days? How *dare* you!"

"I know! I'm so sorry. I had no idea it would affect you that way. Believe me, if I'd known I'd have simply knocked you on the head instead."

"You . . ." Octavia didn't know what to say to that. She just shook her head in amazement.

"But how remiss of me." He gestured proudly over her shoulder. "Miss Nightingale, allow me to welcome you to Hyperborea."

Octavia turned around and let out a gasp of astonishment.

Away in the distance a series of pyramids thrust up from the jungle. They were huge, easily ten times the size of the ones at Giza. And they were stepped, looking more like the South American pyramids than the Egyptian ones. Even from this distance she could just make out vehicles flitting through the air around the huge structures.

"That is Thrace, our capital city. Where I once ruled." He smiled painfully. "We won't be getting any closer, so if you want Mr. Tweed to get a look you should probably wake him."

Without taking her eyes from the sight before her, Octavia reached down and felt her way up Tweed's chest, moving across his face and onto his ear. She tweaked it painfully.

Tweed sat up suddenly. "The gun's on the mantelpiece!" he

shouted. He blinked and looked around sleepily. "My tongue feels like a furry hedgehog is living on it." Octavia turned his head so that he was looking at Thrace. "Ah. I'm still asleep. Jolly good."

He tried to lie down again, but Octavia kicked him.

"Get up, Tweed. We're in Hyperborea!"

Octavia heard herself say it, but she still didn't quite believe it. She stared at the massive city, and she thought, *I'm not here. This isn't real.*

"We're actually not far below London, you know. Thrace lies just to the north of your city."

Tweed stared in amazement at their surroundings, then turned back the city. "How many people live there?" he asked.

"Tens of thousands. It used to be a lot more, but . . . well . . . the sickness."

As if in response to his words, the light suddenly dimmed. It was like a thick curtain had been pulled across the sun. Octavia looked up and saw that *Tak'al* had faded to a dull grey. Small dark spots roiled across its surface.

"Why is it doing that?"

"That is what happens now. It seems to coincide with your busy periods, but it is staying like that for longer and longer periods."

The skiff moved on. Octavia and Tweed watched Thrace recede into the distance like a city swallowed by the dusk. Molock dropped the skiff lower and steered them north over the jungle canopy. Now that Octavia looked closer she could see that a lot of the plants and trees below her looked diseased. The leaves were black, and whole section of the jungle had vanished, the outer edges of these spaces rotting, like gangrenous wounds eating up everything around them.

"You see?" said Tweed. "Kind of makes you sympathize with Sekhem and Nehi."

Octavia rounded on him angrily. "Stop saying that."

"Why?"

"Because I don't like it. It's like you're siding with them, with people who tried to murder me—murder *us*," she added, waving at Molock.

"But . . . I can't help it," protested Tweed.

"Oh really? And would you feel so sympathetic if they had succeeded in killing me?"

"No. I—"

"And will you still be sympathetic when they unleash their weapon? When they've killed untold thousands?"

Tweed didn't answer this time.

"You can understand them," said Octavia, "but that's not the same as sympathizing with them. And if you *do* still sympathize with them keep it to yourself because I don't want to hear it." She turned to face Molock. "And I would like to see my mother. Now please."

He nodded. They flew north for the next hour or so. The dim light seemed to be affecting the skiff. Every now and then it would slow down, dipping alarmingly in the air. Molock would then fiddle with an odd control panel made up of colored stones and the vehicle would reluctantly lift higher and pick up speed once again.

"Did Tesla do this on purpose?" asked Tweed. "Did he know what he was doing when he created the Tesla Towers?"

"No," said Molock, "I do not think he knew. I think he accidentally stumbled upon a means of drawing power from *Tak'al*. He did not question where it came from."

"We have to tell the Queen," Tweed insisted. "It's the only way this will get sorted out. She can send scientists down here. They can work with your own people to find a solution to—"

"No!" Molock turned and glared at them. Octavia was rather nonplussed by this. It was the first time the Hyperborean had shown any real anger.

"This will not happen. My people stay hidden. Do you understand? I will stop Sekhem and Nehi. Somehow. They will be tried for their crimes, and that will be the end of it. The Covenant commands it."

"The Covenant will see you dead," said Tweed.

"The Covenant protects us," said Molock. "We must trust in *Tak'al*. It will see us through these times of trouble."

Tweed didn't say anything more, but Octavia could see the disgust in his face. He hated blind faith. Hated it with an absolute passion.

ᖫᖰ

The shadows over the sun passed a few hours later as they left land behind and flew out over a vast ocean.

Octavia leaned over the edge. She could see silver-pink fish scudding along just beneath the surface. They leaped into the air, soaring over the skiff and showering them with water. At the top of their arc the fish unfurled wing-like fins and banked to the right, flying a good fifty feet before diving into the water again.

She turned her head to find Tweed grinning at the sight. That made her happy. He'd been too serious these last months.

One of the first things she'd noticed about him was how childlike he was. Not childish—although he could be that—but rather, that he looked at certain things with the naivety of a child.

She missed that about him. Truth to tell, it was the first thing she found attractive about him. It was shortly after noticing it that she found herself looking at him and wondering if there could be more.

She was thinking about it again, even after she'd promised herself she wouldn't. But . . . she had a feeling that things had changed. That look in his eyes back in the desert. There was no mistaking that look.

There was something there. They just had to figure out what to do with it.

After another hour or so of travel, Molock glanced over his shoulder. "Come see."

Octavia and Tweed crowded forward. There were a series of bumps on the horizon. As they drew closer Octavia realized that the bumps were actually a whole load of ships. Rafts and boats lashed together with ropes and cables. There were about a hundred of them, maybe more, all of them linked by wooden planks and rope bridges, forming a man-made island miles across.

Octavia could see Hyperborean people going about their everyday lives, fishing, pulling buckets of water out of the ocean, washing clothes. She could even see children running between boats, laughing and screaming as they played catch.

"What is this place?" asked Octavia.

"This," said Molock proudly, "is Hope Springs. The home of many of those rebelling against Sekhem and Nehi."

"Why doesn't the government shut it down?" asked Tweed. "Come and arrest you?"

"They don't know we're here. Nothing around for miles and miles. They don't tend to leave Thrace much. Too busy trying to catch the rebels who stay in the city." He winked and tapped his nose. "Misdirection, you see. They think we're in Thrace causing trouble, but our main body is elsewhere."

There was a narrow lane of water that led into the island, the waterway flanked by two lines of small rafts. Molock set the skiff down in the ocean and coasted into this lane, bumping to a slow stop against one of the boats. He climbed out and helped Octavia up. Tweed followed close behind.

Octavia looked around nervously. Everywhere she turned she saw reptilian faces, their yellow eyes studying them with intense curiosity. The children, especially, seemed delighted to see them, running and leaping over the decks of the boats to land on all fours before them. They seemed more taken with Tweed, taking his hands and prodding his knees and fiddling with his clothes. One of them poked him in the ribs and he burst out laughing.

"Hey! Enough of that. I'm ticklish."

This was the signal for all the children to try to get him to laugh. He shrieked and batted their hands away, and Octavia found herself grinning. *This* was the old Tweed. The one who took delight in the irreverent. As she watched he leaned down and started tickling one of the little girls. She yelped and leaped away.

Octavia shook her head. "They don't seem too frightened by us," she said. "I mean, you'd think they'd be wary of us, by how different we look."

"Oh, but they're used to humans by now."

"What do you mean?"

Molock nodded over her shoulder. Octavia turned and saw a crowd of Hyperboreans watching them. There was movement from behind them and the crowd slowly parted to reveal a lone figure.

Octavia blinked. Her stomach lurched as her brain tried to catch up with what she was seeing.

It was her mother.

She looked different. Thinner, *healthier*. Her skin was tanned, her eyes bright and wide as she stared at Octavia in astonishment. Octavia took a step forward, then stopped, frowning uncertainly, as if she was scared what she was seeing wasn't real.

"Mother?" she said uncertainly.

"Octavia?"

Octavia took a huge gulp of air that turned into a sob and sprinted forward. Her mother opened her arms in wonder as Octavia collapsed into her hug, nuzzling up against her shoulder.

"Mum," she whispered.

And she knew that everything would be all right now. She would be safe. Because her mother was here. And her mother could fix anything. Octavia felt tears rolling down her cheeks. She had done it.

They had done it.

Her mother started to cry and laugh at the same time, stroking Octavia's hair the way she used to. Octavia closed her eyes and let the fear and uncertainty of the past year drain away.

"Octavia," said her mother in wonder. "What are you doing here?"

Octavia tilted her head back and looked up into her mother's tear-filled eyes. "Rescuing you, Mum. What else?"

ᑫᑫ

They sat at a table inside the upturned hull of a large sailing ship. The curved walls arched above them. Holes in the hull let in heavy beams of light that crisscrossed through the air.

Octavia told her mother everything. About what she had been doing since the kidnapping, about how she spent months searching for information on Moriarty, how she met Tweed, the events of last autumn. Everything leading up to them arriving in Hyperborea.

As she talked her mother stared at her in wonder, occasionally shaking her head in amazement. When Octavia told her about the steamcoach chase through the streets of London last year, she actually laughed out loud then put her hands over Octavia's.

"It seems my disappearance has done wonders for the excitement levels in your life."

"Some of it I could have lived without," said Octavia. She sighed. "I missed you, Mum."

Octavia's mother tightened her grip on Octavia's hand. "I know, love. I'm sorry. I've tried so many times to get them to let me go.

They just kept saying it was too dangerous. That they couldn't risk their world being exposed."

"Well, Molock promised. He said if we helped him he'd release you. Then we can go home."

"How . . . how is your father?"

"Not good. He's not handled any of this very well. He thinks you're dead."

The hands slipped away from Octavia's. Her mother looked down at the table, her black hair hanging over her face. After a few moments she looked up and smiled tightly. "Then think how happy he'll be when we turn up on the doorstep."

Octavia did think about it. She wasn't sure *how* her dad would react. He might very well have a heart attack right on the spot.

But to be a family again . . . how nice would that be? Things she used to dislike—being forced to have dinner together, family walks on a Sunday afternoon, her dad playing the piano badly in the drawing room. All those things she once brushed aside as childish she now couldn't wait to experience again.

"Now, tell me more about this Sebastian Tweed fellow. He sounds . . . *singular*."

"Singular. That's a very good description, actually."

She told her more about Tweed, about his social skills, or lack thereof, about his father, the life they had led, and how she thought he was struggling to find his place in the world since he found out he was a simulacrum.

Once she had finished talking she stood up and moved to the door, pushing it open. *Tak'al* had dimmed once again, turning the light grey and purple, almost as if a storm was coming.

Tweed was playing hopscotch with the Hyperborean children. Octavia opened her mouth to call him over, but paused. She leaned against the doorframe and watched him laughing with the kids. One of the smaller boys pushed him so he landed outside his chalked square. Tweed shouted in mock outrage and picked the boy up, holding him upside down and dangling him in the air by his legs. The other children shrieked with delight, the upside down boy the loudest among them. Tweed put the boy down, but then the others quickly lined up, demanding to be dangled upside down as well.

Octavia shook her head and grinned. "Tweed!" she shouted.

He glanced over, a second, upside-down boy swinging around to look at her as well. "Put the child down and come meet my mum."

She returned to her chair to find her mum looking at her shrewdly. "You like him."

"I do. Although he can be very annoying. And frustrating. But he's a good person." Octavia thought about it. "He has a heavy soul. He needs to learn how to carry it."

At that moment Tweed entered the room, rubbing his hands together. Octavia groaned the moment she saw him. He had that slightly manic, wide-eyed look he got when he was in uncomfortable situations.

"Mrs. Nightingale," he said, holding his hand out.

Octavia's mother shook his hand. "Sebastian Tweed. Octavia has told me everything about you."

Tweed looked in alarm at Octavia. "*Everything?*"

"Everything. And I must thank you for helping her track me down. It was very good of you."

Tweed dismissed this with an airy wave of his hand. "Nonsense. Mrs. Nightingale, I think I can honestly say there isn't much I would not do to help your daughter. You . . ." He flailed around for the correct words, and spectacularly failed to find them, ". . . you birthed a very fine specimen with that one," he said, pointing over at Octavia.

Octavia's eyes widened.

"Er . . ." said Tweed. "Not birthed. No. Not quite polite that, is it? Created? *Spawned?* No. *Produced?* Yes, produced. You produced a very fine human being in Octavia." He took a deep breath, looking pleased with himself, then frowned. "Human being? Not very flattering that, is it?"

"No," said Octavia firmly. She couldn't help noticing her mother was trying not to laugh.

"Person? Child? Baby?" He looked helplessly at Octavia. "Oh, whatever. The point is, Octavia Nightingale is a very wonderful person, and I'm sure that's in no small part because of you and Mr. Nightingale. So, well done."

He looked around the interior of the ship, his face turning more serious. "Actually, families and upbringing have been on my mind rather a lot lately, and I came to the conclusion that Octavia would have turned out just fine without you. She's that kind of person. But your input has, I think, given her that extra something." He frowned. "Er, that was a compliment."

"I know it was. And I thank you, Sebastian."

Tweed nodded seriously. "As I said, it has been weighing on my mind recently. Nature versus nurture. Upbringing versus—"

"Sebastian," interrupted her mother. "I've known a lot of people in my day. My work has brought me into contact with saints *and* sinners. I've interviewed murderers and politicians. I've seen unwed mothers who help at the soup kitchen, and killers who find religion. And there is one thing I've learned from all of these people. A single, universal truth." She leaned forward and gripped Tweed's hand. He was rather startled by this and started to pull away, but Octavia's mother held it tight. "Where you come from does not define who you are. You forge that path every day with your actions." She released his hand and sat back. "And if everything my daughter has said about you is true, then you're a better man than most I've known who were born into a normal family."

Octavia stared at her mother in astonishment. She had told her mother everything about Tweed, even her worries about his current state of mind, but she hadn't expected her to actually say anything to him about it.

Tweed, for his part, was staring at her mum with a very odd look on his face. Intense, embarrassed, relieved.

And grateful. Very grateful.

Octavia suddenly realized he had never had this. Never had a mother to tell him his feelings were normal. Barnaby was not the kind of person who would discuss such things. He was already treating Tweed as an adult when he was only five years old. Barnaby saw emotions as weakness, a viewpoint that had been impressed on Tweed from a very early age.

So who was there to tell Tweed that just because he felt it, it didn't mean it was true, that he was better than his fears, that part of life was learning to rise above them?

No one.

Except . . . he *did* have someone. He had Octavia.

That was supposed to be your job, Octavia. You're *his friend.*

She felt utterly ashamed. She had watched him going through all this turmoil, and all she could think about was that she preferred the old Tweed. Yes, she was worried about him, but she hadn't taken that extra step and asked him if he wanted to talk about it. She had failed him.

She turned away to hide the sudden tears in her eyes. She heard him say quietly, "Thank you Mrs. Nightingale. I appreciate that. I really do."

CHAPTER FOURTEEN

The room Tweed had been provided was a tiny cabin inside an old passenger ship tied up along the perimeter of Hope Springs.

He lay in bed that night and stared at the ceiling. He couldn't sleep. Octavia's mother's words kept going round and round in his head.

Where you come from does not define who you are. You forge that path every day with your actions.

Was that true? Could he really look past what he was? Even better, could he really *accept* what he was? Octavia's mother seemed to think so. So did Octavia, but she was different. She'd been there when he found out. She had already accepted him.

He realized he might possibly take that for granted. She was, after all, his only friend, and he had grown so used to having her around that he didn't question her acceptance of him.

The problem was, *he* hadn't been able to accept who he was. He blamed others, he felt sorry for himself, he got angry and lashed out, but what had that achieved?

What if Octavia's mother was right? What if all he needed to feel like he belonged, that he had earned a right to this body, this *soul*, was to forge a path through life that left him proud of who he was.

Tweed smiled and put his hands behind his head. Perhaps he *could* be normal after all.

He closed his eyes. He had grown used to the constant creak and groan of the ship as it rose and fell with the waves. So when the long, slow creak began he didn't think much of it. It was only when he sensed the change in light that he realized someone was opening his door.

Tweed sat up. Perhaps Octavia or Elizabeth had gotten lost. All the cabin doors along the passage looked the same, after all. He tried not to even acknowledge the brief flare of hope that it might be Octavia.

"Someone's in here," he said softly.

"I know."

Orange light flared, crawling across the cold human features of Nehi. She stepped into the cabin. Temple followed after her, quickly closing the door and placing his lantern on the lone table in the room.

Tweed scrambled from his bed, but Nehi pointed a gun at him. It wasn't a Tesla gun. It looked like it was made from brass, with a series of concentric circles around the barrel.

Tweed dragged his eyes away from the weapon and stared at her in confusion. "How are you even here?"

"You mean why aren't we dead? We escaped the collapse. Just as you did. We've been following you since you came down to Hyperborea. You were just too stupid to notice."

"But . . . *why?*"

"The box. Where is it?"

"Box . . . ?" It took him a moment to realize she was talking about the box he had stolen from her room, the one that contained the plans. "The plans aren't in it anymore. Molock handed them over to his people."

"I do not care about the plans," snapped Nehi. "I want the box. Temple?"

Temple quickly searched the room. It didn't take him long. There weren't many places to look. The small table, a closet, and beneath the bed. This last hiding place was where Tweed had put the box. Not because he was trying to hide it, but because he just didn't want to trip over it.

Temple yanked the box out and opened it. Tweed moved a step

closer and saw him flick a hidden switch. A false bottom swung up, flooding the room with bright white light. Tweed squinted as Temple pulled out a glass vial about the size of his hand. He handed it to Nehi and she slipped it inside a leather pocket on her belt. The white light winked out, leaving Tweed blinking away fading afterimages.

"Is that . . . is that a *soul?*" he asked. "In an æther cage?" Everyone knew how the Ministry Mesmers had the ability to take souls out of the human body. Mostly to insert into automata, but also in their top secret projects, the kind that resulted in Tweed being created.

"Who . . . ?" He stopped talking, his mind working furiously. "It was never about the blueprints," he said slowly. "That's Nikola Tesla's soul, isn't it? You took it when you killed him. You," he said, turning to Temple. "You used to work in the Mesmer department. I remember Chase saying something about it when we first started training with him."

Nehi handed the gun to Temple and retreated to the doorway.

"Why?" he asked urgently. "What do you need his soul for?"

Nehi looked at Temple. "Give me a head start, then kill him."

She disappeared into the passage. Tweed frantically searched for a means of escape. There wasn't any. The room was tiny. No room to fight. No room for anything. He sat down on his bed.

"You really are an idiot," said Temple. "We've been one step ahead of everyone the whole time. Misdirection. That's what you learn in the Ministry. Get people looking for one thing while you walk off with the true treasure."

"What are you going to do with it?"

"No. Sorry. I'm not going to stand here and recite our plans while you try to come up with a way to escape. Suffice it to say that a new order is coming. And I for one am glad you won't be here to see it."

Tweed threw his pillow at Temple. It was rather laughable, really. A pillow against a gun. But it hit Temple in the face, obscuring his vision. Tweed ducked and moved as the man pulled the trigger. A burst of orange light sizzled past his head and disappeared into the wall, leaving a smoking hole in its wake. He thought he heard it hiss into the ocean outside.

Tweed grabbed the gun. Temple tried to hold onto it but Tweed dug his fingers savagely into his wrist. Temple cried out, his fingers spasming open. Tweed snatched the gun and tried to turn it on him, but the man had already bolted from the room.

Tweed went after him. Temple was at the far end of the corridor already. Tweed pulled the trigger. A bolt of orange light surged along the passage, illuminating the walls as it went. Temple ducked. The bolt slammed into the wall, spreading out into a puddle of fire. Temple ducked through a doorway, clambering up the steps to the deck. Tweed swore, then ran back to his room, grabbed his blanket, and used it to put the fire out.

He followed Temple outside. It was the middle of the night. *Tak'al* was casting a soft white light over everything, similar to the light of the moon. Temple was scrambling up a rope ladder hanging from a flying machine about ten times the size of the skiff they had used to get here.

Tweed pointed the gun and fired. The orange light flashed into the air, hitting the bottom of the ship. It shuddered, then swung clumsily around. Tweed fired again. This time he hit a structure on top of the ship, the steering room, he thought. Flames flickered and spread. The ship surged forward, then picked up speed and soared away into the sky. Tweed shot at it, more out of frustration than anything else.

There was a commotion behind him. He turned to see Octavia and Elizabeth emerge from below.

He sighed. "We've got a big problem."

"So the blueprints were never the goal," said Molock. "Tesla's soul was. But why?"

"Maybe they need him, but they need him compliant," said Octavia. "He would never agree to create some terrible super weapon for the enemy when he was alive. Maybe they're going to put his soul into a construct. Then they could force him to do their bidding."

"Possibly," said Molock, "but it matters not. This is not your problem anymore."

"What do you mean?" asked Octavia.

"Our deal. You have honored your part. As much as you could. Now it is my turn to honor mine. You are all free to go. I consider you good, honest people, so I can only hope you will respect the law of our Covenant and not reveal anything about us to your people. Will you do that?"

Tweed and Octavia shared a look.

"Uh, we haven't honored anything," said Tweed. "The deal was we help you stop Sekhem and Nehi. We haven't done that yet."

"Yes, but you tried—"

Tweed held up a hand. "Trying means nothing. They have to be stopped, Molock. We want to help."

Molock broke into a grin. "Excellent. I must admit I hoped you would say something like that."

"So what do we do?" asked Octavia's mother.

"We must find out where they are gaining access to your world. It obviously wasn't back in Egypt. They had to blow up the walls in order to get their followers out. It has to be somewhere else."

"How are we supposed to find that out?"

"I have a few contacts who might be able to help."

"Here?" asked Tweed.

"No. Elsewhere."

"But what will you do about this place?" asked Octavia. "What if Nehi tells others about it?"

"I will instruct my people to move. We have done it before. But let us hope we succeed, then I can reclaim my place behind the throne and we can all come home." He smiled wistfully. "Wouldn't that be nice?"

ΩΩ

It was four days later. Tweed was tired, cold, and bored. Oh yes, he was also irritated.

Being cooped up on a small skiff for ninety six hours, (or five thousand, seven hundred and sixty minutes), tended to do that to him. He needed alone time to decompress, to get quiet in his own mind. He craved loneliness with the same desperation he once craved companionship.

It was a bit of a dichotomy, really.

The skiff was skimming low over restless savannah. The grass was long and thin, tipped with purple fronds that made the whole area look like it was covered in heather. Strange creatures that appeared to be a cross between frogs and squirrels leapt through the grass, catching dragonflies the size of Tweed's hand with long green tongues.

At least they were close now. They were headed for a distant brown bump on the horizon, the beginning of a range of sandstone mountains. Molock had told them there was a rebel hideout there, and this was where he hoped to get the necessary intelligence they needed to track down Sekhem and Nehi.

After a few hours, the savannah gave way to scrub, then desert, the flat lands around them rising up into the foothills of the ochre mountains themselves.

Tweed noticed that Molock was looking around uneasily. Tweed scanned their surroundings, but couldn't see anything that might worry him.

"What's wrong?" he called.

"We should have been intercepted by now," said Molock. "Our lookouts should be stationed miles out from the cliffs."

They soon discovered the reason why. A crashed ship similar to the one Tweed had seen Nehi use. It was mangled and shredded, a pile of debris at the end of a deep furrow in the ground.

"They've been attacked," said Molock grimly.

They found more wreckage as they headed deeper into the mountains. Tweed thought he could even make out bodies lying on the ground. Elizabeth joined Molock at the controls and put a comforting hand on his slumped shoulders.

"All these lives," he said. "We were so close. Almost ready to challenge them. We will have to start all over again."

"How many of your people were here?" asked Tweed.

"Hundreds. We picked it because it was defensible. Out of the way."

"There's still hope," said Octavia. "Perhaps some escaped."

"Perhaps."

Molock guided the skiff between the slowly rising peaks. The dusty ground was scattered with scree and dry weeds. He picked a circuitous route, bringing them low into a deep ravine, rocky hills rising up on both sides. They kept well below the lip of the depression, moving slowly. Even here there were signs of battle: large, smoke-smeared holes gouged out of the valley walls. The wreckage of skiffs and larger ships littering the basin.

The ravine narrowed and closed in above them, taking them into a twisting maze that cut through the mountains. The sky was hidden from view as Molock carefully tapped and touched the controls, moving them around huge rock structures that thrust up from the ground, sailing beneath lethal overhangs that sliced across their path.

The ravine finally opened into a wide canyon. A small river wound erratically along the ravine floor, disappearing into the shadows of the mountains.

There was a large village at the edge of the valley. Or at least, the remains of one. Piles of ashes and half-burned pillars showed where houses and huts had once stood. Tweed could smell wet ash in the air, the acrid stench of old smoke.

This is what they do, he thought. *You felt sorry for them, you thought you understood, but these are the kind of people they are.*

Octavia glanced over at him. He could see she was thinking the same thing, the memory of their argument in the skiff fresh in her mind. Thankfully, she didn't say anything.

Tweed looked away and at that moment he heard a deep roaring sound, a heavy noise that vibrated through their bodies.

Then a huge brass and wood ship, looking like some sort of massive whale, soared over the cliffs and dropped heavily into the canyon. Tweed had a brief second to register the gun barrels pointed at them, then a bright surge of orange light was burning through the air toward them.

Molock shouted in alarm and leaned hard on the controls. The skiff banked to the right, dropping toward the ground. Tweed grabbed a seat to stop himself flying over the side. The bolts of energy sizzled past them, scoring the bottom of the skiff, and hammering into the canyon wall. Rocks and stone exploded outward. Stones and pebbles pattered into the skiff and a cloud of dust billowed up into the sky.

Tweed shielded his head and prepared for the second volley, but instead he heard a deep, booming voice echoing mechanically throughout the canyon.

"Sorry! So sorry! Thought you were someone else. But you're not. Obviously. Um . . . hello Molock."

Molock wiped the dust from his eyes and blinked at the huge airship floating in the air before them. Except it really wasn't like an airship. It looked more like a spaceship from a Atticus Pope novel. Tweed reckoned this was what a minnow felt like facing down a shark.

"Solomon Okpara," muttered Molock. There was relief as well as resignation in his voice.

And a small amount of trepidation as well.

"Molock!" boomed Solomon Okpara, striding across the deck of his ship and enfolding the smaller Hyperborean in his massive arms.

Tweed couldn't help staring. Solomon Okpara was *huge*, a massive, solid slab of lizard with a huge gut. He was about seven feet tall, his yellow and red eyes wide with happiness.

"I thought I'd lost you, my friend," said Solomon, smacking Molock on the back then pushing him away to arm's length so he could get a better look at him.

Molock patted Solomon's arms. "Good to see you too, Solomon." He looked around. "What happened here?"

Solomon's face darkened. He moved Molock aside and lashed out to his left, smashing his taloned fist into the closest wall. He then spent a few seconds swearing violently while he tried to wrest his fist free.

"Royal Guard," he said, and spat on the deck. "They came soon after you went topside. Caught us all by surprise."

Molock stepped away, leaning on the railing of the ship and staring down into the canyon. "Any other survivors?"

"Oh yes. We had an hour's warning. We got many to safety. What you see around you is the remains of the battle of those who stayed to defend their retreat."

"How many lost?"

"Seventy-two."

Molock's grip on the railing tightened so much that the wood splintered and cracked. Tweed raised his eyebrows and glanced at Octavia. He hadn't realized Molock was so strong.

Solomon put his meaty hand on Molock's slim shoulder. "Seventy-two lost their lives so two hundred and thirteen could escape. But we will make them pay, brother. We will get you your throne back. We will banish the pretenders and bring peace to the land. Just like the old days, yes? Solomon as your royal guard, ordering many flunkies to do his bidding." He sighed. "Good times."

"Sorry to interrupt the reunion," said Elizabeth. "But I really think we need to start thinking of a way to stop Sekhem and Nehi from doing something monstrous to my people. How are we going to get back to the surface to stop them?"

Molock turned to face them, his face worried. "You are right. Of course. I had hoped to check our maps, the intelligence we had gathered here . . ." he looked around at the wreckage. ". . . It seems we had a wasted journey."

"Not quite," said Solomon.

Everyone turned to face the Hyperborean. His face split into a huge grin, revealing blackened, serrated teeth. "I followed our attackers. Discreetly of course. But follow them I did. Right back to their rather large and heavily defended base, which, I might add, we have absolutely no chance of breaking into. To think otherwise, I say now with a seriousness of the heart, would be insane and death-wishy."

"But insane and death-wishy things are what we do best," said Tweed, rubbing his hands together. He could feel the old excitement growing. The excitement that drove away the doubts and the dark thoughts. "Isn't that right, Songbird?"

Octavia said nothing.

"Ha ha," Tweed answered for her. "That's right."

CHAPTER FIFTEEN

And here they were, three days later, lying in the freezing snow atop the crest of a hill. Below them sprawled a huge, heavily-guarded compound, sheltering beneath a mountain range that soared up into the obscuring clouds. The wind howled around them, swirling the snow around in blinding gusts.

Tweed, who was lying just to Octavia's right, said something.

Octavia pulled back the hood from the thick jacket Solomon had given her. "What?"

Tweed shifted the scarf away from his mouth. "I said it's rather cold, isn't it?"

Octavia favored him with a bit of a glare. He had that look. The one where he was enjoying himself entirely too much for it to be appropriate.

She leaned in close to his ear. "You do realize this is suicide, don't you?"

"Have you got a better idea?" he shouted back.

Octavia clamped her mouth shut, frustrated. The problem was, she didn't. According to Solomon, hidden inside this base was the passage Nehi and Sekhem used to travel to the surface. It was their only route home. And Nehi already had a good five or six days lead on them. She had probably met up with Sekhem already. For all they know, they could have already carried out their nefarious plan, whatever it actually was.

But that didn't mean they should stop. No. They had to go on. They had to at least *try*. There might still be a chance to stop them.

She turned her attention to the walled compound below. The central structure was another of those stepped pyramids, but this one had walkways and bridges branching off from each level, linking the pyramid to other buildings behind the compound walls.

The wind died down slightly and Molock leaned in to them. "I don't want anyone killed," he said.

Octavia, Tweed, and Elizabeth all turned to face the Hyperborean. He shrugged and looked slightly sheepish. "These people are still my subjects. They follow Sekhem and Nehi because they are brought up to obey authority. They are simply doing as they are told. Our weapons all have lower strength settings. We can render them unconscious. The end result is the same. Please?"

"I for one am quite happy not killing anyone today," said her mother. "I'm not sure I would like that on my conscience."

"Fine with me," said Tweed absently, still staring down into the compound. He narrowed his eyes and Octavia followed his gaze. A squad of armed Hyperboreans was patrolling the snow-covered ground in front of the gate.

"Have you told Solomon about your no-kill policy?" asked Tweed.

"I have."

"Was he happy?"

"He wasn't."

"Didn't think so." Tweed sighed. "Look, I don't mean to cast aspersions on your friends, but are you sure he can do this? He seems a little . . . unpredictable."

Octavia attempted to stifle a snort of laughter at the irony implicit in that statement. She was only half-successful. Tweed carefully ignored her.

"It's just . . . this plan needs perfect timing."

"Do not worry. Solomon might appear a bit on the eh . . . rough and ready side, but there's no better pilot in the land. He'll do his job."

"Listen," said Octavia abruptly.

Everyone froze. Off to their left was a pass through the foothills. It led back to a road that cut through the featureless, snow-covered tundra they'd had to cross. Now that the wind had dropped, Octavia could hear a low whine coming from that direction.

"Here we go," said Molock.

They shuffled backward until the rise hid them from view, then they ran diagonally across the hills until they arrived at the tree line they had already picked out as a good place to hide. They hunkered down behind the trees, watching the pass below.

The skiffs came into view a few minutes later. Three large, flat-bottomed vehicles that skimmed slowly above the ground, their beds loaded with supply crates. Solomon had been keeping an eye on the compound, noting their times and routines. He was very contemptuous of them. Overconfident, he said. Arrogant. Never assuming an attack would come. He then launched into a five-minute rant about what he was going to do to the traitors when all this was over.

Octavia almost pitied them.

When the three skiffs were about fifty meters off, Solomon's ship, which he had proudly told them all was called *The Boisterous Lady*, heaved into view, shooting up past the foothills on the opposite side of the pass and dropping into the road with a speed that, frankly, surprised her. She'd been riding on the ship for the last few days, but she had never seen it maneuver as well as it did now.

The Boisterous Lady came up fast behind the skiffs. One of the guards casually glanced over his shoulder, turned back to the front, then did a double take and whirled around, shouting in alarm.

The Boisterous Lady fired her guns, huge beams of white light that smacked into the ground beneath the last skiff. The explosion launched the skiff into the air, flipping it over in a somersault. Crates and boxes flew in every direction, smashing to pieces against the walls of the pass. The skiff did two full flips before landing right side up again, thudding hard into the ground. Fragments of wood and splattered food rained down around it.

The two drivers, who were lucky to be strapped in, quickly patted themselves down for injuries. Then they remembered *The Boisterous Lady*. The driver looked over his shoulder, squealed, then frantically smacked at the controls until the skiff took off again, struggling to catch up with the others.

Solomon picked up speed, sailing over the top of the convoy, casting a bulbous shadow across the road. Octavia heard a high-pitched whining, and then the guns fired again, the white light hitting the wall of the pass. Huge rocks exploded across the road, forcing the lead skiff to stop abruptly. The others followed suit. The drivers pulled out rifles and handguns, ducking for cover and firing up at *The Boisterous Lady*.

Thin beans of orange light pummeled into Solomon's ship, but she shrugged them off as if they were flea bites. Then Solomon's voice roared through the hidden speakers, "Why you no fight back, puny ones? Why are you just sitting there—oh, you *are* fighting back? Apologies. I didn't realize."

The white light around his front most gun built into an ever-growing circle, then burst toward the ground. Earth and rocks exploded into the air, coming down on the heads of the cowering drivers.

"Come on," said Molock.

While the drivers were occupied, they slid down the bank and headed toward the rear skiff, clambering on board. Octavia and Tweed grabbed the flapping leather cover that had been used to cover the crates and dragged it back into place, using it to shield them from view.

Musty darkness enveloped them. Octavia listened as the drivers shouted to each other, firing their guns at *The Boisterous Lady*.

There was more shouting, this time sounding a bit happier. That meant they were into phase two and Solomon had veered away. Which also meant that the compound had seen the attack and was responding.

Sure enough, Octavia heard craft zipping past their position. Then the sounds of running feet. The skiff lifted clumsily off the ground and lurched forward. The drivers babbled to each other in their own language as they headed straight for the compound.

The heavy thrumming of *The Boisterous Lady* flashed by overhead, followed by his pursuers. Solomon would be hovering high above the compound now, firing randomly at the structures below him. This was tricky, because the Hyperboreans were sure to have heavy weapons in the compound, but the plan was for the gate guards to wave the skiffs through the gates without stopping to inspect them.

The skiff picked up speed, bouncing and jouncing over uneven ground. It veered suddenly to the left, sending them all rolling against one another. They shifted abruptly to the right, there was a burst of speed, and the light that had been filtering in through gaps in the covering suddenly went dark. Running feet faded into the distance.

Silence.

"Think it's safe?" whispered Octavia after a while.

"Only one way to find out," said her mother. She sat up and threw the cover back. She waited a moment, then poked her head back under. "It's safe."

Octavia stood up, pushing the covering away. "That was needlessly risky, Mother," she said angrily. "You could have done that without exposing yourself so much."

Elizabeth looked at her in surprise, but Octavia didn't change her expression. She had only just found her mother. She didn't want to lose her again.

"Sorry, love," said Elizabeth. "Won't happen again."

Octavia nodded. Tweed leaped out of the skiff and rubbed his hands together gleefully. "Who'd've thought? It actually worked."

Octavia looked around. They were in a long warehouse, a storage facility by the looks of it. Huge crates were stacked neatly against the walls, barrels and drums piled up to the ceiling. More skiffs were parked in neat rows that receded into the distance.

There was an explosion from outside, followed by panicked shouting. Another explosion, this one close by. Smoke billowed past the doors.

"He *does* know we're in here, doesn't he?" said Octavia.

"He will be attempting to generate cover for us," said Molock. "Trust me, he knows what he is doing. Despite a rather . . . unconventional way of looking at things."

"I like him," said Tweed, checking his gun.

"You would," said Octavia. "You're both borderline sociopaths."

"Octavia!" said her mother, shocked.

"What? It's not an insult. Is it?" she said to Tweed.

He shrugged. "Not really. Pretty accurate, actually. Although I hasten to add, *I* am not the problem. Everyone else is."

Octavia raised her eyebrows at her mother. *You see?*

Tweed waved his gun in Molock's face, causing the Hyperborean to duck away. "Sorry. How do you change the strength on this thing?"

Molock twisted the circular fins around the barrel of the gun. "There you go. Enough to knock them out, but no more than that."

"We should get going," said Elizabeth. "No telling how long Solomon will be able to distract them."

The others checked their weapons, then they moved through the dim interior to the wide sliding doors. Octavia peered around the corner.

It was chaos. Hyperboreans were running in every direction, most of them trying to get under cover while beams of furious white heat rained down on them from above, sending explosions of dirt and billows of smoke around the area.

The Boisterous Lady hovered about thirty feet up, and Solomon's voice boomed around the compound, "Come on, puny lizards. This is all you have for Solomon? I am bored. I crave challenge. Bring me your best fighter. I will battle hand to hand. I will push him to the ground and make him cry for his brood-mother."

"He's enjoying himself, isn't he?" said Tweed.

Molock grimaced apologetically. "Yes, the enforced hiding has not agreed with him. Solomon is a man of action."

Another burst of energy erupted from the ship, hitting a two-story structure off to their left. The building exploded, huge fireballs curling up into the sky. Octavia felt the heat against her face even from this distance.

"Let's go," said her mother, and they all slipped from the hangar. Her mum first, Octavia next, Molock third, and Tweed watching the rear. They moved around the edges of the compound, using the thick, cloying smoke as cover, ducking behind walls and vehicles whenever someone ran past.

They headed for the huge pyramid. It was relatively uncrowded there. Solomon was keeping everyone's attention focused on the walls and gate. They crossed a cleared area in front of the structure and headed into a long narrow passage that led to the door.

When they were halfway along the passage, the door slid open. Five Hyperboreans sprinted out, weapons in hand. Octavia's mother dropped immediately to one knee and fired. Octavia copied her. Orange electricity soared along the dark corridor. The Hyperboreans stumbled to a halt but they barely had time to register their presence before they were wreathed in lightning.

One of them escaped the first volley and returned fire. Octavia was surprised to see he was using a normal pistol, one they must have brought to Hyperborea from their world. A bullet smacked into the wall next to Octavia's head, chips of stone stinging her cheek.

Tweed leaped over her head. He landed in a crouch and fired his own gun. A bolt sizzled along the passage and hit the Hyperborean in the chest. He flew back through the air, hitting the wall with a grunt of pain and sliding to the ground.

Tweed looked at her, his eyes troubled, then he turned and ran toward the entrance before any more Hyperboreans could catch them by surprise.

Her mother leaned in and whispered in her ear. "Your knight in shining armor."

Octavia blushed and got to her feet. "That would be fine if I *needed* a knight in shining armor. Which I *don't*. Because I'm perfectly capable of protecting myself."

"Of course you are. Still, it's nice knowing there's someone out there to watch your back. Someone you can depend on. Doesn't hurt he's quite scrummy."

"Mother!" exclaimed Octavia. "Behave yourself."

They joined Tweed, who was now standing by the open door. There was a long passageway beyond, with doors opening to either side. At the far end was an arch through which she could see lots of lights. But their shape and brightness seemed to indicate the lights were far away. Noises echoed toward them, bangs and scrapes, distant shouting.

They entered the pyramid and sprinted along the corridor. The archway at the end opened onto a balcony that overlooked the huge central space of the pyramid.

"Over there," said Tweed.

Octavia followed his gaze. In the opposite wall of the pyramid was a huge tunnel that sloped down into the ground.

"That will be the passage to your world," said Molock. "It will drop below the mountains, then climb up through the inside. Easier to keep it hidden."

Octavia nodded and studied their surroundings. Right now, they were about fifty feet above ground level. There was a ramp to their left that circled the pyramid wall, and a bank of five caged elevators to their right. They couldn't use the ramp. They would be spotted by the Hyperboreans below. Even the elevators were risky, but they didn't really have any other options.

They hurried to the closest elevator and crowded inside. Molock closed the cage and pulled the lever down. The elevator lurched and started to drop.

They could still see through the bars of the cage. The floor of the pyramid was a frantic swarm of Hyperboreans, some of them jumping into small skiffs and speeding away, others forming into orderly lines while burly officers handed out weapons.

Their view of the floor was blocked every time the elevator drew level with a new floor. Octavia crouched down every time this happened, trying to keep her eyes on what was happening.

When they were about five floors from the ground the armed soldiers moved off to the left. Good. That meant the way would be clear for them once the elevator doors slid open.

They bumped to a stop on the ground floor. But instead of it opening directly into the pyramid, the elevator instead opened onto an enclosed corridor. Molock pulled the cage doors open and they stepped outside—

—to find the orderly lines of soldiers approaching rapidly from the left.

Everyone froze. Octavia thought it almost comical. A tableau of surprise that lasted for the briefest of seconds but seemed to stretch on forever.

The guards acted first. The front two dropped to their knees, allowing those behind them the space to fire. They raised their rifles to their shoulders just as Molock and her mother fired their own guns. Lightning burst out in a wild explosion, crawling across the walls,

223

then arcing and grounding in the soldiers. Their muscles contracted, fingers spasming on triggers. Gunfire erupted, deafening in the confined space. Bullets slammed into the walls and roof, one of them skimming past Octavia's arm. She felt the wind of its passage and fired wildly as she spun around and retreated back into the elevator.

Tweed was already there. Octavia grabbed her mother, yanking her out of the passage. Molock joined them, slamming the cage shut and yanking the lever up again.

"Well," said Molock with a nervous smile. "That was rather close. Um . . . any suggestions?"

Octavia waited till the elevator passed the second level, then pulled the brake. She yanked the cage open and ushered everyone out, then slammed the lever all the way up and closed the doors, letting the elevator resume its journey back to the top.

"Quick thinking," said Tweed. The other four elevators started to rise, filled with soldiers hell-bent on catching up with them at the top.

They pressed themselves up against the wall and waited for them to pass, then used the ramp around the wall to reach the ground floor. Luckily, no one saw them. They hit the packed earth of the pyramid floor and hid behind a stack of wooden pallets.

"Right," said Molock. "We're in. Now—and I realize we should have finalized this beforehand—but do we have a plan?"

Tweed put his hand up. "Actually, we *did* talk about this. And as I recall, we kept arguing."

"Yes, well, *you* did," said Octavia. "But we're not going to get into this now. It's not the time."

"We kind of *need* to get into this now," said Tweed. "It *is* the time. In fact, this is the *exact* time we need to get into it."

Octavia lifted her hand to stop him and glanced around the edge of the palette. The pyramid was about two hundred feet wide. The opening to the tunnel was about a quarter that, and over to their left. They couldn't run the distance. They'd be spotted in a second. But they couldn't hang around here either. She looked up. The elevators had arrived up at the top. Once the soldiers realized they weren't to be found, they'd be back down here to search for them. They had to move now.

"There's no point just sitting here," said Tweed. He slapped Molock on the shoulder. "Come on, old chap. You're the only one that fits in here. Off you go and fetch us a skiff. That one over there will do." He pointed to a skiff about thirty feet away. Soldiers were loading heavy weaponry into the bed of the vehicle. Octavia thought she spotted some kind of grenade launcher.

"Right," said Molock. "Yes. Good idea."

Molock stood up and nervously wiped the dust off. "I'll get the skiff."

"Chop chop," said Tweed.

Molock frowned. "You . . . want me to chop someone up?"

"Figure of speech, old chap. It means hurry up."

"Oh. Right."

Molock moved out of cover, walking nervously toward the skiff. Octavia winced. If anyone took a second look at him, the game was up. He looked like he was a wooden toy.

He slowed down enough so that when he arrived at the skiff the soldiers had their backs to him, trying to maneuver more weaponry off a loader. Molock hopped inside the skiff, then quickly activated the vehicle and turned it around. By the time the soldiers realized he had taken it, he was halfway back to their position.

They sprinted from cover and ran toward him. Molock slewed the skiff around, presenting it side on and almost smacking right into Tweed in the process. They leaped aboard as shouts erupted behind them. The crack of gunfire echoed around the pyramid. They ducked down beneath the lip of the skiff as Molock turned it toward the tunnel.

Octavia peered over the edge. The soldiers were chasing them, firing as they came. But then a second, heavier grinding drowned out the gunfire. A beam of light fell down through the center of the pyramid and speared the floor. The beam grew wider, illuminating the pyramid with daylight.

The pyramid was opening up.

Starting at the very top, each level was sliding back like a child's puzzle, opening wider and wider. Octavia saw tiny figures peering down at them.

Octavia smacked Molock on the back. "Faster!"

Molock tried, but the skiff was so weighed down by the weaponry that it couldn't go any faster.

The tunnel was approaching. Brave (or stupid) Hyperboreans tried to block their path, but they ended up diving out of the way when it became clear Molock had no intentions of stopping.

Two small flying machines erupted over the edge of the pyramid. They plummeted downward, then slowed just before they hit the ground, bobbing in the air then surging toward them with a burst of speed.

They were smaller than the skiff they were using, built for speed more than anything else. And they were already catching up.

The skiff crested the lip of the tunnel, rising up then crashing heavily onto the downward slope. Their surroundings dimmed as they left the bright sunlight behind them.

Octavia peered ahead. The tunnel seemed to go on forever. Their pursuers would catch them in no time.

She turned to Tweed and saw him lifting one of the massive grenade launchers that the soldiers had loaded onto the skiff. There were two more lying at her feet.

Tweed was struggling to steady the long weapon on his shoulder. Octavia helped him, grabbing the end to stop it from tilting forward. The pursuing skiffs ramped over the lip of the tunnel and shot toward them in a burst of speed.

"Do it!" shouted Octavia.

Tweed closed one eye, sighting along the barrel, then he pulled the trigger. There was a *woosh* of sound. The launcher jerked violently in their hands, feeling suddenly lighter.

But nothing happened.

Her mother screamed. Octavia whirled around to see the rocket coursing away in front of the skiff. It crashed into the tunnel wall just as it curved around to the left.

The grenade exploded.

The tunnel wall tore apart. Huge pieces of rock burst outward, careening across their path. Molock veered wildly, sending the skiff left then right as he tried to dodge the falling rocks.

Octavia looked at the launcher in horror, then met Tweed's eyes. As one they both threw the heavy weapon overboard.

It hit the ground, then flipped up and tumbled end over end. One of the skiffs was close behind them, the driver trying to avoid the huge rocks that had fallen in their path.

He failed to spot the launcher.

It smashed into his chest, sending him flying over the side. The skiff veered wildly and smashed into the wall, shattering into pieces that tumbled and spun through the air.

Tweed looked at her in amazement, then broke into a shaky grin. Octavia grinned back.

But there was still one more skiff left. It dodged and weaved around the fallen rocks, the lizard driver glaring at them with cold fury.

They left the falling rocks behind them. Octavia checked the weapons that remained. Two more launchers, plus some rifles. She decided to leave them where they were and instead pulled out her Tesla gun. She'd never fired a real rifle before and didn't want to start now.

Tweed pulled out his own gun and they fired at the pursuing skiff. Their first few volleys missed, but they succeeded in making the driver slow down and drop back slightly.

They lost sight of him as the tunnel turned sharply to the left. Octavia grabbed the seat to steady herself. She turned around to tell Molock to take the corners easy, but the words died on her tongue as Molock drove them into a huge space easily five times the size of the pyramid.

The area was filled with strange machinery—huge drills, gears, poles, even cogs for some truly massive gears. Vast machines were lined up around the walls, the floor covered in metal shavings and chunks of rocks.

And directly opposite them, a huge hole in the mountain face. A hundred feet long and the same again high.

The opening of the tunnel up to the surface.

Molock gunned the skiff forward, heading for the huge bank of elevators that Octavia now noticed had been built at the bottom of the tunnel.

Octavia heard a noise behind her. She whirled around and saw the pursuing skiff heading in their direction. A second Hyperborean was standing behind the huge circular barrel of a gun. He started furiously cranking a lever and the autocannon rotated, spitting bullets out at a terrifying rate.

Everyone hit the deck. Even Molock. Octavia heard the bullets smack into the side of their skiff. Then there was a bump, the sensation of rising upward, a moment of floating . . .

They slammed into the wall. The rear of the skiff lifted up then tipped over sideways, sending everyone sprawling out into the elevator. Octavia hit her head against the wall. She cried out in pain, white lights flashing across her vision. Sounds dimmed, everything slowed. She saw all the weapons tumbling into the elevator with them. Her mother was helping Molock into a sitting position. There was blood on his head. Octavia shook her head, trying to stay conscious.

She blinked heavily, looked around for Tweed. Where was he? She had to make sure he was okay.

She saw him, standing up behind the skiff. It was still on its side, shielding them from the bullets that smacked into its underside. Tweed winced at every impact. Blood trickling from a head wound. Why was he just standing there? He was going to get shot.

He looked at her and opened his mouth, shouting. She frowned. She had no idea what he was saying.

Then everything sped up again. The white light receded from her vision, the sounds came crashing back.

"What?" she shouted.

He took one hand away from the skiff, gesturing upward. That was when she realized he was holding the skiff in position where it had crashed, making sure the bullets didn't reach them.

Octavia looked wildly around. Her mother was trying to stanch the wound on Molock's head. She had her back against the levers that controlled the elevator. Octavia moved her aside and yanked the lever down. The elevator started to move. Slowly, agonizingly slowly.

The gunfire was still coming. It was deafening, a staccato roar that battered her senses, blocking everything else out. The skiff was being shredded. Octavia could see light punching in through holes in the bottom of the vehicle. As she watched, another hole opened up only inches from Tweed's head.

He must have seen it too, because he straightened up and gave it a gentle push.

It tumbled out of the elevator and dropped through the air. There was a heavy crash and the gunfire suddenly stopped.

Tweed and Octavia carefully peered over the edge. The skiff had landed on top of their attackers.

The sudden silence rang in her head.

Tweed turned to her. His eyes were shining with excitement and relief. "They don't look too healthy," he said with a straight face. "Bet they're feeling a little . . . *flat.*"

"Tweed!" said Octavia, shocked. "A little good taste."

"Sorry, sorry. But I bet they're feeling a bit *depressed* about the whole thing."

"Quite."

"They were very determined, weren't they? Took a lot to *squash* their spirit."

Octavia giggled, then quickly put a hand over her mouth to stop it becoming hysterical. She was feeling shaky, glad to be alive, overwhelmed, and terrified. All at the same time.

But still, she couldn't resist one. "You could say they were . . . *dying* to catch us."

Tweed snorted with laughter. They both turned away to find her mother and Molock staring at them with open mouths.

Octavia clamped her mouth shut. "I'm so sorry," she mumbled. "I'm not laughing at them. Just . . . I . . . I can't help it."

Her mother shook her head in disappointment. For some reason that sent her into giggles.

༄

The elevator picked up speed, the walls skimming past in a blur. The four of them sat on the floor, utterly exhausted by the events that had brought them here.

Octavia sat back to back with Tweed, their heads resting against each other. She wasn't sure who had taken that position first, but it felt nice. To feel him so close to her.

It was difficult to judge how far they were traveling. There was no frame of reference. Just the blurred rock that flew past and the cold wind that whipped around them. The tunnel itself was huge, so wide even Solomon's airship could fit into it.

After about half an hour the light changed. Their surroundings brightened, almost imperceptibly at first, then more and more, a bright white light spilling down the tunnel toward them.

They stood up. Octavia suddenly realized that they had no idea what was waiting for them up there. They could very well be rising directly into Sekhem and Nehi's lair. She pulled her Tesla gun out, noting that the others were reluctantly doing the same. No one wanted to fight again, but they might have no choice.

The elevator lurched, then slowed its ascent. They were able to see the actual rocks of the walls now. They slowed even more, and then gradually rose above the lip of the elevator shaft and bumped to a stop.

There was no army waiting.

Instead, there was a cave about twenty meters deep and fifty wide, open to the outside world. A frigid wind brought the tang of snow and ice to Octavia's nose.

They stepped off the elevator and moved toward the exit. As they drew closer, Octavia could see snow-covered mountains in the distance, sharp against a lead-grey sky.

They stopped at the cave opening, looking out onto a freezing landscape. Octavia shivered and pulled her thick jacket tighter. Where were they? The Arctic? Somewhere far to the north, that was for sure. The mountains that surrounded them were craggy and inhospitable. Black, jagged rock was exposed by the biting wind that blew powdered snow from the peaks, sending it swirling into the sky.

"Bit nippy," said Tweed, but his joke fell flat as they took in the hostile landscape around them.

There were two grey metal boxes against the wall. They paused to search through them, finding blankets, rucksacks, tins of food, flasks of water. Everything they would need to trek through the snow.

While the others packed everything into the rucksacks, Tweed hurried back to the elevator. He picked up the missile launcher, then hit the lever to send the elevator back down to ground level. He checked both sides of the launcher, hefted it right side up, pointed it down into the tunnel, and fired.

Octavia watched in astonishment as the missile erupted from the launcher and disappeared from sight. Tweed dropped the weapon and hurried back to join them.

"*What?*" he said. "You don't think they would follow us up here? Of course they would."

As he finished they heard a muffled explosion far below their feet. The ground trembled, and after a few moments a thin cloud of dust drifted up the shaft.

"I suppose we had no choice," said Molock.

"None," said Tweed, pulling his rucksack onto his back.

Octavia did the same. "What do we do now?" she asked. Where were Sekhem and Nehi? Where was the *Albion?* How were they ever going to find them?

Molock stepped out of the cave and looked up into the sky. "I think we go that way," he said pointing up to the left.

The others stepped out of the protection of the cave. The cold stung Octavia's cheeks and nose, stripped her throat raw. But she barely noticed it, because off to their left, moored to the top of one of the largest mountains around them, was the airship *Albion.*

It was still here. They weren't too late.

"Looks like we've got a bit of a trek ahead of us," said Tweed. He glared at Octavia. "And you *know* how I feel about exercise."

CHAPTER SIXTEEN

I t was early morning. Too early. No one should have to rise at such a ungodly hour. It wasn't natural.

Tweed yawned and stared with a glazed expression at the horizon. The rising sun was just visible in the narrow gap between the grey clouds and the rocky ground. Pink and orange light seeped slowly across the sky, growing brighter with each passing minute. Tweed watched it hungrily, the only hint of color in this freezing wasteland.

He sighed when the clouds finally swallowed the sun, the color fading like a half-remembered dream. Only grey, white, and black remained.

It had been about fifteen hours since they'd left the cave, following a path that wound up around the mountain. They knew it was the way to go because of the deep furrows that had been worn into the ground. It seemed Sekhem and Nehi couldn't do whatever they were doing to the *Albion* down there. They had to move their supplies to where the *Albion* was moored above the peaks, safe from any winds that might smash it against the mountains.

Tweed and his companions had slept in a cave signposted by a pile of litter outside the narrow opening. It was obviously used as a resting station because there was even a pile of firewood just inside the entrance.

They had spent a good while arguing about whether to light the fire, but as the night got colder and colder the argument for (we'll die if we don't) won out over the argument against (we might be spotted).

Tweed sighed and glanced up at their destination, still a good fifteen or so miles away. He couldn't see the airship anymore, but they had all marked its position.

Not that they needed to. Just following the path would take them directly to the enemy.

This was something that bothered him. What, when they came right down to it, were the four of them planning on doing when they got there? It was obvious they were going to be vastly outnumbered.

They *could* go in with all guns blazing, but Tweed wanted to avoid that. The truth was, he was still feeling conflicted about the whole thing. Damn it, Sekhem and Nehi *did* have a point, whether Octavia wanted to admit it or not. They—the Hyperborean people— had been treated abominably by his government. Their very source of life was being drained to sustain the rapid growth of the British Empire, and nobody seemed to care.

It made him furious.

But then he would remember what Sekhem and Nehi had done. Killing Tesla, almost killing Octavia, the attack on the rebel camp. These were all terrible, terrible things.

But . . . the thing was, Tweed sort of understood where they were coming from. He didn't condone their actions, of course not, but he *understood* them.

With the Lazarus affair it was different. Homes and Lucien, they wanted power, they wanted to enrich themselves. It was easy to hate them. But Sekhem and Nehi . . . they were protecting their people.

Who was he to judge them for that?

"Penny for your thoughts," said Octavia, appearing at his side. She blew into her hands, her breath puffing into the air.

"They're not worth that much," said Tweed.

Octavia glanced at him, then pulled on her gloves. "You're being all thoughtful. I'm not sure I like it when you're thoughtful. It makes me worry."

Tweed was silent for a while. "Do you really think we have any right to judge them? I mean, after seeing what we're doing to their world?"

Octavia let out a disgusted sound. "This again? *We* didn't do it, Tweed."

Tweed waved his hand in irritation. "We. Us. Them. The Ministry. You know what I mean."

"Of course I do. And you think that makes it fine for them to turn a death weapon against London?"

"Of course I don't think that!" He pulled his hood up. "It doesn't matter. You don't understand."

"Don't patronize me! Of course I understand. Sekhem talked to you. He told you about the pain, the suffering. You feel guilty. Conflicted. So what? Real life is never black and white." Octavia put her hands on his arms and turned him around to face her. "They've been wronged. Yes. But that doesn't give them the right to take other lives. Not even one. As soon as they did that they forfeited any right to my sympathy. I mean, look at Molock. He's in the same position. He's a royal, in charge of his people. But he's looking for a different way to fix this. One that doesn't involve mass murder."

"Hiding away in the shadows is not what I call looking for a way to fix this."

Octavia sighed. "Well . . . no, possibly not. But I'm afraid that's something that doesn't have anything to do with us. It's his decision, not ours."

"You two ready?"

Elizabeth and Molock stood in the path just outside the cave entrance. Tweed nodded unhappily, and he and Octavia followed after them.

Octavia didn't say anything else, which he was grateful for. It was one of those arguments that would just keep going round and round with no solution, and he *hated* that. It offended him on so many levels. There *always* had to be an answer. He wouldn't accept anything else.

They were ambushed a few hours later.

Molock and Elizabeth were about ten paces ahead of Tweed and Octavia. They had already disappeared around a bend in the path.

A few seconds later came the staccato crack of gunfire.

Tweed peered around the curve of the mountain wall. Bullets peppered the ground in front of him, snow spraying up into his face. He saw Molock shove Octavia's mother out of the way. She slipped, banging her head hard on the ground. A bullet struck the rock where she had just been standing.

Tweed and Octavia darted from cover and grabbed her mother's shoulders, dragging her back to safety. Molock followed after, bursting around the corner at top speed. He tried to slow down, but his feet skidded out from beneath him. He fell heavily and slid straight for the edge of the path.

"Grab my foot!" shouted Octavia.

"Wha—?" Tweed barely took in her words before Octavia launched herself forward in a dive, attempting to intercept Molock before he went flying over the edge of the mountain.

Tweed swore loudly and ran after her, landing on his backside and grabbing her foot. He slid with her. He dug his heels in, watching the edge of the path rapidly approaching.

Octavia collided with Molock and his weight sent them spinning off to the side. They hit a bump in the path and flipped, tumbling over and over until they came to a panting, shaky stop in a snow drift.

"That," said Tweed slowly, "was not fun." He gently pushed Octavia's head into the snow. "And don't you ever do that again. What if I didn't have such lighting quick reflexes? You'd be doing a swan dive over the cliff right now."

Octavia spat snow from her mouth. "I had faith in you."

"Did you? Jolly good. I'm glad one of us did."

They pushed themselves shakily to their feet and moved back up the path to join Octavia's mother. She was peering around the corner, studying their attackers while rubbing the back of her head.

"Are you okay?" asked Octavia.

"I'm fine. Just a bit of a knock."

Tweed peered around the curve. Their attackers were . . . well, they weren't people. Not as such. They looked to be some sort of hybrids. Half-man, half-machine. As if someone had given a mad scientist equipment, an unlimited budget, a few people to experiment on, and said "go for it."

The closest was a figure who was literally only half-human. From the stomach down he was all construct, his legs rusted metal with pistons that puffed clouds of steam into the air every time he moved.

Another was a woman missing most of her face. A brass mask had been joined to the puckered, scarred skin. Her one eye was an orb of dark glass.

Another had a set of metal arms, while yet another consisted of the upper body of an ancient man attached to a set of wheels, like a half-mechanical wheelchair.

One standing off to the side of the group had a slate-grey body with a long strip of ridged metal that looped through his chest, out his back, and along the ground behind him. Tweed couldn't figure out what it was until the figure caught sight of him and braced himself in the snow, leaning forward at an angle. Bullets shot from his chest, the long strip jerking and stuttering, empty casings erupting from a hole in his shoulder.

Tweed jerked back, hearing the high whine of bullets striking the rock face.

"Do you think this means Sekhem and Nehi know we're coming?" said Elizabeth.

"Not sure," said Tweed. "There's a cave there."

"A way station?" said Octavia.

"Possibly. Perhaps they're just lookouts."

"That means we must be about halfway there," said Molock excitedly. "We could get there tonight."

"Yes," said Elizabeth. "If we could get past that lot first."

Tweed took another quick glance around the bend, surveying the area. The gunfire started up straight away. He jerked back, then pulled his gun out and adjusted the setting.

"Prepare to be amazed," he said. Then he whirled around the bend, held his arms straight out, and fired his gun.

He didn't wait to see if he hit the target, but jerked back into cover again.

The others were watching him expectantly.

"Wait for it," he said.

They waited. Nothing happened. He smiled uncertainly, gesturing for patience.

Still nothing.

"You missed," called a voice.

Tweed swore under his breath. Octavia tried to repress a smirk, but she didn't try very hard. He pointed at her. "I saw that."

"What?" said Octavia innocently.

"You know what." He sighed. "All right. Second attempt."

He gripped the gun then crouched down and swung around the curve. He fired again, and at the same time the enemy shot at the spot he had been standing during the last attempt. Rock chips stung his face as he pulled the trigger. Once, twice, three times.

He ducked back into cover, then nodded confidently at the others.

A second later they all heard it. A grinding, cracking noise, followed by a heavy thump and the screams and cries of the hybrids, abruptly cut off.

Tweed smiled. He raised an eyebrow and jerked his head to the side, inviting the others to look. They did, tentatively at first, then straightening up moving out into the open. Tweed followed after, and saw that the overhang he had been aiming at had collapsed, the rock and the huge drift of snow that had been resting on top hiding the bodies of the crew of constructs.

They walked through the snowy mountains for the rest of the day. They didn't encounter any more guards or hybrid constructs, something that bothered Tweed a bit, because the kind of people Sekhem and Nehi were, he'd have thought they would have guards everywhere. The fact that they didn't meant either that they were so confident in their firepower that they didn't care, or that they were about ready to set off with the *Albion*. With each passing minute he felt the urgency of what they were doing building and building.

The sun set as they trekked up the mountain path. It was pale and watery, streamers of gold bursting out from beneath the low clouds, turning the sky pink and violet. Everyone paused to watch, an unspoken decision. Breath clouded before their flushed faces as they watched the violet fade to grey, the pillars of gold slowly moving across the distant landscape before gradually winking away to nothing.

Tweed sighed, sorry to see it go. It was at moments like this, similar to those he spent on the roof of his house back in Whitechapel, that his mind finally stopped moving, the barrage of non-stop thoughts and ideas simply . . . slowing for a while.

They moved on, the stars winking into razor-sharp existence above their heads.

An hour or so later, they finally arrived. They rounded a bend in the path to find the *Albion* floating in the night sky. Spotlights danced across the massive airship, lighting it up as if it was on display in some fancy exhibition.

The lights shone up from a huge complex built directly into the mountain, windows hidden beneath overhangs and expertly fashioned to follow the contours of the rock. By the spotlights they could see that the *Albion* had been changed from the first class floating hotel they had traveled on. The safety net that had prevented Octavia and Molock falling to their deaths was gone. And sticking out from the bottom of the hull was a huge metallic structure that cradled what looked at first like a giant's telescope. The device was massive, easily the size of a two-story house.

"Tesla's super weapon," said Molock grimly.

So that was why they needed the *Albion*. Looking at the size of the weapon, it was immediately apparent that it would need something massive to move it. Only the *Albion*, with its Tesla Turbines and massive gasbags, could support its weight.

They stayed in cover and watched the complex. There was no movement on this side of the structure. Everything seemed to be happening on the airship. The spotlights illuminated tiny figures scrambling around on lines and ropes, making what looked like last minute adjustments to the weapon.

The entrance to the complex was a stone door about thirty feet long. After making sure the coast was clear, they moved out from the lee of the cliff and sprinted up the slope toward it, keeping to the edge of the path in the hopes that it would hide them from view if anyone happened to glance out any of the windows.

They arrived at the door and crouched down in the shadows, waiting to hear if any alarm had been raised. Nothing. No blaring klaxon, no shouts of alarm.

"I get worried when things go our way, Songbird," he said. "This all seems too easy."

"Why did you go and say that?" snapped Octavia. "Here I was, thinking the exact same thing, and you know what I said? *Nothing*.

Because saying that kind of thing out loud is a curse, Sebastian Tweed. A jinx."

Tweed looked at her in surprise. "What are you talking about? I was just saying this is too—"

Octavia slapped a hand over his mouth. Tweed's eyes went wide in amazement. "Wha oo oo-in?" he mumbled around her fingers.

"Don't you dare. Are you touched in the head? You never say that kind of thing." Octavia shook her head. "For a smart person, you really can be an idiot."

Tweed prized Octavia's hand away, trying to ignore how pleasant her skin felt against his mouth. "Are you quite finished?" he asked.

Octavia didn't do anything else mad, so Tweed straightened up. "I'll try the door."

He turned as if to walk away, then smothered a quick grin. He glanced over his shoulder. "I'll be right back."

Octavia's eyes went wide. She raised her hands in the air in exasperation, looking to her mother and Molock for help.

Tweed headed for the small panel he could see to the right of the door. It was a basic lever system, nothing complicated. He pulled it down and the concrete door groaned and slowly rumbled along tracks, heading into the wall.

Tweed grinned and put his hands on his hips. The interior slowly revealed itself to them, the light spilling out into the cold night. A concrete floor, lots of space, and two large wheels with heavy treads on them. Tweed followed the treads up, expecting to find some sort of heavy duty machinery. He was rather surprised, then, to find a metal body, incredibly large arms with pistons venting steam into the air, and a thick, solid neck.

The neck had a man's head attached to the top. The man was smoking a cigar.

He stared at Tweed.

Tweed stared back, noting that the hybrid was holding what appeared to be incredibly heavy pipes above his head. (Which looked comically undersized when compared to the body.)

The man puffed on his cigar, sending a stream of smoke into the air, then he spat the cigar out, grinned, and hurled the huge pipes directly at Tweed.

Tweed looked frantically around as the metal pipes—easily the same size as he was—bounced and crashed onto the floor, rolling directly at him.

There was nowhere to go. The sheer cliff face to his left, and the drop to his right. The only option was back the way he came.

He turned and sprinted down the slope. The pipes clanged and thundered behind him, picking up speed on the icy path. He caught up with the others as they ran, and Octavia turned a furious glare on him.

"I *told* you!" she shouted. "Never get cocky. It comes back to bite you in the backside."

In response, Tweed reached out and gave her a shove. She shrieked and went tumbling to the side, falling into a narrow cleft Tweed had spotted on the way up. Problem was, it was only big enough for one, but at least it meant Octavia was safe.

Elizabeth and Moloch were ahead of him, making for the bend in the path. Tweed risked a glance over his shoulder, and immediately wished he hadn't. The pipes were only about ten feet behind him. He wasn't going to make it.

The others slid around the corner, then poked their heads back around.

Tweed saw the look of horror on Elizabeth's face. She opened her mouth to shout, but he was already dropping, skidding along the snow and trying to angle for a rock that protruded up along the side of the path.

He grabbed it, scraping the skin from his fingers and swinging himself around to face back the way he had come. He yelped and snatched his hands back just as the first pipe hit the rock and launched into the air, skimming past just above his head and soaring over the edge of the cliff. Two more did the same, while another trundled down and hit the cliff where Elizabeth and Molock were hiding. It smashed into the mountain, gouging a huge chunk out of the rock, then spun away into the abyss to the left.

A second later they poked tentative heads back around the bend. Tweed waved a shaky hand and pushed himself to his knees. But as soon as he put his hands to the ground he felt a vibration running through the snow.

He looked up to see the massive hybrid rolling toward him. It's enormous claw arms snapped at the air.

"Gonna get you boy!" the head shouted. "Gonna get you and squish you till you burst!"

"Charming," muttered Tweed, straightening up and reaching for his gun.

It wasn't there.

He whirled around, searching the ground. He spotted it down the slope, resting up against the cliff wall next to Elizabeth and Molock.

The hybrid was about fifteen feet away now. The treads spun on the snow, picking up speed.

Ten feet.

Five.

"Bugger," said Tweed softly.

He straightened up just as electricity surged up the hybrid's back, crawling and leaping across the metal plates, arcing up over the man's face. Smoke poured from his ears. The treads froze up and he skidded. He opened his mouth to scream—

—and his head exploded. Tweed jerked away as bits of skull and brain peppered the ground around him. The hybrid's body skidded past him, hit the edge of the path, then tumbled away into darkness.

Octavia stood in the path, her Tesla gun still raised at shoulder height, silhouetted against the light spilling out from the doorway. Tweed stared at her, then took a deep shuddering breath.

Elizabeth and Molock joined him.

"Your knight in shining armor," said Elizabeth as she walked past.

They caught up with Octavia. She gave him "the look." "What are you never going to say again?"

"I'll be right back," He mumbled.

"Sorry?"

"*I'll be right back.*"

"And?"

"This is too easy."

"What?"

"*This is too easy.*"

Octavia patted him on the cheek. "Good lad."

They entered the complex and found themselves in a large foyer from which various doors opened. The floor was scuffed and scratched, evidence of the massive amounts of material that had been brought through.

"We need to find Tesla's soul, yes?" said Tweed. "I think that's the only thing that will stop them at this point."

"What if it's already up on the airship?" asked Octavia.

"That's a very strong possibility," said Molock. "They would keep it close to them, wouldn't they?"

Tweed frowned. "I don't know. Keep it safe, or keep it close?"

"We have to find a way up to the airship anyway," said Elizabeth. "We just keep our eyes open for his soul at the same time."

There were four doors leading off from the foyer. Tweed looked at them. "One each?"

Octavia shook her head. "No way. You'd end up sneaking aboard the *Albion* by yourself and sailing off without us. We should pair up. I'll keep an eye on you."

"Fine." He pointed at the two doors to the right. "We'll take these. We should meet up back here in an hour?"

The others nodded.

"Good. Now remember, if we fail here, then thousands of people will die. So . . . let's not fail, eh?"

Octavia and her mother moved aside to hold a low conversation, leaving Tweed and Molock standing awkwardly nearby.

Tweed watched them, his thoughts going back to his talk with Octavia. "Just so you know," he said, "I still think you're wrong. Hiding away while you hope to come up with a solution is not in your best interests."

"We have thought long about this, Sebastian. Revealing ourselves will only lead to trouble for my people. Keeping ourselves hidden is the path we must follow."

Tweed shook his head, exasperated. "Listen to yourself! Doing nothing is why we're in this mess! Doing nothing is what finally drove Sekhem and Nehi to rise up against you! If you had gone to the Queen, or even the Prime Minister, none of this would have happened."

"You are correct. None of this *would* have happened. Because my people would all be dead." Molock sighed and shook his head. "I do not mean to sound patronizing, but you have the optimism of youth. You think the best of people—"

"I assure you I don't," interrupted Tweed. "People are crap.

Really, they are. But when it comes to bigger things we can really surprise you." He shook his head angrily. "I had this exact same conversation with Sekhem back on the airship! You're both the same, you know that?"

For the first time ever, Molock allowed anger to show through his usually calm demeanor. "We are not the same! How dare you! Those two are going to doom us to a war that will kill us all!"

"Whereas you're going to hide in the shadows in a move that will kill you all. Same result."

Octavia joined them, surreptitiously wiping her eyes. "Ready?" she asked.

Tweed nodded. "I'm finished here."

"As am I," said Molock. He turned abruptly and walked toward Elizabeth. Tweed hesitated, wondering if he should call him back, but decided against it. He hadn't said anything he didn't believe. What did he have to apologize for?

CHAPTER SEVENTEEN

Octavia and Tweed had been moving through the complex for about ten minutes and still hadn't come across another living person. The corridors they moved through were chiseled directly out of the rock. The floors were nothing more than metal grills laid over dusty stone. There had been no attempt at prettying anything up.

"Tesla's soul," Octavia said slowly.

"What about it?"

"If they're using it to somehow build this weapon, shouldn't we destroy it?"

"No," said Tweed immediately. "If we do that, we're no better than Chase. We're no better than Sekhem and Nehi. We don't have the right to kill him."

"Even if it saves others?"

Tweed looked at her, serious. "Octavia, who are we to judge who lives and who dies?"

"Tweed, *someone* has to. I know you don't like it, but hiding away from the decision—"

"It's not hiding away," Tweed snapped. "It's accepting that we have no right to sentence anyone to death."

"Some would say it's survival."

Tweed shook his head. "No. If there is a choice, if we can discuss it like we're doing now, then it is *not* survival. It's playing God. Don't you see? That's what caused all this mess in the first place. The Ministry playing God over the Hyperboreans. Then Sekhem and Nehi playing God to get revenge, proclaiming judgment on innocents. We're not like that. That's not who we are."

Octavia thought about this. She wasn't sure she agreed with that. If one life could save thousands, surely it was that person's responsibility—that person's *duty*—to sacrifice him or herself for the greater good? She would expect no less from herself.

She said as much to Tweed, adding, "I think you're oversimplifying the whole issue."

"No. I'm not. That's the trick, you see? They try to make it sound complicated, but it's not. But you *are* right. Up to a point. It might be a person's duty to sacrifice himself to save others, but it has to be *his* choice. No one has the right to make that choice for someone else. It has to be done freely."

Octavia could see she wasn't going to change his mind. She wasn't sure she *wanted* to. What he was saying was part of who he was. It was what she liked about him, what drew her to him. He had formulated his own views of right and wrong. And he had to figure out for himself if those views were correct or if they were simply naive. Who was she to try to influence that one way or the other?

They turned into a corridor, checking any doors they passed. They were all locked. Another corridor, more doors. All of them locked.

Finally, they found a door that opened. Octavia peered inside. It looked like a workshop of some kind, but it held nothing of interest.

"This is hopeless. What are we meant to do? Just wander around aimlessly until we stumble on something?"

"Any other suggestions?"

Octavia thought about it. "Make our way up top and set fire to the *Albion*?"

Tweed brightened at this. "Not bad." Then he frowned. "Actually, no, I thought we'd use it to escape. I don't fancy being stuck here forever. It's a bit cold, you know?"

Octavia hadn't thought about that. They *did* need some form of escape. So destroying the *Albion* perhaps wasn't the best idea.

They walked on and reached an intersection between corridors. To the left was a set of stairs. To their right—more doors.

"Flip a coin?" asked Tweed.

Octavia was about to answer when she heard footsteps coming down the stairs. They ducked back into the corridor and peered around the corner.

Two elderly men walked into view. Behind them came Nehi. She was pointing a gun at their backs. The trio didn't pause, but kept descending the stairs. Tweed and Octavia waited, and a few minutes later Nehi reappeared, climbing back up to the floors above.

"So who were they?" said Tweed.

"Someone held against their will. Which means they might be willing to help us find Tesla's soul."

They headed over to the stairs and peered over the banister. No sign of any guards. They hurried down to the bottom level and found themselves in an empty room with a single, glass-paneled door leading out. There was a small table in the room, and a set of keys hanging on a hook in the wall.

Octavia peered through the glass. Beyond was a single corridor with prison cells to either side. There didn't seem to be any guards here either, so Octavia opened the door and they approached the first of the cells.

Inside was one of the men they had just seen being led down the stairs. He looked to be in his sixties, thin grey hair hanging down to his shoulders. He was pacing back and forth, but froze when he saw them.

"Who . . . who on earth are you?" he asked, shocked. He took a tentative step forward, gripping the bars. "You *are* real, aren't you? I've not finally gone mad?"

"We're real," said Octavia.

"Why are you locked up in here?" asked Tweed.

"To do their bidding," spat the man. "Why else? You have to get us out of here."

"What do you mean do their bidding? Who are you?" asked Tweed.

"Dr. Johan Strauss."

"You're a doctor?"

"A scientist. We're all scientists."

Octavia stepped back to get a better look at the line of cells. There were another five of them, each holding a single person. Three men and two women. All of them looking haggard and worried.

"They needed people to help them build their weapon," said one of the men. He had a thick, German accent. "We were all taken from our homes. Kidnapped. I am Dr. Faber, from Berlin."

"Mary Campbell. Edinburgh," said another. She looked to be younger. Early fifties, perhaps. Her Scottish accent was soft, easy to understand.

A tiny man whose face was a mass of wrinkles nodded and smiled at them. "Dr. Vladimir Kolotcha, Russia."

"Dr. Jake Ampney. Oxford man, myself," said the youngest of the group. Which wasn't saying much.

Realization dawned. Octavia remembered the article she had been proofing at *The Times* the afternoon Tweed returned to Stackpole's house. "The missing scientists." She turned to Tweed. "Scientists have been disappearing over the past few years, all of them experts in their fields. Another one went missing just last week."

Dr. Ampney raised his hand. "That would be me."

"And you helped them build that weapon?" asked Tweed angrily.

"They threatened our families," snapped Strauss. "What choice did we have?"

Octavia put a calming hand on Tweed's arm. "What does the weapon do?" she asked.

"It is a combination of two of Tesla's weapons," said Dr. Campbell. "His death ray and another that was called the 'Destroyer of Worlds.'"

"That sounds fairly ominous," said Tweed.

"It is. It is an electromechanical oscillator."

Octavia and Tweed looked at her blankly.

"He never perfected it, but Tesla claimed he could use it to set up vibrations in the crust of the earth that would split the planet in two."

Octavia's eyes widened in alarm. "Is that what Sekhem and Nehi are going to do? Use it to . . . create an earthquake or something?"

"Not quite", said Dr. Strauss. "As my colleague said, the weapon attached to the airship is a combination of both. A sort of death ray earthquake machine. Basically, it disintegrates matter. It will eat away at whatever it is pointed at, and the longer it is activated, the quicker its effects will spread. In a matter of minutes it will disintegrate a space a hundred feet wide. Ten minutes, it will devour five miles of the earth. An hour, an entire city will be destroyed."

"*Ja*," said Kolotcha. "And remember, we're talking five miles wide *and* five miles deep. It just . . . eats everything away."

"But they could never complete it," said Campbell. "You see, Tesla put in a safeguard. The machines as he designed them could only be activated by him."

"We thought it was safe to build them," said Ampney. "After all, Tesla would never activate them. We all knew that. We were playing for time, hoping that someone would come and rescue us." He shook his head. "We didn't realize that Sekhem and Nehi had made other plans."

"His soul," said Octavia. "They can use his soul to activate it?"

Dr. Campbell nodded. "It is his essence. The key. And now that they have it, they are getting ready to launch. It was the last thing they needed."

Octavia and Tweed glanced at each other. So now they knew exactly what Sekhem and Nehi were going to do. They were going to point this ray at London and just . . . dissolve it to nothing. And with the kind of time frame the scientists were talking about, very few people would be able to escape. Millions would die.

"Do you know where they keep Tesla's soul?" asked Octavia.

"You're too late," said Dr. Campbell. "All the modifications are complete. They're setting sail within the hour. The only thing to do now is stop them before they launch."

Octavia tapped her foot thoughtfully. "Is there an armory around here?" she finally asked.

"One floor up," said Kolotcha.

Tweed realized what she was thinking. He grinned at the scientists. "How much do you want to make reparations for what you've all done—what you were *forced* to do?" he corrected.

It was Dr. Campbell who answered first. She gripped the bars so hard her knuckles turned white. "Those bastards took me away from my family. My grandchildren think I'm dead. You want help, sonny, you put a gun in my hand and I'll take them on myself."

Kolotcha grinned. "I like you, Dr. Campbell. You have the spirit of a Russian bear! Only prettier."

Tweed turned his attention to the others. "You all feel that way? Because we have a chance to stop this before it's too late."

The scientists all nodded. Tweed ran back to the first room, grabbed the keys, then came back and unlocked the cell doors.

"Which way?" asked Octavia, as the elderly scientists stepped into the corridor.

Kolotcha took the lead, heading up the stairs to the next level. He led them around a few twists and turns, passing glass-walled laboratories filled with half-completed hybrids. Another room had condensation running down the glass. It was filled with stainless steel instruments and tables, and a tiled floor that sloped slightly toward a drain. One wall was simply a bank of closed metal drawers. It took her a moment to realize the drawers were large enough to contain bodies, or at least, body parts. She shuddered and averted her eyes.

"Are those hybrids part of their cult?" asked Tweed.

"No," said Dr. Faber. "They are curious things. They obey like automata but still have enough human brain left to adapt and make choices. Very dangerous creatures."

The armory was a narrow room lined floor to ceiling with shelves, and crowding these shelves was an arsenal of odd-looking Hyperborean weapons. Octavia didn't bother taking any. She already had her Tesla gun, and she was comfortable with it, but the scientists all crowded around and picked the biggest guns they could find. Tweed grabbed a second pistol, identical to the one he had taken from Temple.

Vladimir Kolotcha had chosen some kind of rifle that was taller than he was. He had it resting against his shoulders, but it was so heavy it was slowly pushing him backward. As Octavia watched, he finally overbalanced and slowly toppled into the wall, where he rested at an angle.

"*Ja*, this one, it might be a bit big," he said.

He dropped it and picked up a smaller one, this one the length of his forearm.

Octavia surveyed their improvised squad. Two seventeen-year-olds and five scientists, none of them below fifty years of age. She sighed and locked eyes with Tweed. But if she thought he was going to share her concerns, she was sadly mistaken. His eyes blazed with excitement.

"Are you all ready to kick some evil cultist bottom?" he shouted.

"Damn right!"

"*Da!*"

"Aboot time!"

"*Ja!*"

"Yes!"

Tweed gave her a thumbs up.

Octavia groaned. They were all going to die here. She just knew it.

They left the armory and moved quickly along the corridors, moving up the stairwell to level three. Apparently, there were five levels and then the rooftop where the *Albion* was moored. Octavia glanced at the others, but none of them seemed to be feeling anything but giddy excitement. Weren't they afraid? She was *terrified*.

But then, if she had been kept prisoner for six years, she supposed she'd jump at the chance to get revenge. Fear would be buried beneath a desire for payback.

But Tweed . . . She couldn't help staring at him. He was sliding along the walls, peering around the corners, with his guns held out before him for all the world as if he really was Atticus Pope. She hoped he hadn't finally snapped.

"Tweed," she whispered fiercely. He didn't acknowledge her. "Hoy. Tweed!" He glanced over his shoulder.

"What?"

"You all right?"

"I'm fine. Why wouldn't I be?"

She checked to make sure none of the others were listening. "You're acting a bit . . ." She searched for the word.

"Heroic?"

"No . . ."

"Manly?"

"Definitely not."

"Brave?"

"*No.*"

And then she remembered something. This was sort of how he had been acting that time in the Zeppelin factory, just after they'd been attacked by the Laughing Man and his lightning gun. This *was* Tweed. This was who he was, this was him being normal.

"Mental," she said. "You're acting a bit mental."

"Oh." Tweed shrugged as if this was perfectly ordinary. "You've got to be a bit mental to survive, I reckon."

So saying he winked at her and disappeared into the next corridor. The others followed, and after a few minutes they were crouching outside a set of double doors.

"It opens into a large room," said Ampney, "but it's been used to dump all the stuff that's been offloaded from the *Albion*. Lots of boxes and crates."

Tweed pushed the doors open a crack with the tip of his gun. Octavia joined him and peered through. Light filtered in from somewhere, but not much. As Ampney had said, there were crates piled everywhere. The floor was strewn with books, ornaments, bottles of wine, clothes, old suitcases.

"We were struggling with weight," whispered Dr. Faber from behind her. "We had to offload everything we could."

"*Ja,*" said Strauss. "You should see the other side of the mountain. A pile as high as your Big Ben."

Tweed pushed the doors open and entered the room in a crouch, pausing behind a large crate. The others followed and the doors squeaked as they swung closed again.

Octavia winced, then peered into the room.

Orange electricity soared past her head and burst the doors from their hinges.

A second later the room was a brightly lit confusion of exchanging gunfire. Tweed was lying on the floor firing around one side of the create. Kolotcha crouched above him, firing blindly in every single direction, while Ampney, Campbell, and Faber shot from the other side of the crate. Octavia winced at the sudden heat, the smell of burning tin. She grabbed hold of the top of the crate and pulled herself up so she could peer into the room.

A bolt of energy came directly at her. She barely managed to drop before it soared through the space where her face had just been.

"Surrender!" shouted a voice. "We have you surrounded."

Octavia frowned. She straightened up. *"Mother?"* she called.

There was a pause. "Octavia?"

Octavia moved out of cover. Molock and her mother were leaning around a wooden crate similar to their own.

"You were shooting at us!" exclaimed Octavia.

"We thought you were the enemy. Sorry."

Tweed hurried past Octavia. "We've got some friends," he said proudly.

"So I see. Who are they?"

"Kidnapped scientists," said Tweed dramatically.

"Ah. Are any of them evil?"

"Don't think so," said Tweed. "Why do you ask?"

"Oh, you know. In all those Atticus Pope books, there's always an evil scientist. I mean, we've found the lair, I was just hoping for a scientist."

"Atticus Pope!" Tweed whirled around and grinned at Octavia. "Nightingale. Your mum reads Atticus Pope! How wonderful."

"Yay. Wonderful," said Octavia wearily, making her way for the door in the far wall and the set of stairs on the other side.

The group climbed to the top floor, moving quickly until they came to a final corridor. At the end was one last room, and then a stairwell leading directly to the roof.

Octavia gently pushed the door open. Darkness, then the flash of muzzle fire, the rat-a-tat of gunfire, and bullets ripped into the wall by her face.

Octavia ducked back and slammed the door closed. Bullet holes were sprayed across the corridor wall, but the burst had been badly aimed. She could hear someone screaming at the shooter inside the room.

"I told you to wait! I told you to hold your fire until they'd all entered the room, you stupid pieces of scrap!"

She recognized that voice. It was Temple.

"Guess they heard the little rumpus downstairs," said Tweed. "How many?"

"How many flashes?" Octavia thought back to the terrifying moment. "At least twenty. That I saw. Probably more."

Nobody said anything, but she knew what they were thinking. That they couldn't do this. There were too many.

But if they didn't stop Sekhem and Nehi, then everything they had been through was for nothing. All the people they had hoped to save would die.

"We can do this," she insisted.

"There are too many," said her mother softly.

Octavia opened her mouth to argue, but her mother held up a hand.

"I don't want to lose you again, Octavia. We've only just found each other." She turned to the scientists. "There has to be another way up to the roof."

"There isn't," said Ampney. "If there was, we would be using it right now." He sighed. "I fought in the Crimea, girl. I know you think we can do this, but I have to disagree. There will be deaths if we go through that door."

"There might be deaths, but we also might win. Right?"

"It is possible," he said reluctantly. "But not probable."

"Don't you see?" she said to everyone. "We have no choice. If we do nothing, even if we fail, then they've won." She looked at Ampney. "Did you want to go to war?"

"Of course not. But it was my duty."

"And why is this different?"

Ampney opened his mouth, then closed it again.

"Octavia—" began her mother.

"Hey, where's Dr. Campbell?" asked Tweed.

Octavia looked around. All the scientists were there except the Scottish doctor. "I saw her just now. She was standing right here."

"She wouldn't have run, would she?" asked Tweed.

"Hah!" said Kolotcha. "No chance. Better to ask if she went into the room ahead of us. A fierce woman, that one. She would not run."

"Should we . . . go look for her?" asked Octavia.

There was a noise from the room behind them. Tweed opened the door slightly and peered through. Then he quickly pushed his gun though the gap and fired blindly. Octavia heard clattering and shouting from the other side.

"No time. They're coming at us."

He fired again. Bullets peppered the door in response, forcing everyone to duck against the walls.

The gunfire stopped. But another sound replaced it. The sound of running feet, coming from along the corridor. Running feet, and swearing. In a Scottish accent.

Dr. Campbell sprinted into view waving a bag furiously over her head.

"Where have you been?" asked Octavia.

Dr. Campbell took a huge gulp of breath and held the bag out. "Remembered seeing these back in the armory. I think they might be grenades."

Ampney took the bag from her and peered inside. He held one up. It was round, made from metal, about the size of her clenched fist, with Hyperborean runes circling it.

Molock peered at it. "Yes, that is indeed a grenade."

"That would kill them," said Octavia.

"Might do," said Ampney. "Depends where it's thrown."

"Do we really have time to worry about that?" asked Strauss. "You think they're worried about killing us?"

Octavia chewed her lip. He had a point. What if—

She heard a noise and turned to find Kolotcha standing by the door looking guilty.

"What did you—?"

She was cut off by a huge explosion from the room beyond. The doors slammed open, sending Kolotcha sprawling. The shock wave struck the rest of them, sending them staggering back. Octavia's ears rang. She used the wall to steady herself.

"What did you do?" shouted Strauss.

"Sorry," said Kolotcha, wincing and wiggling a finger in his ears. "I thought it might have been a simple concussion grenade."

"I don't think it was," said Tweed, peering through the door.

Smoke poured out into the corridor. The dim lights in the room flickered—those that were still working, anyway. Octavia could just see that Kolotcha had thrown the grenade to the right, while most of their enemies had been on the left.

No one was left standing. Some were sprawled, unmoving, while others were groaning, trying to pull themselves to their feet.

Now was the time to move.

She glanced over her shoulder. "Ready?"

The others nodded uncertainly. They hadn't really recovered from the shock of the blast, but there was no time. This was the only chance they'd get.

"Let's go."

She pushed the door open, firing her gun ahead of her. Blue lightning streaked through the smoke, blowing wooden crates apart. The
others joined her and formed a line, firing into the dimness. One
of their shots hit a hybrid, wreathing him in orange electricity, his
limbs shuddering then seizing up.

Some of the cultists had made it to their feet and were moving
backward, heading for the door that led to the roof. It looked like
they had sent the hybrids ahead of them, so the constructs had taken
most of the damage from the grenade.

The cultists fired their guns as they retreated, but they were confused, disoriented. Octavia and the others kept up a steady barrage
of gunfire, blue and orange light mixing, climbing up the walls,
crawling across the floor, grounding itself into anything that was
metal.

The cultists finally made it to the door, then turned and bolted
up the stairs.

Octavia paused on the threshold. The stairs zigzagged upward.
No one was waiting for them. They hurried up the stairs, arriving at
an open door that led directly outside.

Octavia could see some of the cultists scrambling up ropes that
hung from the *Albion*. Octavia fired wildly through the door. She
missed, but one of the cultists still on the rooftop turned and glared
at her. Temple.

He shouted at the others, waving at them to return fire while
he tried to grab a rope. But it shifted just out of reach. The *Albion*
was rising. Temple jumped a second time, but the rope was getting
farther and farther away. He screamed at the airship.

Tweed shot through the door, narrowly missing Temple. He
swung a furious glare at them, swept up his gun from where he'd
dropped it, and returned fire. They ducked to the side. Tweed put

his guns around the doorframe and fired blindly. The others followed suit, shooting wildly into the open.

That was when Octavia noticed the strange white glow that reached them through the door.

"What's that?" she shouted, straining to be heard above the gunfire.

Then, slowly, one by one, the guns outside fell silent.

They peered outside. Their eyes were drawn immediately upward. The huge lens that hung below the *Albion* was glowing bright white.

"They've activated the death ray," whispered Strauss, fear evident in his voice.

Temple was standing directly below it. His face was bathed in light, his hands outstretched to either side.

And then he started to scream.

His skin flaked, sloughing away from his head, floating into the air like ash. His hair fell away and burst into tiny flames.

Octavia watched in horror. His skin boiled away, revealing muscle and sinew. Then that bubbled, vanishing in clouds of steam to reveal the bones underneath. He dropped to his knees. A red puddle formed around him, then the bones collapsed and disintegrated, crumbling away and vanishing.

The area around him started to fragment in the same way, the stone of the roof melting away like ice.

The scope of the death ray expanded, creeping outward, stone disintegrating like sand funneling into a hole. More cultists were caught in its grip, as were some of the hybrids who had made it up to the roof. Their metal frames rusted in an instant, flaking and bubbling as if touched by acid.

The hole in the roof was ten feet across. The other cultists had realized what was happening and were running back to the stairs.

Octavia thought that was a very sensible idea.

"Run!" she shouted. "Out! Out now!"

No one needed a second warning. They sprinted down the stairs, back into the room where the grenade had exploded. Light appeared above them. Octavia looked up and saw a hole forming in the roof, simply appearing and expanding. It touched the wall and the hole carried on growing, devouring everything in its path.

The death ray was moving faster, picking up speed. The group sprinted through the corridors, the compound collapsing all around them. Dust hung in the air like a choking mist. They ran down the stairs, holes appearing at random all around them. It was like some kind of nightmare. A nothingness that spread and ate anything it touched. And this was what they wanted to do to London? The thought drove anger through her body, gave her an extra burst of speed. She helped Dr. Campbell over a fallen roof beam. She could hear screams close behind them, screams that were abruptly cut off.

They reached the front atrium, where the huge hybrid had charged Tweed. They sprinted through the entrance, slipping and sliding on the snow outside. They kept going, moving as fast as they could.

They made it to the bottom of the slope, taking shelter behind the curve in the mountain wall, then turned back to watch.

The complex was almost completely gone. Dust and smoke hung heavy in the air and Octavia was thankful for that. It should have masked their escape. The area where the complex had once stood was now a vast depression, a gouge in the mountaintop. There was nothing left to show that anyone had ever been there. Just an empty crater.

The *Albion* still hung in the air. As they watched, the white light underneath it flickered out. Silence dropped over the mountains. No screams, no cries for help, no moans of pain.

Nothing.

The Tesla engines flared to life and the *Albion* turned around in a slow circle. It moved forward, gradually picking up speed as it flew west.

They watched till it was a speck against the grey sky. No one said anything. What was there to say? They had failed. London was as good as finished.

Not only that, but they were likely going to die as well, stranded out here in the frozen mountains.

There was nothing else to do but trudge back the way they had come. Her mother came to walk next to her. She put an arm around Octavia's shoulder, and Octavia slipped hers around her mother's waist.

"Just don't say 'you did your best,'" said Octavia.

"I wouldn't dream of it."

They walked in silence for a while.

"But you did," said her mother. "We all did."

"Not much of a comfort for the people in London, is it?"

"No," sighed her mother. "No it isn't."

They passed the bodies of the hybrids, buried beneath the snow, and toward late afternoon arrived at the crevice where they had spent the night. Without talking, they all headed inside. This time they lit a fire straight away. There was no need to hide from anyone anymore.

Night fell, and the stars burst into glittering life. They huddled together and slept fitfully, rising early the next morning to continue their trek.

They were heading back to the entrance into Hyperborea. Octavia wasn't sure why. They had destroyed the elevator with the last rocket launcher. It wasn't as if they could go back down.

But it was the only place they *could* go.

They were about an hour away from the cave entrance when they heard the noise, a dull booming that echoed around the mountainside. It went on for a while, accompanied by the screeching of metal, then the crump and rumble of falling snow. An avalanche, perhaps?

They picked up speed, curious to know the cause.

They found out soon enough.

The Boisterous Lady hung in the air above what used to be the cave entrance leading to Hyperborea. The ship was terribly battered, the sides scraped and shredded, huge dents in the metal where rocks had hit it. The entrance to the cave itself had collapsed, rock and rubble now piled up high, sealing off the entrance completely.

Octavia stared at the ship in shock. She wondered briefly if she was seeing things, but then Solomon's voice boomed over his speaker system.

"Hallo over there. Solomon wonders if you might need a ride somewhere? Excuse the lateness of my arriving, but some silly person destroyed the lift shaft and I had to blast my way up. Very time consuming! You want to come? I have hot drinks and chocolate. Lots of chocolate."

"Chocolate?" said Dr. Campbell. She looked speculatively at the others, then elbowed them out of the way and set off at a run.

The others soon followed.

CHAPTER EIGHTEEN

T he wind whipped Tweed's hair around his face. He bared his
teeth into the gale, grinning like a maniac. Then he remembered that this kind of thing annoyed Octavia, so he quickly stopped.

He looked guiltily around and saw her flying her pod off to his
right. Was that starboard or port? He wasn't sure. He tapped the controls, his pod banking, and dropped beneath her. The waters of the
channel weaved briefly into view, then vanished again, replaced by
heavy grey clouds as he pulled up on her right.

He waved.

The battle pods, as Solomon called his escape craft, were surprisingly easy to steer. Just a stick control, the slightest touch of which
sent you spiraling left or right, and a lever to control speed. That was
it.

They had two seats, front and back. They'd mounted a gun in
the rear of each pod so that one person could drive and another could
shoot.

And Tweed had a feeling they were going to be doing a lot of
shooting. They were half a day out from London now. It had taken
them four days of travel, with Solomon coaxing every last bit of speed
out of *The Boisterous Lady*. The Hyperborean was convinced they
would be able to catch up with the *Albion*. It was too heavy, he said,
too cumbersome. No match for his beautiful ship.

They hadn't quite caught up with it, but they *had* made good
time. Tweed didn't think they were too far behind.

But would it be enough?

At first there had been some discussion about why they even had
to learn to fly the pods. Octavia had raised the point that if the *Albion*

flew into view above London and started firing a Tesla death ray at the city, the Ministry would respond. They had to have their own airships and weapons to fight off an attack.

That was when Dr. Strauss told them about the invisibility devices. The same technology they had encountered on Harry Banks's constructs had been brought to Sekhem and Nehi by Temple. The scientists had adapted the devices to the *Albion*.

Which meant the airship and the death ray itself was invisible. No one would know where the attack was coming from.

Tweed glanced over at *The Boisterous Lady*. Molock was waving at them from the railing. Tweed wiggled the lever, the pod dipping left and right in response. Molock gestured for them to head back aboard, then he pointed over his shoulder.

Tweed dropped the pod beneath the airship and saw that land was visible in the distance.

They were back in England.

The Boisterous Lady crested the white cliffs. Tweed stared down at them, then nudged Octavia, who was leaning on the railing next to him.

"Hey, Songbird. Do you think we're 'proudly cresting' the white cliffs of Dover? Or are we sort of *limping* over them?"

Octavia gave him half a smile. "Guess we'll know in a little bit, won't we?"

"Yeah." Tweed sighed. "I suppose we will." He turned his gaze back to the grey clouds. Snow was falling again, covering the familiar countryside with a comforting, suffocating blanket that hid the truth of what was to come.

"Do you really think they'll go ahead with it?" he eventually asked.

She searched his eyes. "*You* don't, do you? You think they'll realize what they're doing is wrong. That they'll have an attack of conscience."

Tweed shrugged uncomfortably and broke eye contact. He did sort of think that. No, he *hoped* that. Everything Sekhem and Nehi were doing, it was out of pain, hurt. Surely they'd realize that killing millions of innocents wasn't the answer.

He had to hope.

He stared into the distance, watching the hills and towns roll by beneath them.

About two hours later, he saw the smoke.

At first he thought it was just the clouds, or perhaps the normal smoke and steam that gathered above the city.

But it wasn't. Wavering plumes of thick, oily smoke drifted above London.

He stared at it in shock, then ran to the trapdoor and shouted below, "They've started! We're too late!"

The others rushed onto the deck. As they drew closer to the city they could see the smoke was coming from where the Houses of Parliament had once stood.

The buildings were gone. Just . . . *gone*. The old Big Ben was nowhere to be seen. All that was left was a smoking hole in the ground, a hole that was slowly expanding.

As they watched in helpless horror, London Bridge buckled. It sagged, and then the supports disintegrated and the entire structure dropped slowly into the Thames. The weight of the bridge sucked the water under, and a few seconds later it erupted upward again in a dark fountain that flashed into steam as soon as it touched the death ray.

There was no doubting anymore. Sekhem and Nehi were going to kill everyone in London unless they were stopped.

"Come on," called Tweed, running for the hold where the pods were kept.

The others followed him into the dim underbelly of the ship, pulling on their flying goggles and strapping themselves in. Only four pods in all. Tweed and Octavia in one, Elizabeth and Molock in another, Faber and Ampney in the third, and Campbell and Kolotcha in the last. Strauss was staying behind to help with the hull-mounted guns while Solomon flew the ship.

Octavia took the gun, not because Tweed was better at flying than her (at least, that's what she said—he reckoned differently) but because she was a better shot than he was. (They knew this for a fact, unfortunately. They'd had a competition.)

Solomon pulled a lever and trapdoors in the hull fell open. The pods dropped. Tweed let them fall for a few seconds, then thrust the lever forward to build up some speed.

They peeled away from the airship. The other three pods dropped into the sky, then banked and veered to either side. They headed straight for the Houses of Parliament. Tweed squinted into the clouds. There. He could see the disturbance in the air, the same as when they were chasing the constructs. It was actually harder to notice against the clouds, probably because the *Albion* itself wasn't moving. No one else would even know it was there.

"Remember the plan!" Octavia shouted behind him.

He nodded. It wasn't *much* of a plan, if they were being honest. The others were going to act as a distraction while Tweed and Nightingale snuck aboard. They'd been chosen because they already knew the layout of the airship.

Tweed pushed the acceleration lever forward as far as it would go. The pod lunged ahead, shaking violently with the strain. The air howled in his ears. He pulled back on the steering stick, trying to gain some height. This was going to be tricky. They needed to hit the *Albion* from the bottom, but that was kind of difficult when they couldn't really *see* the bottom.

They were about a hundred meters from the airship when the ornithopters suddenly appeared, blinking into existence as they exited the invisibility field cast around the *Albion*. He heard the distant rattle of gunfire as they picked their targets.

Octavia swung her own gun on its pivot and fired solid slugs of energy at the ornithopters. Bullets zipped past their pod. Tweed banked, trying to keep moving so he wouldn't be an easy target.

Kolotcha and Campbell dived straight in, aiming for the closest ornithopter and firing madly. Their shots skimmed the wings of one of their attackers and it dropped through the air in a crazed corkscrew. Tweed tilted the pod slightly so he could see it crash into the waters of the Thames far below.

Tweed pulled to the left, hoping to avoid the battle and slip past unnoticed. But two ornithopters peeled away and came for them. Tweed turned slightly, moving side on to give Octavia a chance to fire. Her shots sliced through the air, missing their pursuers and disappearing into the clouds.

The ornithopters drew close, sticking to their rear. Tweed tried to shake them. He pulled up and they followed. He dropped, then banked. They did the same.

He got desperate, trying to twist and fall at the same time, skimming over the water and rising up about a hundred feet back along their path. He thought his pursuers would both follow. One did. The other slowed almost to a standstill, which meant Tweed brought his pod back up directly in front of him.

Tweed found himself staring into the barrel of a gun. Except it wasn't just one barrel. It was another of those autocannons. One of the cultists furiously cranked a handle and the barrel spun, spitting out bullets directly at them.

THE OSIRIS CURSE

Tweed pushed forward on the stick, but he wasn't quick enough. Bullets peppered their side, cutting holes in the metal flank and barely missing Tweed's leg. He cut all power and dropped straight down. Octavia pulled the gun back and fired up at the ornithopter's belly.

Her shots struck home, ripping a hole right through the orni-thopter. It somersaulted backward then dropped like a stone, trailing black smoke in its wake.

"Good shot!" Tweed shouted, pulling up. He craned his neck around to see where the second attacker was. He tried to see past Octavia's head, but she stiffened suddenly and pointed behind him.

He whipped around and saw the ornithopter coming straight at them, the craft's wings folded back in a diving position. What was the idiot doing? There was no way he could pull out of such an attack. Folding the wings was for when the craft were parked.

He was going to crash into them.

"*DUCK!*" screamed Octavia.

Tweed dropped his head and felt heat sear his neck as Octavia fired the gun. There was a scream, abruptly cut off. He looked up to see the ornithopter, smoking and on fire, heading straight for them. He yanked the lever to the side. The pod banked right. The ruined ornithopter scraped along the bottom of their pod, sending them spinning into the clouds.

Tweed managed to steady the craft. He quickly looked around. There were no more attackers coming for them so he aimed straight for the wavering spot that signaled the location of the *Albion*.

He slowed down as they approached, eventually moving at no more than a crawl. He stared intently upward, nudging their craft slowly up.

And then the wooden underside of the hull faded into view.

Tweed blinked, then realized they had entered the field given off by the invisibility generators. Octavia tapped him on the shoulder and pointed to a spot on the hull.

"Over there," she shouted.

Tweed nodded and moved the craft forward. When they drew close he saw a trapdoor in the underside of the airship. But there was no way to open it from this side.

"Drop lower a bit!" she shouted.

Tweed did as instructed and Octavia fired the pod's gun at the trapdoor. It burst away into the ship, leaving a gaping opening in the hull. Tweed guided the ship forward and Octavia undid her safety harness, stood up, and leaped into the *Albion*. A moment later she poked her head out again.

"Come on then!"

Easier said than done. This was the tricky bit. Tweed undid his own harness, then balanced the steering stick with his knees. He reached up, but he wasn't close enough to grab the lip of the trapdoor. He'd have to stand.

He looked around at the clouds and mist all around him. Off to their left the others exchanged gunfire with the cultists. He watched Elizabeth fly her pod beneath an ornithopter, Molock shooting it from beneath. The enemy vessel burst into flame and spiraled out of the sky. Then Dr. Campbell flew through the thick smoke given off by the explosion, heading straight for two more ornithopters. Kolotcha stood up in his seat, firing widely into the sky. Tweed could see, even from this distance, that he was screaming defiantly into the air as he did so.

A bullet struck him in the chest.

Tweed cried out in horror. Dr. Campbell took her eyes off the ornithopters to see why Kolotcha had stopped firing. She saw the Russian slumped over in his seat and grabbed his arm. He was still alive, barely. He looked up and gripped her hand.

Both ornithopters opened fire on their pod, the bullets ripping it to pieces in seconds.

Tweed squeezed his eyes shut, turning quickly away. He didn't want to see that, didn't want to see them die. He took a deep breath and looked up to see that Octavia still had her head hanging out of the trapdoor. She had seen everything.

Tweed furiously wiped tears from his eyes and stood up in the pod. He steadied himself, then jumped toward Octavia. His fingers curled over the edge of the trapdoor, but his foot banged against the pod as it dropped away below him. He lost his grip and ended up swinging wildly, the fingers of one hand the only thing preventing him from falling.

Octavia grabbed his arm, steadying him. He reached up and caught hold of the hatch with his free hand. He waited a couple of seconds to catch his breath, then pulled himself up.

He stood up and looked around, avoiding Octavia's gaze. He didn't want to see her pain, didn't want her to see his.

They were in a narrow space between the floor of the airship and the actual hull. Tweed had to bend over so as not to hit his head. Toward the center of the space was a protective metal casing that dropped through the hull and rose up into the ship. The death ray. They hurried over, but the metal was thick and solid. They tried to fire their guns at it, but the electricity just skittered off the metal like oil on water. They weren't going to disable it that way.

Octavia led him to a second trapdoor that led up into the *Albion* itself. Into a store room, to be exact. The store room led out into a dim corridor. There were no lights lit anywhere. They paused in the doorway, listening. But all they could hear was their own breath.

They made their way through the airship, moving quickly up through the levels, drawing closer to the Bridge. That was where the scientists said they had built the controls for the death ray. That was where Sekhem and Nehi would be. They didn't encounter a single soul along the way. The airship was abandoned.

They arrived at the final set of stairs leading up to the bridge level. Tweed glanced at Octavia surreptitiously as they climbed the steps and moved quietly along the wood-paneled corridor. He had a plan, but he knew she wouldn't go for it. He had to do this carefully.

"Remember when Sekhem tried to make me choose between you and Molock?" he whispered.

"Yes."

"Do you remember what I said if the situation were reversed? That I'd want you to do what was right? Not to save me because I'm your friend, but to do the right thing?"

"I remember. I also remember you couldn't make that choice yourself."

"Because I honestly didn't think he would do it. After talking to him in his room . . . I don't know, I thought I understood him."

"But you didn't."

"I suppose not. But what if it was a choice between you and saving thousands of lives. What would you want me to do?"

Octavia didn't answer at first. "Why are you asking me this?" she said slowly.

"I just want to know," he insisted. "What would you have me do?"

"What was right, I suppose. Thousands saved in exchange for my life? It's not really complex."

"But only if you gave your permission," insisted Tweed. "That's what I'm always trying to say. No one has the right to make that choice for someone."

"I suppose . . ."

"I'd be the same," said Tweed quickly. "My life for thousands? Easy choice."

"Tweed—"

"Shh." Tweed held up his hand. Octavia paused. "Sorry," he said after a moment. "Thought I heard something."

A lie. But he didn't want Octavia to ask him anything more. He'd put it in her mind now. That was enough.

He checked his gun. "You ready?"

Octavia took a nervous breath. "As I'll ever be. Do we have a plan?"

"I thought making it up as we went along *was* our plan."

She smiled at him. He winked, then they hurried along the last ten feet of corridor, pausing before the door that led into the bridge. The last time Tweed had been here was to bring the captain and his crew their tea and coffee. He wondered where they were now. Had they made it off the *Albion* when Sekhem stole it? Or had they been among the unlucky ones who plummeted to their deaths in the desert? What about Violet? Had she made it?

He gripped the gun tightly, then carefully pushed the handle. He opened the door slowly, peering inside.

The interior of the bridge had changed. There was a new console in the center of the floor, replacing the globe of the world that had been there before. The console held a few levers and a view screen showing a grainy sepia image of London.

It also held Tesla's soul.

It was inserted into a slot in the center of the console, its white light spilling out over the brass and wood.

Sekhem and Nehi stood over the console, staring at the screen. Nehi muttered something and pulled the lever down, but Sekhem put a hand over hers.

"Slowly, my sister. We must make them suffer. They must taste the fear."

They entered the bridge, guns extended before them. Octavia moved to the right and Tweed to the left.

"Move away from the console," said Tweed.

Sekhem and Nehi spun around, both of them drawing thin swords from scabbards hanging at their waists.

"How did you get here?" snarled Nehi.

"Move away," said Tweed, louder this time.

Sekhem stared at him, eyes narrowed. "I don't think so, Mr. Tweed."

"I'll shoot you."

Sekhem reached out and rested his hand on a button. "Shoot me and I'll push this button. It turns the power of the death ray up to maximum and locks it there. What you might call an insurance policy. For when your people finally boarded us and tried to shut it down. The two of us might die, but we'll take London with us."

"You've proven your point," said Tweed. "There's still time to stop this. To salvage the situation."

"There is nothing to salvage!" shouted Nehi. "You killed my children. Your people will die in return."

Tweed's eyes opened wide. "Your children . . . ?" Tweed remembered when Sekhem was first telling him about *Tak'al*, about how the sickness was killing his people. He had stopped short when he mentioned his sister.

"My sister's son was one of the first to die," said Sekhem. "Then her daughter. It was why we took the crown from Molock. He was not *doing* anything. He was just standing by and letting our children die!"

Tweed's hand dropped. He stared at Nehi. He could see the pain there. The agony of a mother losing a child. Even though their faces were different it was all in the eyes.

"Tweed?" said Octavia.

Tweed dropped his gun on the floor.

"Tweed?" said Octavia, more insistent this time.

Tweed ignored her. He took a step forward, then another. Sekhem and Nehi both pointed their blades at him.

"What are you doing?" snapped Nehi. "Stay back."

Tweed kept walking until the points of the blades were only a few inches away from his chest.

"I'm so sorry," he said. "So sorry for what happened."

"I do not need your sympathy!"

"I understand now. Finally. Why you are doing this. But you must still see it's wrong. Your children *died*. Think of all that pain you are feeling. You are going to inflict that same torture on how many others?"

"They deserve it!"

"They don't. They're innocent. Like your children were. There is a way forward from here, Nehi. A way to fix this. To heal your people." He looked at Sekhem. There was doubt in his eyes. The slightest flicker. He moved his hand away from the button. Nehi saw it too.

"No!" she screamed. "Sekhem. They must pay for what they have done. Remember Alabeth? The dead in the streets. The sick calling for your help. Whole families, rotting in their homes, still clutching each other in death. And it's all because of them!"

Sekhem's face hardened. Tweed saw him reach out for the button again. He sighed. He had tried.

"Octavia?" he called. "Remember what we just talked about?"

"What—?"

Tweed reached out and grabbed the two blades hovering before his chest. He felt their sharp edges slice into his palms. Sekhem and Nehi stared at him in surprise, then tried to pull the blades out of his grip. He winced in pain, feeling the blood well between his fingers. But he kept hold.

"Do it, Octavia!" he shouted. "Shoot me!"

"What?" Octavia screamed. "Tweed, *what*?"

"Shoot me! My life for London. Remember?"

"No!" screamed Octavia. "Tweed, I won't!"

Tweed gritted his teeth as Sekhem and Nehi tried to pull the blades away. The razor sharp blades sliced even deeper into his flesh. He looked over his shoulder at Octavia.

"My . . . choice . . ." he said, trying his best not to scream at the pain.

"Tweed . . . I don't . . . I can't—"

"I can't hold this much longer, Songbird. Please."

Then he heard the snap of electricity and his whole body was slammed with something monumentally heavy. He screamed as the blue lighting surged through his body, down his arms, into the blades, and into Sekhem and Nehi. They cried out, the three of them caught in a deadly cage of lighting. He could smell burning, could hear a hideous buzzing in his ears, like gigantic bees eating him from the inside. Sekhem looked into his eyes, and the last thought that went through Tweed's head before his heart stopped beating was:

He understands. He respects my choice.

Octavia watched in horror. There was a huge, terrifying *bang*, and all three of them were thrown into the air. Sekhem and Nehi hit the wall and slid to the floor, unmoving. Tweed flew back toward her and landed heavily at her feet.

Octavia ran frantically to the console and yanked Tesla's soul out of the machine, disabling the death ray. Then she spun around and dropped to her knees next to Tweed. Smoke rose from his clothes. His skin was deathly white.

She put her head to his chest. Nothing. No heartbeat.

"No, no, no," she sobbed.

She straightened his body, then joined her fists together and pushed down on his chest. One, two, three, four. She stopped, tilted his head back, then leaned down and blew air into his lungs.

She listened again for his heartbeat. Still nothing.

"Come on Tweed, you bastard."

She pushed down on his chest again, then blew air into his lungs. Nothing.

She did it again. And again. For five minutes, Octavia compressed Tweed's chest and blew air into his body, but nothing she did made any difference. Tears streamed down her face.

"Tweed, come on! You can't leave me here on my own. I need you!"

She hit him again. And again. Still nothing.

Octavia stood up and looked helplessly around. She didn't know what to do.

So she kicked him. Hard. And screamed at him.

"You wake up now you selfish bastard! You are *not* leaving me behind!"

He didn't move. His face was grey.

Octavia cried out in anger and dropped to her knees, bringing her fists down as hard as she could onto his chest.

The thump echoed around the bridge.

And Tweed surged up into a sitting position, sucking in a huge gulp of air and knocking his head against Octavia's in the process.

He looked around in a daze. He rubbed his chest gingerly, then turned his pale face to Octavia and touched his forehead. "Ow," he said.

Octavia stared at Tweed in amazement, then grabbed his jacket and yanked him into a fierce kiss.

They held the kiss for quite a long time. Tweed's hand came up and tenderly cupped her face.

Then Octavia broke off and slapped him. Hard.

"*Ow!*" He looked at her in amazement. "What the *hell*, Songbird?"

"Sorry. But you deserved that."

"What for?"

"For dying."

"For . . . Wait, I . . . *died?*"

"For about five minutes."

"How . . . ?" he rubbed his chest again then looked at Octavia. "You . . . ?"

She wiped her eyes and nodded, smiling.

"Bother. You're probably going to hold that over me now, aren't you?"

"Oh, yes," she said, suddenly laughing through her tears. "Without a doubt."

He nodded. "Thought so. Give me a hand."

Octavia helped him up. He limped over to check on Nehi and Sekhem. They were both dead. He arranged their bodies, crossing their arms over their chest.

"There's something outside we need."

He guided her to the door.

"What?" she asked.

"It's in the corridor."

Octavia looked into the passage. There was nothing there. Tweed gave her a small shove. She staggered out of the bridge and turned to look at him in amazement. "Hey . . ."

"Sorry, Songbird," he said.

Then he closed the door.

Tweed locked the door and headed for the steering controls.

"Tweed," Octavia shouted, "what are you doing? Tweed?"

He ignored her, thinking back to when he had seen the pilots steering the *Albion*. He pushed the levers that fed the Tesla Turbines, then spun the huge wheel to turn the ship toward the south.

He'd thought about this for days now, wondering what he was going to do when they got to London.

He knew now.

He'd been stressing about who he was. How he hadn't earned his place in the world. He knew he had to do *something*, something that would make him feel like he belonged. Belonged in the human race.

Elizabeth's words came back to him.

Where you come from does not define who you are. You forge that path every day with your actions.

He'd stopped Sekhem and Nehi. He'd earned his body, his soul. He'd earned his place.

But it didn't end there. He could still help others. Molock was wrong. If Hyperborea was revealed to the world, if the reason for their *sickness* was revealed, people would help.

There would be no war.

He knew this with a certainty he had never felt before.

The *Albion* heaved slowly around and left London behind. What had Molock said? Thrace, the capital city of Hyperborea, was north of London. And as he recalled, south of Thrace there wasn't a thing. Just empty grasslands.

So . . . about here should be fine.

He stopped the *Albion*, then turned to the death ray. He picked Tesla's soul up from where Octavia had left it on the console and inserted it into the slot.

Then he pulled the lever, powering up the weapon.

Tweed took out his watch and flicked the lid up. Ampney said that for it to burn through the crust of the earth it would take about ten minutes.

He pushed the button to fire the death ray, watching on the view screen as the invisible beam hit the ground. He felt the vibration through the soles of his boots. Stones and rock exploded upward in a massive geyser of dirt, then burst and vanished into dust.

"Tweed! You better not be doing what I think you're doing!" shouted Octavia.

Tweed moved to the door. "I have to, Octavia. Don't you see? They'll have no choice. The government will *have* to come up with another way to get power. The sickness will stop."

"Tweed, this could lead to war! Molock said—"

"Molock is wrong! The same way Sekhem and Nehi were wrong. He's scared. That's fine. He fears for his people. But this is the right thing to do."

"Tweed, don't you see? You're doing exactly what Chase did. What Nehi and Sekhem did. You're making choices for people without their blessing. You can't do that."

Tweed paused. She was right of course. He was being a complete hypocrite. But . . . he was so sure this was right. If only everyone else could understand . . .

He still had time to stop it. He headed back to the console, checking the view screen. The hole in the ground was massive, half a mile across.

No. This was the right thing to do. If saving lives meant he became like Barrington Chase, then he would just have to find a way to live with that.

He watched the screen and waited until he saw the barest wink of light far, far below. Then he switched the machine off. He took Tesla's soul out of the console and carefully put it aside, making sure it was safe.

He unlocked the door. Octavia stood there, glaring at him angrily.

"What have you done, Tweed?"

"I . . ." Tweed looked over his shoulder, suddenly uncertain. "I . . . I don't know yet."

Octavia grabbed him by the arm.

"Come on. You'd better contact your father. You've got some explaining to do."

∞

It was about seven hours later.

They were standing around the massive hole Tweed had created. It had been cordoned off by the police and the Ministry was doing its best to keep curious onlookers back.

Queen Victoria peered into the hole while her nervous advisors and bodyguards hovered around, ready to grab her should she slip. The surviving scientists, Octavia's mother, Molock (in his human guise), Tweed, Barnaby, and Solomon all stood in a respectful semicircle around her. Solomon also wore a human guise, that of a huge, bearded man with a booming voice. It fitted his personality perfectly.

Tweed was leaning on the railing that had been erected around the hole. He had been looked over by a doctor (at Barnaby's insistence) and was actually holding up remarkably well for someone who had been dead for five minutes.

And oddly, he seemed the better for it. He seemed more at peace within himself. Octavia wasn't sure what it was, but something had changed in him.

"And you're saying there is a whole civilization below us?" asked the Queen. "An entire race of beings who we have been . . . killing with our need for power?"

"That's about right, Your Majesty," said Tweed.

She looked at him, then her eyes flicked to Octavia. "You two have a remarkable talent for seeking out trouble and bringing it straight to me. You are like cats presenting their owners with half-eaten corpses." She sighed. "And the Ministry knew about this?"

PAUL CRILLEY

"No," said Barnaby. "I had no idea."

"Well, you wouldn't. You've only been there a couple months."

"Barrington Chase knew," said Octavia. "He was part of a secret group within the Ministry that made sure word of the Hyperboreans never got out."

"Interesting."

"And Temple was a spy," said Tweed. "Sekhem and Nehi's man on the inside. He told them where Tesla was. I reckon he hired Harry Banks to steal H. G. Wells's invisibility devices. Banks just decided to keep a couple for himself. Use them on his constructs."

Queen Victoria looked at Barnaby. "Barney, has Banks been picked up yet?"

Barney? Octavia and Tweed exchanged an amused look.

"Not yet, Your Majesty. But it will be done before the day is out."

The Queen nodded and turned to Molock. "And you, my man. You are the King of your people?"

Molock started to bow, but she held her hand up. "No. I do not entertain people who are in disguise. Your true face, please."

Molock looked surprised, but he nodded. A second later his face rippled, the skin darkening, hardening up, until his true lizard face was looking at the Queen. She didn't even blink, although her guards and retainers all gasped and took a step back.

"And your friend?"

Molock waved at Solomon and his face likewise melted and reformed. He bowed low.

"Your Majesty. I am your humble servant."

"Thank you both. For helping to stop these . . ." Octavia could see she was picking her words carefully. ". . . terrorists from causing lasting damage between our people."

She stepped closer and looked disapprovingly at Molock. "However, I do wish you had come to us directly when this problem

283

manifested. I assure you, we had no idea, and I know Tesla had no idea either. We could have joined together and come up with a solution."

Molock frowned. He glanced briefly at Tweed. "I . . . I am sorry, Your Majesty. I feared for my people, as any good ruler would. I hoped our scientists would be able to come up with a solution that would not necessitate any . . ."

"Meetings?"

"*Wars*. I fear our people are too different to . . . to mingle. I would dearly love to be proven wrong, but I thought that if a meeting could at all be avoided, then it was best to do so."

"Yes, well, there's nothing we can do about that now, is there?" said Queen Victoria with a sidelong glance at Tweed.

At least he had the decency to look embarrassed.

"Well now," said the Queen. "Busy days ahead, King Molock. Delegations must be formed, ceremonies of greeting, and dare I say it, embassies in each of our cities?"

Molock exchanged bemused looks with Solomon. "Is that it?"

"What did you expect? A declaration of war? Despite what you may think, we are not a bloodthirsty species." She nodded at the rescued scientists. "We already have a think tank created to look into this power source of yours. We will do what we can with poor Tesla's soul. God knows what is left of him, though." She pulled her coat tighter about her body. "Start off as we mean to go on, King Molock. Cooperation and friendship. We will send our best doctors to your cities to see what can be done about this sickness. If you will have them, of course."

"Your Majesty, we . . . we would be very grateful."

"Good. We will get this sorted, Molock. Trust me on this." She smiled. "And once it is all behind us, we will start with the cultural exchanges. I'm sure both our worlds will soon look rather different."

Again, the sideways look at Tweed.

"Whether we wanted them to or not."

EPILOGUE

They watched from across the street.

Octavia's mother glanced over her shoulder, but Octavia made shooing motions with her hands. She could barely contain her excitement.

"Come on," she said nervously. "Hurry up."

Her mother reached up and knocked on the door. Octavia reached out and gripped Tweed's arm. He placed his own hand over hers, a calming gesture.

The door opened.

Her father stood there, staring at his wife. Octavia could see that he didn't recognize her. Not at first.

He stepped forward, looking intently at her face.

Then his eyes widened. He reached out hesitantly, as if unsure she was real. Her mother grabbed his hand and held it to her cheek.

Her father leaned forward and swept her mother up into a tight embrace. They wrapped their arms around each other and didn't move.

Octavia blinked the tears away and averted her eyes, leaving them to their moment. She saw Tweed hastily rub his own eyes and she grinned at him.

"What?" he said. "I've got something in my eye."

"I never said anything!"

He put his arm around her. "How do you feel?"

Octavia rested her head against his shoulder. "Happy. Content. You?"

"Like I belong. Like I've earned my place."

"Idiot," said Octavia warmly. "You never had to earn your place."

"I did," he said seriously. "I needed to earn my soul. But it's done now."

"Good. No more feeling sorry for yourself, right? Because there's seriously nothing more unattractive and tiresome than a man feeling sorry for himself. Promise?"

"Promise."

"Good."

A hansom cab slid around the corner ahead of them. It slewed wildly in the slush, almost flipping over before the automaton got it under control again.

The cab skidded to a stop right next to them. The door flew open and Barnaby leaned out.

"Get in."

"Can't," said Tweed. "We're going to dinner." He locked eyes with Octavia. "We have a few things to talk about."

Octavia winked at Tweed, laughing when he flushed instantly red. Oh, this was going to be so much fun.

"No time," said Barnaby. "You know how H. G. Wells's invisibility technology was stolen?"

"What about it?"

"That wasn't the only thing that was taken."

Tweed and Octavia shared a troubled glance.

"What else?" asked Octavia.

"His time machine. Come on. You're wanted at the palace."

They climbed into the cab and it sped off. Octavia glanced out the window and saw her mother and father heading into the house. Octavia smiled, then turned back to face Tweed.

His eyes were blazing with excitement.

"The game's afoot, Songbird."

ABOUT THE AUTHOR

Born in Scotland in 1975, Paul Crilley moved to South Africa when he was eight years old. He was rather disappointed to find out that Africa was not at all like the Tarzan movies he watched on Sunday afternoons and that he would not, in fact, have elephants and lions strolling through his backyard. He now lives in a small village on the east coast of South Africa with his family.

He also wrote the Invisible Order books, and penned the upcoming humorous Middle Grade zombie series, Deadbeat Diaries. When not writing novels he works in South African television. He also freelanced on the MMO Star Wars: The Old Republic and recently wrote a comic miniseries for IDW Publishing.